An Ellora's Cave Roma

www.ellorascave.com

Hideaway

ISBN 9781419960819
ALL RIGHTS RESERVED.
Hideaway Copyright © 2006 Denise A. Agnew
Edited by Sue-Ellen Gower.
Cover art by Syneca. Photography by Darrell King.

This book printed in the U.S.A. by Jasmine-Jade Enterprises, LLC.

Electronic book publication October 2006
Trade paperback publication August 2010

With the exception of quotes used in reviews, this book may not be reproduced or used in whole or in part by any means existing without written permission from the publisher, Ellora's Cave Publishing, Inc.® 1056 Home Avenue, Akron OH 44310-3502.

Warning: The unauthorized reproduction or distribution of this copyrighted work is illegal. Criminal copyright infringement, including infringement without monetary gain, is investigated by the FBI and is punishable by up to 5 years in federal prison and a fine of $250,000.
(http://www.fbi.gov/ipr/)

This book is a work of fiction and any resemblance to persons, living or dead, or places, events or locales is purely coincidental. The characters are productions of the author's imagination and used fictitiously.

HIDEAWAY
๘

Trademarks Acknowledgement
ಏ

The author acknowledges the trademarked status and trademark owners of the following wordmarks mentioned in this work of fiction:

Glock: Glock, Inc.

Chapter One

"Each subsiding century reveals some new mystery: we build where monsters used to hide themselves."
— Henry Wadsworth Longfellow

☙

He was a dead man.

He could feel danger's hot pursuit on his neck. His breathing came hard, heart threatening to pound from his chest, his legs pumping as he ran full speed through the forest. His grip on the firearm stayed tight. He couldn't afford to lose the weapon. Tree branches impeded his flight, slapping at his head and torso, threatening to scrape and bruise.

He leapt over a root and his feet landed with a crunch in the pine needles covering the forest floor. Somehow he'd escaped, though fragmentary memory refused to form coherent thoughts. Images flashed through his mind with startling speed like dark nightmares. Stark. Terrifying. Out of bounds with his knowledge. The natural world ceased to exist. The supernatural demanded control.

He ducked beneath a branch, jumped over a ditch. Dirt fell away under his feet. With a growl of defeat, he slipped. His arms windmilled as he struggled to stay upright. Recovering his footing, he plunged into another full-speed run.

Behind him, the growling returned. Low. Menacing. Taking the courage he possessed as a man and throwing it into disarray.

Not much farther now. His goal, his refuge came. If he made it to the room, at least he'd have temporary shelter.

Hot breath gusted from the creature behind him, heavy footsteps echoing.

Faster. Must run faster.

A huge impact thudded into his right shoulder and then collided with the side of his head. With a muffled grunt, he staggered under the blow, tried to stay on his feet. Failed. Ground rushed up to meet him, and pain assaulted his right shoulder and head on the way down. He tried to tuck, to fall as he'd been taught. Instead, he sprawled, all legs and arms as he smacked into the ground on his injured side. Stunning pain catapulted through him and his vision faded to a thin strip as dizziness rolled over him. He couldn't move, stunned by shock. His eyelids flickered as consciousness dimmed. Evil would claim him, and frustration and anger leaked through the thought. Weakness threatened.

Fear rose inside and gnawed at determination. She was there too, in harm's way. Damn it. He couldn't let anything happen to her. His soul ached at the thought.

He would protect her.

He would die for her.

A growl echoed in the forest, and a shadow fell over him. He blinked his eyes open with one last effort. What he saw then he wished he could forget. What he saw then seared itself on his soul. With a final grasp on coherence, he uttered the only words to describe how he felt about what looked down on him.

"Fuck you, cretin," he said.

* * * * *

Ivy's heart thudded with a soul-deep dread she couldn't contain as Latimer crossed the expanse of the ballroom and—

"Dreck!" Gina Aames stopped typing and glared at the laptop computer with pure scorn. "This is crap."

She hated this. She knew better than to lambaste herself this way. Every book on creativity she'd read reminded her *ad nauseum* that the best way to stifle creative juices was to criticize the work before completing the story.

Other concerns pushed her into critical thinking. Why had she agreed to write an anthology story? She ached to write *Hideaway*, a romantic suspense. She'd written a synopsis for the historical, "Jade Promises", something she hated down to her marrow to write. The synopsis had sucked the life from her tale. She regurgitated the damn thing nine times before her brain turned to mush and she gave it to her agent.

"I'd rather eat maggots," she said.

She looked up from her laptop, grateful for generator power that kept electricity operating. She glanced out of the large windows of her friends' cabin and sighed. She wanted to settle down, enjoy the isolation and just write. Write with power, passion, and everything she couldn't seem to revive for the good of her career. She detested the malaise that wrapped around her. She wanted to feel proud of the twenty pages she'd banged out by the wee hours of the night, but this morning she suffered from even less inspiration. Last night's burst of creative energy had come unexpectedly and with gratification. Her eagerness this morning came to little or nothing. *One paragraph that sucks.*

Gina stared at her computer, the sense of time running, hurrying to run somewhere while she agonized. Making the characters do what she wanted seemed damnably impossible. Weariness spilled over her. She sighed and gazed out of the window across the way in the living room. Of course, she couldn't make the characters breathe because they had no life of their own. They'd stopped talking to her. Reassuring herself that most authors ran into some form of writer's block over the course of their careers, she tried harder. A few sentences bled out onto the page.

"More dreck."

Her fingers hovered over the backspace key. She thought about deleting but didn't. She needed to dump this tendency to try to make the manuscript perfect on first draft.

"Spit it out. Get it down on paper."

She shifted in her chair and reached for the diet cola she'd opened not long ago. After a long sip, she placed her fingers on the keys—

She stopped. Something didn't feel right. She moaned and leaned back against the hardwood chair. Outside, wind rustled the tall pines around the large A-frame retreat. A staggering array of beauty lay in front of her. Jagged mountains rose with blue and green majesty against a cerulean sky and black clouds. A green tinge to the clouds disturbed her, as did the way the trees remained untouched by wind. It was far too still out there. Rarely did the clouds around here turn tornado green.

Disappointment and frustration battled inside her. She didn't want to pretend anymore that she understood what she was doing. Confusion stirred her mind the longer she tried to find inspiration. Maybe she could forget writing today and try to relax with one of the ten paperbacks she'd brought with her. It wouldn't take her an entire month to read ten books since she read most of the time when she wasn't writing. Her friends didn't have a television in their cabin. Gina had set her digital recording system on her television back home to record a month's worth of favorite programs she didn't wish to miss.

One more time she watched the landscape, hoping to catch a look at wildlife. Instead, the approaching thunderheads looming dark and thick caught her attention. A shiver ran down her spine, and unease she couldn't recall sensing in months threatened her peace.

No. She couldn't let the isolation make her imagine things. Just because she spent time alone didn't mean the boogeyman would appear out of the woodwork. Regardless of common sense, her instincts sent blatant fear catapulting into her bloodstream. She took a deep breath and attempted to calm her racing heart.

"Nothing bad is going to happen."

Okay, bad things could occur beyond her control. The saying "shit happens" came directly from that realization, no doubt. Keeping her thoughts on her problem historical romance, she stood and walked around the living area and hoped inspiration would arrive.

She concentrated on deciphering the critical area in her book that would bust the block keeping her creative flow under wraps. Bad characterization? No motivation? Loose plot? Her brain scrambled like eggs as she spun through scenario after scenario. Frustration ate away at her hard-won self-confidence.

"Don't whine," she said. "You've done this before, you can do it again. It isn't going to kill you."

Yeah, it might this time.

If only it was the right time of year for snow. She could head out to the nearby Love Point ski resort, or strap on her snowshoes and follow that somewhat dubious trail into the wilderness. Yes, that would do it. She craved an adrenaline hit. Too much time passed since she'd skied, skydived, went horseback riding and rode some rapids.

She stopped in her tracks.

She heard a strange-pitched sound. A groan? No. A cry for help? God, she hoped not.

Renewed apprehension skated over her senses as she returned to her pacing. Any minute now, her muse would bounce back and take charge. No more meandering. Success lay around the corner. She half believed it when she sat down and started typing.

That's it. Don't let the boogeyman get you.

She laughed. Good.

A few seconds later, she stopped typing and listened. Sun left weak light bands across the tinted glass of the windows. What brought her repeatedly to stare out this window other than the scenic beauty?

The answer wouldn't come.

A faint cry echoed in the atmosphere outside.

She groaned and put her hands over her eyes. "Don't be neurotic, Gina. There's nothing. No one is out there. It's your imagination."

Lightning illuminated the windows, fire-hot and close. She flinched as thunder cracked viciously over the cabin. Ominous dark thunderheads continued to build, menacing with the low-hanging darkness and green tinge that signaled danger. Their presence made her twitchy. Thunderstorms in the Colorado Mountains could arrive without warning for those holed up inside a massive cabin with their noses totally buried in a manuscript.

Ironic she should fear thunderstorms when she feared little else.

Gina sniffed as one tear slid down her left cheek. She wiped away the sign of weakness. No. Crying wasn't a weakness. It signified genuine emotion. An ability to love, live and learn. She glanced back at the screen, and realized staring at one bleak, forlorn paragraph wouldn't bring her another word. At least not for long. Disappointment boiled inside her.

Think of pleasant things. She closed her eyes and tried to imagine a beautiful stone pathway paving the way through an array of bright flowers. Gina inhaled deeply. Yes, that was it. So much like the path she'd followed on a beautiful island off the coast of Ireland when she'd visited fifteen years ago, before she met Ryan. She could almost see the flowers and smell them.

Ireland. Oh, yes. She'd loved it there. Nine days on a tour bus hadn't provided her the total picture of the country, and she craved to return.

There you go. She needed something as inspiring as Ireland. Even the Rocky Mountain high didn't give her what she needed. What did she require?

Irish.

She didn't mind bringing *him* into the picture. Just thinking about Ryan "Irish" Ahern should inspire the most prudish or dried-up spinster into palpitations. She was starting to feel an awful lot like a thirty-three-year-old prune these days. Her hormones hadn't completely abandoned her. But as the now popular saying went, she wasn't that much into them. Deadlines and other writing concerns had siphoned the libido from her life. She drew in another deep breath and relaxed, bringing Ryan into her mind's eye with sweet, slow attention.

She imagined standing on the path, a cool wind tossing her short hair. Out of the blue, Ryan materialized.

Unexpectedly, a cough left her throat and broke the spell. She opened her eyes. Two weeks ago, laryngitis made talking almost impossible. She'd rasped through the days, drinking hot tea with lemon and sucking on natural herbal drops when necessary. Her throat never became sore, and she remained thankful for that. After a couple of days here, her throat problem eased considerably. At least she could talk with not much of a rasp. A close friend, Tara Crayton, had teased her and proposed that her silence could represent a blessing in disguise.

"You need a good, long breather," Tara had said two days before the planned month-long sojourn to the cabin.

Gina had agreed, cognizant her grueling deadline schedule demanded energy…something she lacked these days.

"You're looking rested," Gina had said to Tara.

Tara had smiled, her eyes bright and dreamy. "Preparing for the wedding has been crazy, but I'm enjoying every minute of it."

Gina still envied that glow in her friend's expression. She understood Tara's happiness—her upcoming marriage to hunk Marcus Hyatt.

"I'm so happy you've agreed to be a bridesmaid," Tara had said.

Gina was too, although twinges of envy crept into her thoughts from time to time. If anyone had a chance at happily ever after, Tara and Marcus could accomplish that sought-after goal.

Gina didn't know if a man like Marcus would enter her life, but if he didn't, she wouldn't despair. She found the world and her career fascinating and fulfilling enough.

Lightning seared the air, thunder slicing the atmosphere with a serrated edge. A squeak left her throat as she flinched. Time to shut down the computer. She backed up her files on a memory stick, then removed the stick and powered down the computer.

Heavy knocking on the front door jolted her nerves and she gasped. Her heart tripped over her lungs as she stood. Paralyzed with indecision, Gina stared at the door. No one but the cabin owners, her agent, and Tara knew she was here.

She frowned and headed for the door. She put one hand on the chain lock then stopped. The door didn't have a peephole.

She leaned her ear against the thick wood door and put force into her voice as she asked, "Who is it?"

Another thump hit the door, hollow and disturbing. She licked her lips, her heart pounding like a triphammer.

"Who is there?" Gina asked with conviction.

When she received no answer, she wondered if a bear or other large creature had found its way to her door. Gina didn't know which to be afraid of—human or animal interference.

She undid the deadbolt and left the safety chain hooked. Slowly, she inched the door open and peered around the side. A head of thick black hair appeared at foot level. Not a disembodied head, but one attached to the big, gorgeous body lying on the porch. A body belonging to a man she'd know anywhere.

Ryan Ahern had materialized right from her fantasy straight into reality. "Oh my God."

He moaned and she undid the chain to open the door completely. Ryan flopped onto his back, half in the door and half out, his eyes closed. He clutched a nasty-looking firearm in his right hand. Stark fear gripped her.

Stunned into immobility by Ryan's abrupt appearance, Gina stared at him.

"Shit," she murmured as she knelt by his supine body and felt for a pulse in his tanned throat.

A steady beat under her fingertips sent a sigh of relief between her lips. Glancing over his formfitting blue T-shirt and worn blue jeans told her nothing about his condition. No blood. No tears in his clothing. The weapon gripped in his hand like a lifeline shouldn't have surprised her—he'd joined the same government agency Tara's fiancé Marcus belonged to. Was Ryan on assignment?

Thunder growled, and moisture scented the air. She had to remove him from the elements. Placing one hand on his stubble-rough cheek and one on his shoulder, she tried to rouse him. Damn, but his muscles felt solid. Big and invincible. She palmed down to his muscular chest and her breath caught as he heaved a soft moan. Laced with pain, the sound worried her. Nothing mattered now but making certain he was all right.

She placed both hands on his chest. "Irish? Come on, Ryan. Wake up."

His eyes popped open, and he sat up so fast she toppled back on her ass with a squeak and grunt. His eyes, mountain-sky blue and ringed by thick black lashes, latched on to her without remorse. An angry gaze pinpointed her like a laser. A weird little thrill tumbled in her belly at the intensity in that expression. She'd become so used to warmth and acceptance in his gorgeous eyes—the fierceness in his gaze startled and aroused her in a whole new way. Wow. She'd had rare glimpses of his kick-ass-and- take-names personage years ago, but this glaring, forceful man startled her. She stood rapidly.

"Who are you?" His voice, a raspy, deep sound tinged with a hint of Ireland, always sent tingles straight to her stomach.

"Who am I?" Her echo sounded incredulous. "We've known each other for a long time. How can you ask that question?" He blinked, his gaze turning a bit unfocused and confused. "I found you lying on the porch up against my door. Did you hit your head?"

He scrambled upright, his muscles fluid as a panther as he came to his feet, still in possession of the gun. He towered over her, his gaze laser strong. He swayed and his eyelids flickered as he leaned one shoulder against the doorjamb. While he defined black Irish with his tousled, collar-length black hair, blue eyes and normally pale complexion, he'd acquired a tan in the last couple of years during the summer.

She approached him as she would a wounded animal. "Ryan, why don't you sit down?"

He glared at her then his eyelids flickered again.

"Oh, no you don't," she said in alarm, afraid he'd pass out. Quickly, she went to his side. Ignoring the gun he still clutched, she slipped under his arm. "Come on. Lean on me." To her surprise, he did as told. She staggered under his weight as they wove their way to the leather couch. She eased him down. "Here. Lie down."

She expected him to protest, but his gaze turned foggy. He slid sideways onto the pile of pillows, his eyes closed. She scooped his heavy legs up onto the couch, and he sprawled in a male abandon both defenseless and primal. He still possessed the weapon, his arm lying over his stomach. God, if she tried to take it from him—no, that wasn't a good idea. She hurried back to the front door and closed it, then returned to the couch.

Apprehensive about touching him again, she got down on her knees beside the couch. Slowly she brushed a tangle of thick hair away from his forehead. She gently touched the pulse point in his throat. His pulse beat rapidly under her fingertips. She didn't see any blood or obvious bruising.

"Ryan? Ryan, can you hear me?"

Worried, she stood and went to the kitchen to get a cold cloth for his forehead. She had to try to rouse him and obtain medical attention. Reaching into a small cabinet, she retrieved a cloth and then went to the sink to wet it. After soaking it thoroughly and squeezing the cloth out, she turned around.

"Oh, shit!" she gasped, startled.

Ryan stood not that far away, just beyond the kitchen counter, weapon in hand. Muscles tensed, he represented uncompromising masculinity. Once a soldier, always a soldier described him.

No one compared to Ryan Ahern. Every line of his body boasted tensile strength and sinew. Corded muscle bunched, flexed and made sensual promises. She recalled one day when she saw him chopping wood during the summer. Raw power had drawn her eyes to the long lines and distinct masculinity in each powerful swing as he brought ruthless metal down into wood.

"Ryan, what happened? Why are you here?"

He turned toward the front door with a jerk then stalked in that direction. He swept the door open and surveyed the wilderness outside. He closed the door and locked it with a firm click, engaging the chain.

"Damn it." He rammed the deadbolt home. "This might not hold for long once it finds out where I am."

"It?"

He continued to stare at the door, as if expecting something to crash through it any minute.

Fear returned as she watched his broad back ripple with strength. "Ryan—"

"Lady," he said as he swung back toward her, "we don't have time to play games. We're in serious trouble."

Exasperation displaced her fear. She put the wet washcloth down on the side of the sink. "What is going on?"

He jammed one hand through his hair, causing wild strands to stand up. She'd never seen Ryan so untamed and pumping with action. In a weird way, she responded to his bravado, his keen intensity.

He paced to the towering windows across from the desk, and she followed. "Where are we?"

She almost ran into him when he turned to face her. "My friends' cabin. You know them. Linda and Aaron Fieldman." She shook her head and put her hands on her hips. "Why am I telling you this? You know who I am and where we are."

"No," he said with soft intensity that packed more heat than if he'd growled at her. He took a quick survey of the room. "I don't know jack."

Without thinking about it, she put one hand on his upper shoulder. Tension defined his muscles and heat radiated from him. "If you'd explain what's happening—"

"No."

She withdrew her touch at his harsh tone.

Under his tough exterior beat a heart of gold, yet his eyes flashed with heat, a challenge. Danger lurked inside him, a feral presence animalistic and bold. A flush burned her face as she watched him. Embarrassment made her look away. She couldn't banish her girlish reaction, this silly demand from her body and heart. His hard, lean lines and sculpted sinews showed supreme physical conditioning. The T-shirt delineated well-honed biceps, carved strength of pectorals, and flat, muscled stomach. Lower down, his jeans outlined narrow hips and muscled thighs. Oh, yes. She remembered seeing those legs in shorts during the summer. Hard, powerful, sexy limbs.

Hideaway

In an uninhibited moment, her imagination played a picture. His thighs between hers, his hips churning, thrusting, powering his big cock deep into the grip of her wet, hungry depths.

Warmth flushed her cheeks. Thank heavens he couldn't read her mind.

All six-feet, three-inches of male testosterone dwarfed her five-foot five-inch frame. He'd always made her feel dainty and feminine, but fear rose up and grabbed Gina. A creepy feeling rippled over her skin.

His gaze flicked over her rapidly. "What's your name?"

"Gina. Gina Aames."

"You got a phone in here, Gina Aames?" he asked, his voice hoarse.

"Just a cell phone. Why?"

Ryan's mouth twisted in comprehension, his flint-hard gaze not softening in the least. "No landline?"

She crossed her arms as irritation rose. "No. In case you haven't noticed, we are in the back of beyond around here."

Lightning flashed violently, but he didn't seem to notice the electrical storm. Thunder crashed.

He closed his eyes and took a deep breath. "Fuckin' bloody hell."

"You're scaring me," she said, not too ashamed to confess.

He opened his eyes, and she thought she saw his gaze soften. "I'm not going to hurt you."

She nodded. "Of course you wouldn't hurt me. I trust you with my life."

There wasn't another man on the planet she could admit that to or believe.

He frowned. "How the hell do you know my name?"

Then it hit her. Ryan had always enjoyed pulling practical jokes on his friends, her included. Amusement belted her so hard she snorted a laugh. "Irish, I ought to kick your ass. I can't believe it. You really had me going there for a moment. Is this some kind of initiation you have to do for that organization you work for?"

His brows lowered, and his glower stirred something oddly primitive inside her. Damn if she didn't like this hard edge he'd acquired, even if he had scared the pants off her a minute ago.

"No, damn it. This isn't some sick joke." He snapped the words, and his harshness made her take a step back.

Oooookay. So maybe he didn't know her. Maybe this wasn't an Ahern standard joke. Amnesia? After all, she'd found him unconscious. If he couldn't remember anything, wouldn't he be more confused? Frightened even?

No. Not Ryan. He'd survived perilous situations in the Army, and nothing fazed him.

"I've never seen you wound up like this." She laced her hands together, nervous. "Okay, I take that back. The day we met over ten years ago. You rescued me from that bully. Remember?"

Recognition flickered for an instant in his beautiful eyes then disappeared like a puff of smoke. "No. I don't remember."

When he took a few steps nearer, she caught the unique sandalwood and bergamot aftershave mixed with male sweat that always drove her libido into a lather. His tantalizing scent made her recall the countless times she'd savored his nearness.

"There was this guy when I was in college." She looked down at her stocking feet and felt the cool hardwood floor. "Mike McDougal. He took an intense dislike to me for no reason I could ever figure out. You had the same chemistry class and sat in front of us. After class one day, he started following and harassing me. Calling me names. You offered to walk me to my dorm every day, and you told him to keep the hell away from me or you'd bust his ass. How could you forget that?"

God, please. Don't let him forget that.

He shook his head. "I don't recall shit."

He advanced, and he wore dark and dangerous so well, Gina felt her resolve falter when he stood within six inches of her. Seeing him cool, a virtual stranger raking her with a suspicious glare, scared Gina down in a new deep, dark way she'd never felt before. His blade-sharp gaze drank her in with merciless purpose. Nothing would escape his ruthless resolve, and she knew from experience he never backed down or gave up when he believed in something strongly enough. She couldn't look away from the one man she trusted above any other in the world. Unsettling emotions battered her from all sides. Gina admitted the overwhelming fascination wending through her. She'd seen many handsome men, some who might have crossed over the realm into mind-blowing, knee-buckling gorgeous. Ryan blew her mind even after ten years.

She cleared her raspy throat.

"Are you on an assignment?" she asked, and hated the tremble she heard in her voice. "Are there some creeps after you?"

"I need that cell phone." His quietly deadly voice stirred wisps of hair on her forehead. "Now."

Rankled by his impervious and demanding tone, she sighed. "It's in my purse. In the bedroom upstairs."

She turned to leave, and he followed.

"Don't try anything." His hiking boots squelched over the flooring.

She glanced back at him as she reached the stairway. "That's corny, Ryan. Like a line from an old movie. Can't you do better than that? And put that gun away, would you? It's making me nervous."

He tucked the gun in the back of his waistband, and she felt better.

She reached for the banister as she went up the stairs, but her foot slipped on the runner. A gasp left her as she fell backwards. Two powerful arms went around her waist, and she landed against his firm chest. Heat flared in her body as Ryan kept her pinned to his chest and hips.

His breath fanned across the hair at the top of her head. She'd always appreciated his strength, but somehow this encounter felt different. Rife with possibility. Confused and frightened, she clasped her hands over his forearms. The power beneath her fingers sent ripples of sensual awareness curling low in her stomach. His energy felt potent and ready for anything.

Disturbed by the sensations stirring deep inside, she said, "Ryan? You can let me go now."

When his voice came again, it rasped with that sexy, husky Irish nuance she'd always loved. "You all right?"

"Of course. I'm just nervous. You're acting so strangely."

He released her immediately, and she headed upstairs with him trailing behind.

She headed down the wide hallway, and somehow sensed his curiosity as they passed family photographs on the walls.

"You're not in any of these photos," he said.

"Like I said, it's not my home. I'm staying here for a month."

"Housesitting?"

"This is my friends' summer retreat. They've loaned it out to me while I write." They came to the open master suite door, and she walked inside.

"Nice place," he said with a hint of derision.

Indignant at his tone, she said, "So you've got a personality change to match your amnesia, is that it? I've never known you to be a snob."

"It was a casual observation, not an indictment."

She didn't know what to say.

A weird nervousness passed over her as they came into the normally sunny, but rustic western-designed area. The king-sized bed dominated the roomy retreat. A large master bath at one end, and a huge walk-in closet at the other, plus a small sitting area to one side completed the room. Yes, this place was lavish, but her friends had worked hard for their money and had designed the place.

Thunder rolled with violence over the cabin. She hated storms like this with nerve-bending noise and even nastier intentions.

The storm is the least of your worries, Gina. Right. One of her best friends in the whole world had gone wiggy on her and the more time that went by, the more frightened she became.

Her purse lay on the bed and she dug through it. She came up with a small package of nuts, a lipstick, her wallet—ah, there. Finally the phone. Before she could turn it on, he pulled it from her hand.

"Take it easy," she said.

Instead of dialing, he gave her a once-over that seared her to the core. She stared back, disconcerted. The man standing in front of her remained her good friend, but he'd changed in an indefinable way that disturbed her and turned her on in an uncanny combination. In fact, he'd always possessed an alpha edge that sparked erotic feelings within her.

Rich red highlights gleamed in the black hair that tossed around his head in thick waves and just touched the back of his collar. She liked his hair grown out—though his buzz-cut in the military hadn't detracted from him one bit. *Hell, face it, Gina. The man looks fantastic no matter what.* No woman alive would call him a pretty boy. Nope, Ryan's slightly large nose, well-carved jawline and handsome mouth complemented the rest of his uncompromising masculinity. Standing there now, he reminded her of an Irish warrior ready to kick some serious ass. His broad chest heaved up and down, as if he squashed strong emotion.

"What is wrong?" she asked. "Why are you staring at me like that?"

He shook his head. "Listen, I won't hurt you, but I don't know who you are. I need your cell phone so I can call for backup."

"You've got the phone. So use it." Her words came out sharp-edged. "And when you finish telling your agency buddies what you're doing, just add that you're scaring the shit out of me."

She sat on the bed a minute and then leaned over to grab her athletic shoes. She shoved her feet into the shoes and tied them, then rose from the bed and stomped out of the room.

Ryan's lips parted as a retort came to his lips. He followed her back downstairs to the living area. He stopped near the coffee table, anger churning inside him in a way he didn't understand. She turned toward him, her hands on the back of the leather recliner not far away. He tried to quell the pounding ache in his temples. When he'd come to lying across this woman's foyer, the first thought that popped into his pounding skull was how damned pretty she was. She had softness in her curves, a delicacy in her small frame that made her seem more petite than her true stature. Her full breasts, small waist and rounded hips looked nice in her short-sleeved pink polo top and her denim jeans. Then he'd started to lose consciousness and the angel had supported him when he thought he'd fall. When he'd awakened, distrust had returned.

As she stared at him, he felt his weapon poking him in the back where he'd stuffed it into the back of his jeans. Where was his shoulder holster? He knew he was supposed to have the Glock, and he knew something horrible had pursued him through the woods for some distance. He even understood he worked for the premier government agency that dealt with supernatural threats to the world. The SIA. Special Investigations Agency.

But bugger if he could recall *what* he'd been running from or why. *Shit*. He couldn't even think of his name until she told him.

Ryan. It sounded foreign to him.

Had she called him Irish?

Yeah, he knew that he'd been born near Belfast in Northern Ireland and had come to live with an aunt in the US for good when his parents died in a terrorist bombing. Pain speared through his head and he winced. *Jesus, Mary and Joseph*. Someone else close to him had died in the bombing. He'd only been seventeen.

Yet he didn't know his own fucking name, and he couldn't remember the beautiful creature called Gina. How screwed up was that?

She claimed to know him.

Or did she?

Her shamrock green eyes showed no deceit. Her small nose, sprinkled with freckles, made her appear about sixteen. A short crop of red-gold hair framed her heart-shaped face in a way that stirred his blood.

It was too good a coincidence that she knew who he was, and he'd stumbled into her doorway. Too large a coincidence that he would run from an unknown enemy and turn up at her cabin.

Something was seriously fucked up here.

Her neat eyebrows pinched together, and she placed her small hands on her hips. "Do you plan to stare at me for the rest of the day, or call for help?"

He looked down at the small silver phone clenched in his hand, understanding that he needed to summon serious reinforcements. A wave of the shakes hit him, and nausea made him wince. Whom did he call? What number?

Chapter Two

"Ryan?" The woman who called herself Gina frowned. She walked toward him, and when she reached him she clutched one of his biceps. "Maybe you'd better sit down."

Her small hand gripped him as if she expected him to fall on his ass.

He gave in to the dazed sensation making mush of his determination to stay strong. Shit, maybe he had done some damage to his head. No. He couldn't show more weakness. Not until he knew if he could trust her. He forced his shoulders into a clear line.

"Yeah," he said as she drew him toward the large brown leather sectional couch in the expansive living area.

Pounding in his temples increased. He hated this. Agents didn't succumb to infirmity of any kind on assignment. An unusual and wrenching anxiety hit him in the gut. When he sank down on the couch, she settled close beside him. He drew in a deep breath and her subtle but pleasant scent teased. Familiarity tantalized. Okay...so maybe he did know her. At least he recalled her gentle fragrance. His groin stirred and just like that, his cock stood up and took notice.

Despite the headache, his body wanted hers badly. How the hell could arousal blindside him when he knew he'd been through a traumatic, adrenaline-spiking event not long ago?

Bingo. That explained it. Wounded or not, the reeling, feral alertness he felt with her had an explanation. Battle-hardened warriors sometimes returned from combat with a hard-on the size of Mount Olympus. She represented nourishment for his sexual needs. Friend or foe, as a woman she gave him a savage erection. In other words, he needed to fuck to drain off high tension.

It sounded barbaric, but physiologically it sometimes happened.

Lightning flashed across the sky, accompanied by a horrendous crash. She jumped and gasped. Her grip tightened on his arm. Rain slashed violently against the huge windows as the sky darkened.

"They didn't say anything on the radio about this weather coming in today," she said.

"Can't harness the weather." He glanced out at the angry skies. "Mother Nature does what she wants, when she wants."

"Yes."

He heard the nervousness in her voice, and she sounded as if she were recovering from a cold with her croaky tone. When her fingers stayed tight with tension on his arm, he placed his hand over hers involuntarily. Her gaze clashed with his, and heat flared. Molten need sliced into his stomach. The understanding in her eyes said she sensed it too.

Her gaze dropped down, and Ryan knew the second Gina saw his erection. She couldn't miss it. A pink flush rose into her neck and cheeks. Her gaze darted away. Well, okay. He couldn't help her embarrassment, and yet he couldn't feel disconcerted either. His jeans weren't tight, but they fit him well. No way could he mask the full-blown and fixed reaction to her femininity.

Damn. Maybe he had a deeper connection to this woman than he thought. His fingers tightened on hers. With a soft gasp he could barely hear, she drew her hand out from under his.

"This is dangerous," he said without meaning the monster that might lurk outside.

"Oh?" Her tone came out soft and startled. Her eyes widened. "Did you remember something?"

"Yeah."

Again, she touched him, pressing his shoulder, her touch sending quicksilver flashes of desire direct to his groin when he should concentrate on keeping them safe. He strained through the fog in his brain. He couldn't allow certain emotions to cloud his judgment. Fear. Uncertainty. A need for an anchor. Desire. A craving to take her sweet mouth and forget the mission...whatever that mission may be. Ashamed of his weakness, he shrugged off her gentle touch. He dared glance her way, and the hurt in Gina's eyes surprised him. He steeled himself against her.

"We're in danger," he said. "I'm not sure from what, but that locked door may not keep it out when it gets here."

He couldn't mistake the quiver in her slight frame for anything other than apprehension.

"What do you mean by *it*? Don't you mean who?" she asked.

"My brain is half fried, but there are uncooked spots that recall every detail. I was running in the woods from something fucking vicious." A vision swirled into his head and made him jerk. He closed his eyes, trying to capture light, sound, whatever he could to return to his memory. "There's a nasty stench in the woods. I hear snarling. Heavy footsteps running behind me. I'm hiding here and there, where I can." He tried to nudge another memory to the surface, but it refused. "I've lost the creature temporarily."

When he opened his eyes, discord shone in her eyes and mirrored her emotions back to him. Thunder roared and rain battered the high windows, thwarted but determined to create a terrifying loneliness in his heart. He couldn't recall ever knowing insecurity like this before.

"You must be kidding." A breath pushed out of her, a sigh vibrant with disbelief. "Are you saying there is a wild beast out there?"

"You could say that."

"A mountain lion or bear?"

"I'm not sure. Whatever the hell it is, it attacked me and sent me running."

Yeah, he hated admitting to the running part.

Her gaze scanned him. "I don't see any bites or claw marks or blood. You must have run extremely fast to escape a mountain lion or bear."

Disbelief in her tone made him flare. "Yeah, I'm an extremely fast runner. I remember that."

Anger topped his list of feelings, and other than her insistence and his suspicions, he had no reason to feel pissed-off. Unless, of course, he was hacked because he'd failed a mission. Because now that he was here with her, the creature could come in this cabin and hurt a civilian.

Self-recrimination pierced his armor. *Son of a fuckin' bitch.* He had no right to sit around with his thumb up his ass and put her life at risk.

Renewed determination worked past his physical ailments. No, he knew in his gut he never quit. Ever. "Don't worry. I'm not going to let anything happen to you."

His last sentence cemented it for him. He knew it down to his marrow. He knew in his instincts she wasn't a bodily danger to him. Only an emotional one.

A shiver passed over her slim frame. "No, you never quit. It's one of the things I've always admired about you."

Pleasure, fragile and teetering, warmed the cold knot in his heart. He allowed gratification to swirl inside him for a few seconds then put it away.

"This...this whatever I encountered is powerful." He pulled the weapon out of the back of his waistband and checked it. "It's been fired twice and recently."

His hand trembled as he placed the gun down on the coffee table in front of him and laid the cell phone down next to it. Ryan didn't like the Glock far away from him, but he also didn't care for the unsteadiness in his grip. "Something strange is out there."

Damn, he didn't want to admit to that either.

"Strange? As in paranormal?" Her eyes brightened, as if he'd hit a live wire inside her eager to explore.

"Maybe." He slanted a doubting glance her way. When she didn't mock him, he continued. "You believe in the supernatural?"

"Of course." She tilted her head to the side like a curious kid exploring fascinating concepts. "You really must have lost your memory not to recall that I'm fascinated with the paranormal."

Cold dread sank into his stomach. He understood that he sensed the unnatural and had done so his entire life. Having an inkling of certainty gave him new confidence.

"It's beyond paranormal. We're talking deeply fucked-up evil," he said. "The kind people see in horror movies."

She blinked, and he saw when his words penetrated on a visceral level. The spark of excitement in her heart-shaped, pretty face diminished. He liked rocking a woman's world, but not this way.

"Do you recall anything else about your encounter with the entity?" she asked calmly.

Automatically, he closed his eyes and drew in a deep breath. He reached out with his mind, to beyond the semi-safety of the cabin, into the darkest woods. But, he couldn't sense anything specific at the moment. Only blackness cloaked his thoughts when he tried harder.

He cleared his throat. "It's raw fear palpitating with its own energy, a life malevolent and ugly. Whatever I fought draws energy from people's fears to create special nightmares just for them. Maybe it takes their dreams and makes those a reality."

Again, her beautiful green eyes tangled with his. "A ghost?"

"Nothing that benign. I don't think I can describe it. You'd have to...encounter it. Know it." Damn it, he'd drawn an innocent into danger with his stupidity. Anxiety twisted his gut. "If you're my friend, and I knew this evil was hunting me, why did I bring it to you?"

She shook her head. "Please, don't blame yourself. You don't have your memory back yet. You have no idea what your original plan was."

He made a chopping motion with his hand. Frustration spilled out in his words. "Damned right. If I leave to try and draw the danger away from you, you're vulnerable and without protection." He raked his fingers through his hair. "This whole situation is Tango Uniform."

She grinned a little. "Tango Uniform?"

"Tits up."

Her smile broadened. "You never were one to mince words."

"Sorry."

She crossed her arms. "There's nothing to be sorry about. I know you'd never knowingly draw me into danger, so there has to be a good reason why you showed up here. And I'm not helpless, you know." She sighed. "You always were a little overprotective."

He could feel protectiveness within himself—a driving necessity to guard her growing stronger by the second. It twisted in his gut. "I didn't mean to imply you are helpless." Okay, so he'd admit something else. "I'm scrambled. I'm trying to get my bearings."

As thunder crackled outside, a haunted, pained look crossed her face. Worry built along with his other anxieties. She said she'd known him over ten years.

"I was in the military, wasn't I?" he asked as he stood and walked to the big windows to look out on rain-soaked wilderness.

She smiled a little. "Yes."

"What branch?"

"The army."

Instead of peppering her with more questions, he started a relentless walk back and forth over the floor. The long living area, with its hardwood floors, polished Tuscan tables, and impeccable taste showed whoever owned the cabin had wealth. Yet he felt uncomfortable here, as if the structure possessed another ingredient he couldn't define. He shrugged away the incomprehensible and misdirecting thought. He couldn't recall anything throwing him off as much as being here with her in the mountains in a cabin that made him feel exposed.

"How do you stand this?" he asked, still pacing.

"Stand what?"

"The glass. This massive A-frame structure makes me feel like I'm a tiny mite in a cathedral. Doesn't it diminish you?"

"I never thought of it that way. I came out here for isolation, and it's certainly good for that."

He couldn't take the tension he felt in the air, his body responding continuously to hers and his mind baffled by feelings.

"Son of a bitch," he murmured.

"What?"

"I'm not used to inaction."

"No, you're not."

"It's all crap in my head." He snapped the words, impatience rearing inside him. "I need to sort it out. It feels like I have fucking sawdust for brains. Just keep out of my head a minute, will you?"

"What?" she said again, her brows drawing together in consternation.

"You're sitting there looking so delicious, all I want to do is—" He managed to grit his teeth and hold back. He stopped pacing and turned toward her, his fists clenched at his sides. "You're a distraction."

She heaved a deep breath then stood. "I don't know what has crawled up your ass, Ryan Ahern, but I'd appreciate if you wouldn't take your bad attitude out on me."

Snapped to attention by her aggravation, he paused and then walked slowly toward her, coming around the coffee table until he stood close enough to smell her fresh scent. Attraction sucker-punched him, and he gave in to the exotic lure ebbing and flowing. He reached up and traced his fingers lightly over her jawline. A quiver rolled through her body. A flush turned her pale complexion a delicious pink. He'd be damned if she was afraid of him. No, her reaction said the opposite. Her pupils dilated. Her lips parted and tempted him. He wanted to lean down, taste her and thrust his tongue inside to explore. Arousal pulled his balls up against his body and his cock into drill-hard attention. He wondered if her nipples would be pink or dusky rose or maybe brown. Fuck, what he wouldn't give to know.

Her gaze came up and trapped his. *Be blunt. It's the only way to operate.*

"Is there something else between us? I've got to know, because it's driving me crazy," he asked.

She allowed her arms to drop to her sides. "Like a fight? Well, we have fought before, but we always make up."

"As in the way lovers make up? Because what I'm feeling now says we have some pretty powerful sex between us."

Chapter Three

"No. That's ridiculous," Gina said with a soft, almost winded voice. Her eyes widened. "We...um...we're just friends."

Just friends, eh? Ryan didn't believe it, but if she wanted to play that game, he'd let it stand for now. If they were platonic only, she wouldn't respond to him this powerfully, and he wouldn't be interested in backing her up against a wall, stripping her clothes off and nailing her. With an unknown threat outside, he couldn't explore a sexual adventure with her anyway, no matter how much his body demanded.

She turned away from him quickly and sank back on the couch. He followed and half expected her to shift away when he settled close beside her.

"Ryan," she said softly. "Aren't you going to use the phone?"

Frustration started eating away at his gut. "I don't even know the phone number I need to call."

"I can take care of that. I have a friend in the SIA. Marcus Hyatt."

A man. Unreasonable, stupid jealousy surged into his chest and damned near closed off his breathing. "Is he your boyfriend?"

Her eyes widened, and the gnawing uncertainty devouring him nudged upward a notch. Her lips parted. Her pretty mouth, touched by a hint of pink lip gloss, drew his attention for too long. He slammed his concentration back into the fold.

A brilliant smile sent an added glow to her eyes. "No. I met his significant other, Tara, at an art class a few months back. By extension he's my friend now too."

"Do I know him?"

"That's how you joined the SIA. You met him and Tara through me. You haven't worked at the SIA that long. About three months."

Three months? That was all?

"Marcus is an agent?" he asked.

"Yes. He was in the military, too. Only he was a Marine."

A grin warmed her entire face, and her concern would comfort any man with half a hormone. He gathered it to him like an intoxicating drug. She shifted on the couch, and her scent touched his nostrils and caused arousal to sift through him like fine grains of sand. He yielded to the sensation.

Gina reached up and touched his face, her expression open and vulnerable. Surprise rocked through him when he detected somber worry in her face. "Let me see your eyes."

"What?" he asked, hearing gruffness in his tone.

"I'm no medical professional, but you were unconscious. Do you remember hitting your head?"

"No."

He let her see his eyes. A comforting sensation warmed his center as anxiety deepened her gaze. If she faked caring about him, she had one hell of an acting ability.

"What's the verdict?" he asked.

She released his chin. "Your pupils look equal." She shifted closer and tangled her fingers in the hair at the back of his head.

He narrowed his gaze on her. "What are you doing now?"

Her fingers slid through his hair. "Searching for an injury."

Ryan reached for her wrist and gently tugged her touch away. Heat tingled through his palm and fingers. "I don't need nursing. I need answers."

She sighed. "Where are you going to find them?"

He shook his head and met her gaze point-blank. "Hopefully, I'll find out something soon. If I don't, we're cooked."

"Like I said, we can contact Marcus Hyatt. He'll know what to do. He'll be worried about you."

He shook his head. "I'm okay."

Her cinnamon-shaded eyebrows quirked upward. "By the way, where is *your* cell phone? Since you joined the agency, you always have that weird-looking phone with you."

He wanted to curse vehemently, but didn't. "My I-Doc. Damned if I know. My boss will have my ass for losing it." He stared at the other cell phone on the coffee table and willed it to resurrect memories. Then his gaze cleared and he turned a smile on her. "Hey, at least I know what an I-Doc is."

Gina sat there, flabbergasted by the last few minutes of heart-exploding sensations. Being around him today was like dealing with dynamite. He'd thrown so many soul-deep, searching looks and electric-hot gazes her way, she was flushed, trembling, and tortured with a desire to launch into his arms and kiss him.

Tension and primitive strength bled off him in a wave. When he'd touched her face, she'd almost turned to useless mush on the spot. He must have real amnesia, because she didn't think the Ryan she knew would have asked her such a bold question about their sexual status.

Her heart did that silly pitter-patter thing. The one that never failed to happen when he tossed a full megawatt grin her way. "Don't smile at me that way. Entire legions of women fall at your feet whenever you do that. But I'm not one of them."

Surprise mixed with a smidgen of torture winged through his eyes. "Yeah? Why not?"

His question flummoxed her. "Why? Like I said, we're only friends."

He turned that full gaze upon her, the one that stopped traffic, caused hot flashes and guaranteed a thousand fantasies. "I say again. *Why* are we only friends?"

She didn't answer because she didn't have an explanation that satisfied her.

He cleared his throat. "You have a boyfriend? A husband?"

Soft and husky with sensual nuance, his voice demanded answers. Flustered, she stammered her answer. "Neither. You and I are just not…we're not each other's type."

Sure, keep on telling yourself that, Gina. If he isn't your type, why does your heart refuse to acknowledge the truth? Why doesn't your body stop reacting to him on an overwhelming level?

"What about me? Do I have a woman in my life?" he asked.

"No…I mean, not that you talk about. You might have a girlfriend, but if you do, you haven't mentioned her to me."

He nodded, and she wondered if her answer satisfied Ryan's suspicious frame of mind.

His right arm went over the back of the couch, and the intimacy took her off guard. A woman could become damned intoxicated by his nearness and unable to defend against a hunger too deep to name. Feelings bombarded her she didn't understand, almost as if they didn't belong to her. His nearness overran any harmony she'd erected and replaced it with fireworks. Her belly fluttered with clear attraction, her heartbeat sped up and she couldn't remain neutral. She inhaled deeply, trying to unravel the tight hold he kept on her libido. It didn't matter—Ryan Ahern had hijacked her gonads a long time ago, and she didn't know how to recover them.

His eyes, deeper than any ocean she could imagine, shone with clear doubt. His gaze darted from side to side and her heart sank. Even though his eyes had always held warmth for her, this strange combination of healthy interest in her and yet distrust ate a hole in her heart.

"You still don't totally trust me, do you?" she asked.

He didn't answer, his eyes mysterious and filled with secrets.

"Give me one good reason, other than the fact you don't remember me, that you shouldn't trust me?" she asked.

She walked on a tightrope while he allowed this information to cook in his cerebellum. "Rules are rules, and that's one thing for certain about SIA. You're not a part of the case."

"Didn't I become part of the case when you fell on my doorstep?"

"That's not the way it should work."

She sniffed. "What was I supposed to do? Leave you lying out there?"

Sharp intelligence always showed clearly in his eyes, and a clonk on the head hadn't changed anything. "Don't put words in my mouth, Gina."

Her name on his lips sparked a sensation of soul-deep connection, a vulnerable and electric vibe she wanted to explore. Had always wanted to understand. "So I'm supposed to stay fat, dumb and happy while you plot what to do next with a case you don't know about, without a memory, and with some so-called threat outside ready to make hamburger out of us?"

A laugh erupted from him, the sound clear, melodious and arousing. "That's dramatic, isn't it? Believe me, I want to think of a way to get you out of here."

His gaze warmed considerably, and it rocked her. Admiration. An exotic blend of appreciation and interest. Damn him. He made her want to smile and enjoy him the way she always had with the "other" Ryan. He disarmed her too easily.

"That's the old Ryan I know talking."

"And you like him better."

Okay, you're well armored, girl. Just tell him the truth like you always did before. "Of course. He trusted me."

He went silent, as if digesting this information. "Would you trust a man you'd just met?"

"You haven't just met me."

His eyebrows knitted together, and he switched gears. "I'm sorry I was harsh earlier. I was...off balance. Afraid."

Afraid?

That did it. Fragile anger shattered under his confession. She wanted to keep the wall erect and pretend he couldn't harm her ego or heart no matter what he did. Which, of course, was a blatant lie.

Tiny lines formed between his eyebrows. His grim expression summoned her to probe into his psyche. To fish out the secrets he couldn't tell her. She wanted to break down his defenses in a perverse desire to see him helpless in front of her.

Oh, shit. She'd gone around the bend for the last time. Time to forget sex and revisit what mattered.

"This amnesia worries me," she said. "You need to see a doctor."

One corner of his well-formed mouth moved into a sinful, delicious smile that came and went in a flash. "Are you always this motherly?"

Just with you. "I'd be this way with anyone who fell on my doorstep with amnesia and maybe hidden injuries. But no one in their right mind would ever call me motherly."

He smirked. "I didn't know it was an insult."

Thunder ripped the heavens as rain continued to pound the cabin. He leaned against the couch back, wrapped in annoyance and radiating potency she couldn't define in a few words. She'd always admired his self-containment, his ability to control his emotions when need be.

No, what you really want, at least once in your life, is to see Ryan lose it over something.

She realized that other than the time he'd defended her from that McDougal bully, she'd never seen him snarl, shout or otherwise come unglued.

Maybe that explained why the unusual intensity in his eyes made her hyperaware of him and made her want things from him more outrageous than the fantasies running through her head late at night before she fell asleep. She'd seen his physical reaction to her earlier and it rocked her sensibilities. She'd ached deep inside as she realized he found her attractive. Oh, yes. He'd had one big hard-on because of her, and the knowledge stunned her.

She didn't want an unclear relationship with Ryan, but since he'd arrived today she noted how the relationship changed. At least on his side. When he'd walked toward her with that prowling, feral stare, she knew something altered between them…big time.

"Call this Marcus Hyatt," Ryan said out of nowhere.

She picked up her cell phone and called Marcus at home.

A female voice answered on the second ring. Gina smiled. "Hi, Tara. This is Gina."

"Gina!" Tara's warm enthusiasm always made her feel welcome. "It's been a while since we talked. I was telling Marcus we should have you over for dinner soon. You and Ryan."

"Sounds good. Tara, something very serious has come up. I need Marcus' help."

"Of course. What's wrong?" Tara's pleasant voice turned serious.

Gina stood and started pacing where Ryan had left off not long ago. "Actually, it's Ryan who needs his help the most." Gina explained to her friend what happened. "He doesn't remember me, or Marcus or you. But there are a lot of things he does recall."

After her initial surprise and concern, Tara said she'd get Marcus, who was in the garage doing car work.

Once Marcus took the phone, explanations went quickly. Marcus' voice turned sharp. "Is he injured?"

She almost blurted that she was worried as hell about Ryan, because she was. "Not badly. At least he won't admit to it. But I think he must have been hit on the head or fell. That's why he has the amnesia."

"Or he had some other mental trauma."

"He insists he's not hurt, but he was unconscious."

"He's damned stubborn." Irony filled Marcus's voice. "Maybe I can refresh his memory."

"I'll hand him off to you."

She gave Ryan the phone. Ryan's brows knitted together as he frowned.

"She says my name is Ryan Ahern, but I don't recognize the name," Ryan spoke into the phone, "and she says I know you."

As the conversation continued, Ryan explained how an entity or beast had chased him. While the concept sounded crazy, even to her, she trusted Ryan implicitly. If he said Martians had landed, she'd believe him.

As lightning sliced through the heavens and wind gusts caused tall pines to whip back and forth, Gina could almost imagine she'd been caught in a horror movie and didn't realize it yet. When she awakened this morning, she never imagined the unwanted adventure lying around the corner. That the escapade would feature the man she'd fantasized about for ten years...well, that was almost too much. Seclusion with Ryan in less dangerous circumstances sounded romantic and intriguing. This situation challenged her confidence, her sense of safety.

Safety? Was she losing her edge? She'd jumped out of airplanes, parasailed, skied on some of the most perilous slopes and never allowed herself to fear.

Until today.

Okay, she'd never encountered an amnesia victim before. What she knew about it could fill a thimble. Sighing, she turned away and headed to the kitchen on the other side of the wide-open living area. She needed a dose of hot tea.

While she heard tidbits of Ryan's conversation with Marcus, part of her didn't want to know the contents. She'd rather keep it out of her peaceful world, the one that included writing like a madwoman and achieving dozens of finished pages.

Whom was she kidding?

No, a desire to write lay in tatters while Ryan tromped around the cabin, bristling with high-gauge energy. As he talked to Marcus, he prowled the far side of the room like a caged lion at unease with captivity.

"The what?" Ryan asked. "The Shadow Realm? What the hell is that?"

Indeed. She wondered too.

Ryan stopped at the fireplace mantel. He stared at pictures of her friends and their family. Two young, healthy people with a two-year-old boy and a ten-year-old girl. She'd looked at those photos often since she'd arrived here, and longing stirred within. She couldn't define the gnawing feeling, so she channeled it into her writing. Her friends' situation represented something idyllic she could only visualize, but perhaps never know.

The teakettle banged against the gas burner too hard as she set it down. He glanced at her. She smiled feebly. Nerves tightened her shoulders, and she groaned at the sudden pain. She felt his eyes on her again, but didn't look up. She'd tensed, muscles in her upper arms and shoulders so rock-hard she felt she might snap in two from the pressure. She wanted to roar that he didn't have any right to disrupt her quiet time away from reality. She dared another glance at him, and sure enough, he was staring at her. A fine, low stirring coiled in her belly and sent warning signals directly to her brain. She must have lost her mind from sometime this morning until now. How could she find him so irresistible when their lives might be in danger from some unknown source?

She realized her internal dialogue forced her to miss everything else he'd said to Marcus.

"Hello? Marcus, you still there?" When Ryan apparently didn't get an answer, he glared at the phone. "Fuck. *D'anan don diabhal!*"

The Irish Gaelic slipped from his lips with the swirling, flowing accent that made the language sound so mysterious and beautiful. She'd heard him utter the Gaelic curse that meant "damn you" on a couple of occasions. She winced. Was this the warrior personality at work she'd never seen until today? A man of hard, ruthless edges?

Ryan turned away from the mantel. He strode toward the kitchen side with confidence in every step. The vigor and confidence coming from him put her composure to shame. If she'd lost her memory like this, she'd feel fear down to the marrow. Admiration gained strength inside her.

She retrieved two large cartoon character mugs from the cabinets. He put the cell phone down on the dark blue granite countertop. Glad for the barrier between them, she waited for him to speak.

"I lost the call. Line went dead," he said.

She frowned and didn't say anything.

"Arty the clown and his sidekick Pucky," he said suddenly as he looked at the mugs.

"That's right."

"Children's mugs?"

She shrugged. "I figured we could use some levity."

He grinned, and the superheated arousal blossoming inside her rolled the thermometer into high mercury. She'd never experienced an explosive reaction to Ryan quite like this before. Gina pressed her hands flat on the cool counter surface.

"I'm worried," she said suddenly to sidetrack her mind away from crazy attraction.

"About what?"

"This whole situation. It's weird."

"I know." A sigh came from deep in his chest. "But we'll figure this out."

"Marcus couldn't jog your memory?"

"No."

"Did he have any advice for what we should do?"

"He didn't get to tell me much before the line went dead." He tried redial on the phone. "There's a message saying all circuits are busy or not operating at this time."

She shook her head. "Cell phones are unreliable out here with the mountains surrounding the area. I'm surprised you could get a call out in the first place."

"Marcus suggested an extraction team come in and take me off the case since my memory is half shot. I agreed, even though I don't like the idea of failing on the case."

"You didn't fail. You're injured."

He grunted. "Any extraction team will take a while to arrive. Crappy weather has created major problems up and down the mountain range. Roads have washed out in many places. We're on our own for now."

He scrubbed a hand through his hair, and she wanted to reach over and feel those silky, thick strands between her fingers again.

"Aren't you worried about the creature?" she asked. "Then again, you never gave much credence to that sort of stuff anyway."

His expression turned wry. "I remember briefings about the cases SIA handles, including the supernatural ones. I might be skeptical, but I'm not a total disbeliever."

"That's news to me. You used to be very cynical about anything paranormal and you'd tease me if I mentioned it."

He tilted his head to the side. "And you say we've known each other over ten years?"

"Yes." A pang of sorrow pierced her. "Maybe not as well as I thought."

"Everyone changes."

She sighed. "You're right. There are some things you don't know about me either."

Again, warmth sparked and flared in his eyes until she felt enclosed in the glow. "How well do we know each other? You say we're only friends, but have we ever dated?"

A flush filled her face. "No."

"Why?"

Ryan put his hands on his hips, the world in his eyes. God, she could barely stand to look at him. Not because of defect or dislike, but for the bold assessment that insinuated they had touched, kissed, loved in some cherished fashion she knew never occurred in reality.

Oh, she'd dreamed it often enough.

"Gina?" he asked softly.

"Don't you think the answer to that should wait until we get out of this situation?" His gaze captured hers and held it. So he wanted to stare her down, eh? Well, she wouldn't play that game with him. "What else did you find out from Marcus?"

He swallowed hard, his Adam's apple bobbing. "He repeated what you told me already. Then he explained that I went out on this case with veteran agent Jimmy Fowler." He placed both hands on the counter and hung his head. He stared at the counter. "I don't remember him. Our assignment involved tracking a creature with extraordinary abilities. Something from a place called the Shadow Realm."

Tara had told her Marcus had a mysterious life with SIA, but Gina never imagined the secret world could bother her.

He glanced around. "Is there a basement or cellar in this place? Somewhere we can lock up and hold down the fort if danger gets closer?"

She shivered at the notion and rubbed her arms. "They've got an extra bedroom in a small storage cellar. It has some stuff we could pile against the door if we needed it."

"Marcus said there are weather cells coming our way. Rain is forecast heavily into tonight."

She glanced at her wristwatch. "It's only two o'clock."

"Yep."

"We could drive out."

"Not advised. If we are stuck on Baker Ridge we'll be in a world of hurt. That road is treacherous."

She scowled. "You remember that?"

"Yeah, I do. I remember certain things…just not everything and just not what brought me here in the first place." He went silent and thoughtful, as if he might crack the hard shell around his memories to discover the truth.

"There's a weather radio in the master bedroom," she said.

"I'll get it. Where is it in the room?"

"The top shelf of the walk-in closet."

He departed, his confidence keeping her fears more at bay.

As Ryan left, the teakettle screamed. Gina turned and used a potholder to lift it from the stove and pour boiling water into the mugs. She took frustration and confusion out on her tea bag, dunking it relentlessly in and out of the steaming water.

She was forced to acknowledge a glowing, fierce need that demanded attention like nothing else she'd encountered. She drew a deep breath and released it slowly. *Regroup.* What did she know?

Some crazy monster lurked out there in the woods. The man she had powerful feelings for was stuck in this house with her for hours. She could take this as an ideal situation where she could spend time with Ryan. Alternatively, she could keep her sanity and take heed of their dire state.

He returned quickly with the weather radio. Within minutes, they had a full weather report from Denver that confirmed what Marcus had told Ryan.

Resigned, she decided to give it the old college try. "Okay, if we aren't getting out of here soon, what do we do to defend ourselves from this...this entity?" She gave a soft, derisive laugh. "I can't believe I'm thinking or saying this."

"You know the SIA deals with paranormal threats."

"Not exclusively."

"Most of the time."

She nodded. "All right. But a supernatural being was chasing you? It seems too absurd."

"Maybe it's improbable to you because if you give it credence you'll be afraid. Is that it?"

Anxiety rippled through her. "No. I have faith in you as an agent. But even you're not invincible. No one is."

His eyes narrowed and her gaze snagged on his sinfully long lashes. Her stomach collected butterflies and her heart picked up speed. She thought she detected a flickering of the man she'd always known. Warmer, concerned and curious.

"I don't suppose you'd have that faith if you didn't trust me to extract us from this in one piece," he said.

Her throat tightened and her voice went a little raspy. "Of course."

"Even though I've lost part of my memory?"

"You're still the same man I've known for over ten years."

Did she believe that? Not exactly. This dangerous, on-edge man bristling with expectancy vexed her. She felt an excitement and overruling intoxication that eradicated her common sense. She wanted to reach across the counter, cup his face and reassure him.

Kiss him until he recollected the times they'd shared. But if he regained his memory, he might turn away...say he wanted nothing more intimate than friendship.

So? She'd be right back where she'd always been. A good buddy.

His large hands spread out on the counter surface. She turned to the pantry and put away the tea box. When she swiveled back to him, concern shimmered in his eyes. She snatched up her mug for a satisfying gulp of tea and stared at him.

"We need to barricade in the basement until this is over. I'm not taking any chances with your safety. Something in my gut tells me that's the only way to protect you," he said.

His eyes blazed into hers until molten feelings threatened to bubble to the surface. Whether she wanted it or not, his protectiveness blitzed her courage to resist him and the raw, pent-up emotions inside her. The chemistry between them ensnared her as much as his enthralling attention. Words tumbled through her mind. Gratification and amazement. Safety and uncertainty. She wasn't sure she understood the attentiveness and intimacy his touches, his looks conveyed.

"Do you trust me?" he asked.

She smiled. "Of course. I told you that earlier."

One corner of his sinful mouth curved. "I guess I needed to hear it again. I wouldn't blame you if you didn't."

His humility mixed with vulnerability surprised her. She'd never known Ryan to show uncertainty. On the contrary, his battle-hardened psyche often resembled a cool, almost emotionless façade when he wanted it that way. While she'd always admired his vigor, this smidgen of modesty and need awakened smoldering feelings. Some women would have read his admittance as weakness. She saw it as a new Ryan. One she liked even more.

"You're a fascinating guy, Ryan. I don't think I'd ever get tired of trying to decipher you."

His mouth hardened into a thinner line. The old Ryan returned. "Whatever is out there, we'll survive this." He turned away and looked around the massive living area. "Where's the entrance to the basement?"

She rounded the kitchen island and headed toward the other end of the kitchen. "Not where you'd expect. It's right here against this wall."

She patted a dark wood doorway that matched the other cabinets and nestled in one corner.

He strode over. "Damn. That's clever. They wanted it to look like the pantry, I'll bet."

"That occurred to me too, but I never thought much about it."

He examined the other wooden doors in the kitchen. He twisted the polished brass doorknob on the basement door and it held tight. "I hope you have the key for this."

"It's in this drawer." She rummaged through one of the kitchen drawers. "Here."

She handed him the small key ring.

She didn't try to squelch the unusual exhilaration inside her as he opened the door. They stood at the top of the stairs to the basement and Ryan's gaze centered on the heavy door construction. "This is made to look like wood, but it's steel. Your friends wanted this cellar for protection. Not storm protection, either."

Suspicion centered on his handsome face, and her impatience won out. "Don't look like that."

His gaze narrowed. "Like what?"

"As if you think my friends have a weird motivation for having a storm cellar. A lot of people do."

He shook his head. "Not like this. Many people put together shelters for bombs or tornados. This is more secure. Look at these locks. It's for keeping something out."

"You haven't even looked inside yet."

An indulgent grin spread over his mouth. She couldn't recall the last time she'd experienced this out of balance sensation with either a man or a situation. She didn't give in to unfettered or unreasonable emotion.

"Have you been down here?" he asked.

"Well, no. I guess they never saw a need to show me, and I never asked."

"They told you where the key was at least." He flipped the light switch on just inside the doorway. "Let's take a look."

While she felt odd invading her friends' personal spaces, she followed him. Intuition told her Ryan might be correct about the cellar. Why else would her friends have ignored showing her this room? Did they harbor a secret?

As they clunked down the wide wood steps, she said, "Maybe they have a good reason for keeping this place under wraps."

"Such as?"

"Personal reasons."

He laughed softly, and the husky chuckle sent frissons of heat down into her belly. "Like what? A sex-toy drawer? Or a porno flick collection?"

She made a scoffing noise at the same time her face heated violently. "Ryan."

He laughed softly again, and the liquid sound sent pulsating heat flooding through her. As a writer she imagined things most people didn't, and a vision of a drawer filled with dildos, condoms and butt plugs popped into her head. Had he ever used a sex toy? Used one on a woman? Her imagination almost sent her gonads into atomic meltdown.

"I can read your mind," he said.

Chapter Four

"What?" Gina's voice almost squeaked.

"You're wondering if you can stand to be in the basement with me for a few hours until help comes."

She cleared her throat, relieved he hadn't really read her mind. God, she didn't know if that would be embarrassing or an amazing turn-on. Emotions rolled together, a soup filled with one part fear and one part curiosity.

Oh, hell. I'll never get that picture out of my head now. Ryan holding a sex toy. Ryan pushing a sex toy inside me. Ryan sliding a butt plug into me ever so slowly.

A huge flush filled her face, and she hoped he didn't notice it.

They reached the bottom of the stairs, and she managed to waylay her out-of-control fantasies. He turned just as she missed the last two steps. A startled gasp left her as involuntary panic leapt into her. His arms caught her against his chest. Her hands landed on his shoulders.

A lopsided grin touched his mouth, and his arms tightened around her back and waist. Smoldering and fierce, his gaze was dauntless. "Are you doing this on purpose?"

"What?" she managed to gasp out.

"Falling into my arms. This is the second time."

The rock-solid muscle touching Gina sent her brain into short circuit. Her breath fluttered erratically. Embarrassment mixed with a desire to stay enveloped in powerful arms and drink in his enticing scent. She dared a glance into his melting eyes. Swirls of electricity danced and sparked inside her.

She pushed out words with effort. "Don't flatter yourself, Ryan."

His gaze changed from amused to liquid hot, and in a millisecond, his cock hardened against her belly. Her lips parted as rising tension whipped around them. Hunger centered low in her loins and stirred a frantic fire inside her mind and body. Her gaze lowered from his searching eyes to his mouth. The mouth she'd never kissed but longed to explore for so many years. Frantic desire flooded her senses.

"We don't have time for this." His voice went husky and deepened, and his arms kept her braced against every inch of highly conditioned male body. "We need to haul supplies in here asap and get locked down."

His sensible words penetrated the sensual fog in her brain, but his reasonable dismissal also pricked her feminine ego. "Let me go."

He released her, and part of her regretted losing his secure embrace.

She turned away from speculation to view the basement. "This isn't bad for a storm cellar."

"I'll say." He paced off the comfortably sized room.

About twice as large as the master bedroom upstairs, the area divided into a bedroom section, small eating area and a workstation. A checked white and blue comforter lay over a brass queen-sized bed. Two bed stands with simple brass lamps graced either side of the bed. An inexpensive, light-colored pine chest of drawers stood nearby. A door on one side of the room was probably a closet.

They moved about the room, navy carpet muffling their footsteps as they inspected. On the other side of the room sat a tan-colored desk and chair along with a radio on a table, a large chest along one wall, a small refrigerator and a huge black safe.

"They must keep their important papers and valuables here," she said, reaching out to touch the safe.

Ryan opened the fridge. "There's water in here, but we'd better bring down food."

They made a few trips down to the basement, arms loaded with blankets, extra pillows, food and additional provisions. Gina started to feel claustrophobic in the windowless room. Vents allowed air-conditioning or heating inside, and she had a control to regulate airflow, but unease crawled inside and wouldn't leave her alone.

"I don't know about this," she said as he headed for the top of the stairs.

"Got your purse and the cell phone?"

"Yes."

"Have everything else you'll need?"

She started up the stairs. "My laptop."

She brushed by his body and his warmth fried her ability to think straight. She snatched her laptop and other computer implements off the dining table and made her way downstairs. Nervous energy pumped in her veins and angry butterflies did cartwheels in her stomach.

Chill. I just need to chill. I can't afford to become so nervous I make myself ill. We'll be safe in the basement.

What she understood intellectually didn't seem to make a dent emotionally.

"What are you thinking?" he asked once they'd loaded everything downstairs and stood in the kitchen. "You look worried. Everything will be all right."

She shivered and rubbed her hands up and down her arms again in nervous habit. "How can it be? We're trapped and there is some weird…something out there." She pointed to the windows.

He came up behind her and squeezed her shoulders. With slow precision, he kneaded the tense muscles in her shoulders. "You worry too much."

Damn, she hated when people told her she shouldn't feel a certain way. She turned on him and broke his grip. "Oh, do I? Well, pardon me if hearing that some crazy-assed Bigfoot is after you doesn't just fall right off my radar. Besides, what do you know about me? You can't even remember our friendship or the last ten years of your life."

He didn't have the decency to look stunned by her outburst. His implacable male stoicism stayed in place.

"You're right. There's a lot I need to learn about you. Things I want to know." Warm and gentle, his voice took her off guard.

Oh, good. She couldn't be pissed at him if he kept this up. Mr. Concerned. Mr. Accommodating. The Ryan she thought she knew the last decade had morphed into a tough but amazingly tender guy.

"I'm thinking this is the weirdest situation I've ever been in, but it's probably standard operating procedure for you," she said.

He placed his hands on his hips. "How do you know?"

What did she know about his life? "You're right. I don't know what you do when you come back from a mission." She scratched her forehead. "Do you fall onto the bed and sleep the minute you get home? Unpack? Take a shower? Get a whiskey or a glass of wine?" She gave a small, sarcastic laugh. "Maybe I don't understand you at all. Maybe the last decade has been an illusion."

He seemed to digest this information without flinching. "You're angry. Why?"

Her voice shook. "Because you've done this transformation and it...it scares me."

He nodded and watched her, seemingly digesting the information. He scrubbed his chin with his hand, and said, "By the way. Where the hell do I live?"

"On the outskirts of Denver. You have a nice-sized older home."

"Pets?"

She tried to imagine him snuggling a kitten and couldn't. "No. You're not home enough. I could see you with a bullmastiff or a regal German Shepherd, though. They'd suit you. Or maybe a Rottweiler. It would go with your Roman centurion persona."

He let out a bark of laughter. "Roman centurion?"

She blushed. She'd almost given away her deepest fantasies about him. Without a doubt, he'd look fantastic with that armor, that short skirt-like thing showing his muscular legs.

She gulped. "Never mind."

"Oh, no. You're not stalling. What did you mean?"

She struggled for a quick explanation. "Rottweilers are a very old breed. They go back at least to Roman times. I can picture you as a Roman soldier. It fits you. Brawny. Tough. Battle-rough and horny."

Oh shit, Gina. You didn't just say that.

By the slight grin on his mouth, she'd used her out-loud voice. "Horny? Well, I know from my reaction to you that I sure as hell am horny."

Oh God. Yes, his reaction to her earlier would have cemented the indisputable fact if she didn't already know.

His tongue flicked over his bottom lip. "Have you been to my house?"

Flummoxed by his change of direction, she almost stuttered. "More than once. You've had parties there before."

Skepticism flickered in his eyes. "I'm a bleedin' party animal?"

"No way. I've never seen you drunk. You're too restrained for that. And other than your job, I wouldn't call you extroverted. You have a small circle of friends rather than a ton of acquaintances."

"Do I have hobbies?"

She nodded. "You used to play the bodhran. It's a traditional drum in Ireland."

"I know what it is." He repeated the word, this time sounding it out in Gaelic. "BOWR-awn. I don't recall playing it."

"You haven't played it much lately. Once you joined the army and then the SIA, that seemed to wipe out much of your leisure time."

Ryan's eyes clouded, as if he didn't know what to believe. "And you're telling me we've never hooked up?"

Her lips parted in surprise at his insistence. "Why would I continue lying to you? I told you, we've never had a romantic relationship."

He grinned. "Romantic, eh? What about just sex?"

Just sex. A flush heated up her entire body. Considering her penchant for adventure, why *hadn't* she just hooked up with him? Sex with Ryan would be the ultimate knee-buckling, mind-blowing adventure.

"God!" She stomped out of the kitchen, frustration eating at her. "I never knew you had such a dirty, one-track mind, Ryan Ahern."

"Yeah, I'm trying to find out what makes me tick."

Oh, she could play the outraged one, but his blunt honesty today refreshed her. "You know, maybe you're right. I've all but given up on knowing you on a deeper level. I've always been assured of your undying friendship, but I never expected to someday discover these nuances and angles about you. It's nutty and yet weirdly fascinating."

He threw back his head and laughed, and the tension in her shoulders eased. Other than some ribald jokes they'd shared and some comments he'd made here and there, she didn't know squat about his almost nonexistent sex life. Though she'd certainly wondered on more than one occasion.

"You think sex is dirty?" he asked.

She turned back to him. "No. You seem obsessed with pressing an issue between us that doesn't exist. Maybe I should hit you on the head and see if the old Ryan returns."

He stalked toward her, invading her space. "And the old Ryan never asked you about sex or feelings?"

"Well..." She swallowed hard. "No."

Looking puzzled, he didn't press her any further on that particular subject. "Do I date?"

She snorted a soft laugh. "I don't know. I doubt it."

He looked indignant. "Why?"

"Think about it. Your lifestyle isn't conducive to maintaining a dating relationship." Gina trained her gaze on the landscape outside, flinching when sheet lightning blazed through the dark clouds and electricity crackled with a loud boom. "Because you wouldn't be in this job if you didn't need the thrill. And that type of exhilaration doesn't come from staying a homebody and the normal things in life."

"It's a nasty job, but someone has to do it."

"Yes, but this job of yours isn't for everyone, Ryan. It's dangerous, hard work." Gina heard the derision in her voice and wished she'd restrained it.

"You don't sound happy about it."

"Am I happy about you going out there and getting your ass shot at on a regular basis? No."

"That's a bit theatrical, don't you think?"

She shrugged. "How do I know? I can only guess at what you experience on a mission. Marcus has given me hints, and so have you, but most of the time you keep the sneaky Pete stories to yourself."

He grunted. "Sneaky Pete. Now that's a saying I do remember."

"You told it to me."

He smiled sardonically. "Uh-huh." They went silent for a moment before he said, "You're not happy about my dangerous missions, are you?"

With nonchalance, she waved one hand. "It's your neck in a noose, Ryan. I've known since the first day I met you that you were your own man. A woman wouldn't get in the way of your ambitions. That would cramp your style."

"Shit," he said with conviction. "You make me sound like an unfeeling bastard."

"Part of you is. Sensitivity and empathy don't necessarily figure into combat, now do they? Especially not when you're chasing ghosts and goblins around the world."

He edged closer, his focused attention wearing away at her composure. How did other women resist him? Or did they?

"Have you tried?" he asked as if he'd read her mind. "Did you want to be with me, and I let you down?"

Holy shit. Wanting to be with him? Oh, yes. Had the amnesia completely opened the tight-lipped man she used to know?

"Have you ever been jealous of me with another woman?" he asked before she could speak.

Surprise spiked high inside her. Imagining hordes of adoring young woman flocking around him, wanting his sexual potency...that didn't surprise her. No, it ate at her gut with a sharp fork. Poking. Prodding. Demanding she acknowledge feelings she'd hoped she'd packed away. Okay, so she couldn't ignore him. He stood too near, his body heat radiating toward her and his masculine energy generating arousal inside her.

She felt his scrutiny and dared to glance his way. Sure enough, he threw her an I'm-the-tough-soldier gaze that said two things that stirred her most primitive feminine instincts. Like it or not, the take-no-prisoners, I'd-like-to-fuck-you expression on his face hit her full force. Her nipples peaked tightly, and her breath quickened. Heat swirled in her belly and warmth penetrated deep between her legs.

Did she imagine that devouring, yearning glint in his eyes?

Oh, wow. Maybe not.

"Gina? What are you afraid of?"

She moved away before he could shift any closer and went to stand near the huge front windows. Rain lashed against them with fury. Eerie wind squealed around the house, adding to the bizarre scenario. Fall was coming soon, but summer kept an unyielding grip on this mountain retreat. She stood under the high peak of the cabin roof and closed her eyes. Maybe if she stood there long enough, perspective would come back and she wouldn't feel this soul-wrenching confusion around Ryan.

Why was she afraid? She'd wanted him close for so long, and now he approached her, acted as if he desired involvement, she wouldn't let him near.

He sighed. "Damn, you're making me forget the mission."

Anger blotted out the haze of need she felt. "Oh, really? If you're so worried about the mission, then you should do whatever you can to accomplish it, right? If you need to leave then do it."

Frowning, he approached until they stood a few inches apart. Her breath caught at his proximity. She fixated on Ryan's stern, well-carved mouth before chancing a look into his eyes. Determination and stubbornness burned there. So did a quality she didn't dare hope for—a heat that said he liked being this near.

"I can see you out there," she said impulsively. "In the elements, dodging the bad guys and bullets. There's desert around you and the wind is blowing, and you have some sort of automatic weapon slung over your shoulder, the wind is picking up and sand is shifting." She sighed. "It looks good on you. It's what you do."

"Did. I'm not in the military anymore."

She put her hands out to her sides in a so-what gesture. "This job isn't that much different, is it? I've heard a rumor there's even an elite band of warriors...former regular military or recruited fresh, that work for the SIA. They go on black ops. That's the sort of thing you should do, Ryan. You need the adrenaline, the thrill."

She couldn't berate him, because she enjoyed an on-the-edge feeling now and again herself.

"This storm is kicking our ass and taking names. We aren't going anywhere until this storm breaks and Marcus gets a team in here." His voice turned liquid and husky. "I'm not leaving you here. Anything could happen."

Independence flirted with the overriding satisfaction that at least the old Ryan appeared to remember how much he'd cared for her. Longing made her wistful for another scenario. Ryan lying naked on that big bed in the master bedroom. The fireplace flickering with warmth and sensual promise. Her belly stirred low and deep. She ached for him.

"You're some kind of man, Ryan. Always looking out for me."

"Always?" he asked.

A piercing howl erupted around the cabin. Gina started violently. "What the hell was that?"

Recognition darted into his eyes. He pulled the weapon from his back waistband. "If it's what I think it is, we don't have long."

Another wail, a war cry and hungry beast in one, resounded around the large cabin. A heavy thump landed on the doorway, and she jumped.

He stepped in front of her, weapon ready and clutched in both hands. "Get into the basement." His voice was rough and commanding. "Now."

"But—"

"Do it."

"What about you?"

"Right behind you. Run! Now!"

Fear bolted through her as she sprinted for the basement door. Glass shattered as a growl pierced her ears and filled her soul with heart-shaking panic.

Ryan's rapid footsteps echoed behind her. "Hurry!"

She hurtled down the stairs. The heavy door slammed behind her, locks engaging rapidly. At the bottom of the steps she turned and saw Ryan secure the last lock.

Heavy weight slammed against the door at the same time a bloodcurdling cry erupted. Tense and shaking, she couldn't move. Heart thumping a staccato beat, she shook from within.

Ryan stood halfway up the stairs, weapon trained on the door. Rapid-fire thumping against the steel and unearthly screeches made the hair on her arms prickle. Her chest heaved up and down with fear, her palms sweaty and her stomach pitching back and forth with the worst fear she'd ever experienced.

Then the lights went out.

Chapter Five

"Ryan!"

Gina heard his footsteps taking the rest of the stairs, and the mad beat of angry fists continuing an assault on the door.

Rooted to the spot, she tensed and waited.

"Gina?" Ryan's reassuring voice, jagged with concern, reached her a moment before his hand found her arm and he pulled her away from the staircase.

The pounding on the door continued. "Oh my God," she whispered, unable to believe what had just happened. "What is it?"

"You'll never believe it."

"Sure I will." Her voice trembled. "Humor me."

"Shhh."

"I can't believe this is happening." She knew her voice wobbled, but at this point, she didn't care.

"You're a writer. You have the imagination. Believe it."

She wanted to smack him, but her jarred nerves wouldn't allow anything but stunned trepidation to snake through her veins.

"Easy," he said as he rubbed her arm. "It's going to be okay."

Relief filled Gina as his strong arms surrounded her and brought her hard into his big body. As the cacophony went on, the creature's wrath evident with every shriek and batter of its fist, she buried her face against his shoulder and waited. She crumpled his T-shirt in her fingers, clutching on to the one security she possessed.

His breath puffed against her hair as he held her securely, his exertion evident. Other than his quicker breathing, he didn't give indication of fear. What she wouldn't do to have that immovable strength.

The pounding abated, the pissed mumblings and growling diminishing. Within a few seconds, heavy footsteps marked the creature's retreat. Her fingers continued to grasp at his T-shirt. Her heartbeat eased, her stomach stopped flip-flopping, and her breathing slowed. Ryan cupped the back of her head, his other arm bracing her about the waist. Within his powerful embrace, her fear eased.

When she shivered, he murmured, "It's all right."

"I've never been so scared. God, you must think I'm a wimp."

"Hell, no. You're one brave lady."

She gave a watery sniff and a laugh. "Yeah, right. Is that your way of thanking me for not letting out with a girly scream?"

A soft laugh rumbled up from his chest, and the vibration under her fingers felt wonderful. "Yep."

"You know how to compliment a woman, Ryan."

"My pleasure."

His grip didn't loosen, his hands starting a gentle smoothing motion over her back.

"If you tell me that was some rabid Bigfoot, I think I'm ready to believe you now."

"I don't remember what it looks like, but I sure as hell remember that scream and that weird roaring sound."

"What would I have done if you hadn't been here?"

"Yelled like a banshee and barricaded in here just like we are now."

Reaction hit her, a shivering that attacked her body as she realized the implications. "No. I think I'd be dead. If you weren't here..."

"Hey." His big hands moved over her back then coasted up her shoulders and neck to cup her face. "Don't shortchange yourself."

Two tears escaped and dripped down her cheeks. The generator safety lights turned on and gave the room a pale, almost sepia glow.

Embarrassed by the tears, she released her death grip on his shirt and wiped at her face. "Ignore me. I'm pathetic."

Instead of doing as she suggested, his gaze glowed with slow-burning, hungry need. "Are you kidding me? It's impossible to ignore you." A smoky, husky nuance entered his voice. "You're way too much trouble."

A slow grin touched her mouth, but the serious glow in his eyes erased her appreciation for his humor.

"Is that an insult or a compliment?" she asked.

"Mmm."

His noncommittal male grunt came a few seconds before he lowered his head and his mouth touched hers. Warm and searching, his lips caressed with gentle urgency. Molding and shaping, the sensation of his mouth brushing hers sent shivers of tingling longing into her breasts. Her nipples hardened into beads, aching as his chest crushed hers. Heat darted into her lower belly, moist need gathering as arousal demanded attention. Ensnared by the sudden kiss, she didn't respond or move. Her mind did a happy dance, a wild, heart-shaking recognition that she'd wanted this for months. Hell, for years.

Then she woke up to reality. Though her arms were trapped against him, she shifted, and he loosened his grip. She palmed his broad shoulders then slipped her arms around his neck.

Sounds magnified. Their breaths mingled, and she heard his breathing grow harsher. Her lips responded to his sliding, gliding, relentless pressure. He explored and cajoled, the kiss not yet ravenous, not yet demanding everything from her. She plunged her fingers into his hair to feel the glossy, thick strands graze and slide across her fingers. She inhaled deeply his intoxicating scent, the masculine aroma sending wild spirals of awakening through her stomach and lower. Her body moistened, preparing for a first male thrust, a demand to enter her body and teach it a rhythm she'd never experienced.

She'd had two lovers before, but this was…this was more. Hotter. Deeper. Faster. So agonizingly forceful. If he made love to her, it would drive those two men from her memory forever.

Opening her mouth to fit more closely to his kiss, she felt his arms tighten. Her breasts crushed against his chest. Down below, his cock turned into a spike of male command. A pillar against her belly, his erection heralded what would come, what she wanted with a shuddering realization that rocked her to the core.

A soft moan left her throat as his tongue thrust into her mouth. *Yes, yes, yes.* She'd dreamed of this. Longed for his deep, unrelenting kiss for what seemed an eternity. Thrust after thrust mimicked the rhythm she longed for between her legs. She knew a fierce, unrelenting drive to complete her most primal needs. Now that he held her, nothing in her imagination prepared her for her sharp response. Right there, right then, she wanted him. Tortured by a tension she couldn't wait to release, she moved. Her nipples prickled tightly as she whimpered and tasted him the way he tasted her. Heaven rippled around her, through her as if the fire igniting inside her might choose to erupt like a long-dormant volcano.

His cock's steady pressure against her stomach made her crave a conclusion, and made her desire his thickness driving hard and deep between her legs. Wetness gathered and moistened her folds as an ache grew in her pussy clear to her womb. She shifted and his hands cupped her ass. Palming her ass cheeks, he squeezed. The steady rasp of his tongue over hers startled soft moans from her. Her tongue brushed with small licks along his until he kissed voraciously, a creature unable to hold back and wanting no resistance. Her fingers plunged into his hair again, and the silky texture tormented her sensitive fingers.

She ached inside with a feral intensity that begged for detonation. They needed this moment to banish pent-up stress and an overwhelming passion denied for too long.

Ryan thought he'd died and found nirvana. Battle lust or not, he ate at her mouth like a starving man. His cock hardened painfully against her, and he wanted to find the nearest wall and fuck her standing up. His body and mind pulsed out a continuous desire.

Take her. Now. Now. Now.

Mindless, he kissed her once, twice, three times. Each kiss came at a fresh angle, each hot breath and needy rasp for oxygen recognition of how close to the edge he'd come. When the beast crashed into the cabin, his single thought screamed that he must take Gina to safety. Holding her in his arms brought a million memories to the surface, all of them ramming into his brain for access. He shoved them away and enjoyed. Whatever it took, he would give her pleasure and remove the horrendous fear that brought tears to her eyes and a shaking to her limbs so savage he ached with fear for her.

Her mouth tasted of tea, her tongue hot and silky. His body reacted with primitive fervor, his hands cupping her round, beautiful ass cheeks and squeezing. Her small hands pushed into his hair and caressed him, then moved down to palm his stubble-rough face. Anticipation speared straight to his gut. Blood pounded in his ears, his pulse rushing through his veins and his skin so hot he might melt. Her fingers dug into his T-shirt, twisted it, released it, then squeezed his shoulders in a relentless search.

If he'd harbored any doubt earlier that she wanted him, that changed permanently. He broke the kiss and buried his face in the side of her neck.

Her breath puffed out in a great draught. "Ryan."

"Mmm." He licked along the sensitive notch between neck and shoulder. "You taste wonderful."

Gina shivered as his sweet words, husky with need, pierced her ears. His touch set her on fire. She gasped as he peppered her neck with tender kisses. His hands coasted everywhere, caressing her shoulders, her back, her ass with possessive strokes she wanted never to stop. Quivering in his arms, she surrendered to temptation. Seconds later his hand searched, slipped under her shirt. His fingers located the front clasp on her push-up bra and the clasp came loose with a snick.

They hung on a precipice, and she didn't care. She wanted him. She desired his caresses and yet she feared what they'd bring next. More craving. More longing. More intoxicating happiness she couldn't resist.

She'd risk all for this man, and with that knowledge threw away her last reservations.

His hot palm cupped her right breast, and she wriggled and gasped. He caressed the globe, his big hand shaping, plumping. His tongue slid over one side of her neck in a lingering lick. He nibbled his way with feathering kisses until he reached her collarbone. Still he kept her breast prisoner, gently kneading. Her nipple ached, and she wanted him to touch her there. She kept her eyes closed, the better to feel his caresses. Heat spilled over her face as he pressed tender, reverent kisses to her collarbone. His tongue dipped into the hollow of her neck and she shivered and moaned. He peppered kisses upward until he tasted the other side of her neck with quick kisses.

Pleasure arched through her breast as he found her nipple and brushed over it with his fingers. *Oh! Oh, yes.* She writhed, whimpering as pure delight escaped her. She couldn't restrain the fire or the giddy enjoyment.

"Fuck, yes," he rasped with a caveman roughness.

At his unchained response, moisture dampened her folds. If he touched her private center now he'd find irrefutable evidence she wanted him with a liquid, incredible force. Internally she begged him, her litany a scream of pent-up wants and needs.

God, just touch me.

Gina's head dropped back on a sigh, and she surrendered to whatever came next. His fingers swept over her nipple with light brushes, then he clasped it between his finger and thumb and pinched gently. She gasped and shivered at the delicious feeling. Continually he twisted the nipple, then released his grip on her waist long enough to cup both breasts in his hands. Pleasure hardened her nipples to tight points that begged for more. His fingers tormented and plucked, danced across her flesh with steady pressure. He tugged the nipples with tender resolve. Gina wanted more—his lips tasting, licking, circling her flesh until an orgasm burst inside her. She clutched at his shoulders. His mouth followed along the curve of her neck as his fingers continued a ceaseless assault on her nipples.

As his hands drifted along her body with incessant motion, and showing her exquisite gentleness she'd never experienced from a man, time seemed to stop. She'd figured time warping during passion was a cliché, and even when she wrote it in her romance novels she didn't believe it. With a flash of knowing, she understood why she'd written about love for ten years. She'd believed in her spirit that a man could mean that much to a woman and a woman to a man. She'd acknowledged happy couples with silent joy and envy. Now she recognized this connection had found her and had been a part of her life for a decade. The revelation broke like a huge wave.

Pleasure cascaded over her body along with overwhelming desire to give him what he needed. Cherishing the tenderness he displayed, she moaned softly when he took another kiss. Relentless, his tongue delved into her mouth and caressed, as if he wanted to learn her depths. She shook as the intimacy encased her in a sweet and wonderful world she'd never expected to experience in her lifetime. For kissing him, enjoying his touch was as much about being with him and sharing as it was sexual delight.

She palmed his pectorals and savored hard contours and unyielding muscles. God, he was so strong. Hunger drove her touch down to his hips as she dared to linger low on his waistline close to his tight butt. Boldness called to her—she could reach down and cup that long, thick cock. She'd show him what her pussy ached for, what her whole body demanded. Before she could do it, though, he tensed his arms around her and kissed her furiously. She tasted demand, a reckless passion in his embrace. As if he'd been torn from her arms a millennium ago and returned this minute.

She could have stayed happily cocooned in this miraculous world.

The generator lights flickered and threatened to extinguish.

With a gasp, he broke from the kiss. Ryan heaved a deep breath, dizzy from tumultuous feelings inside him. Raging need to protect her ate away at his defenses. Though the creature outside retreated, Ryan didn't know what would happen next. The uncertain state of the lights jerked him into total awareness.

Rock-hard and aching, his cock begged for conclusion. His arms went taut around Gina. Emotions battered at his mind. Lust. Hunger to taste her longer, harder, deeper until neither of them could do anything but writhe naked on the bed and mate like beasts. He'd never wanted to take a woman with such unyielding passion before.

Gina's eyes softened with unmatched sweetness. He saw attentiveness and caring in those eyes that spoke to a hollow spot inside him. He ached to discover answers behind that pit of loneliness. Through his loss of memory popped a revelation.

Desolation had haunted him in the past. He knew that as much as he knew his shoe size. He'd hidden it deep inside where no one would learn the truth. Standing here with this woman erased that painful void. She filled him in ways he didn't know he needed. He couldn't recall, in the amnesia-ridden cells in his brain, whether Gina or any woman before her created this crazy roller-coaster passion. It frightened him more than flying bullets.

Mesmerized by the fragile lines of her face, he brushed her nose with his lips in a quick, teasing touch. With eyes and hands, he mapped the woman in front of him. Her skin, a fresh peach so perfect he wanted to lick it. Her mouth, a nourishing berry so damned sexy. God, she made him ache. Tasting her nipples and sucking her clit would be fucking bliss. Fear brandished a sharp knife. If anything happened to her because of him, he would never forgive himself.

He eased away from her embrace. "No. I can't do this right now."

A puzzled frown touched her mouth. "Do what?"

His weapon dug into his back and reminded Ryan why they hid in the basement. He turned away and removed the weapon from his waistband. After placing it on the dresser, he turned back to Gina.

How the hell did he say this without hurting her feelings? "We can't get involved."

He saw her stiffen, a scarcely perceptible rigidity to her shoulders. Remembering how her skin tasted under his tongue as he'd kissed those shoulders kept his cock hard. He wanted to groan. He wanted to throw off his convictions and take her.

She nodded. "Then why..." She shook her head and gave a muffled, almost appalled laugh. She reached under her shirt and refastened her bra. "Never mind. We're safe here and that's what is important for now."

Something raw flickered through her eyes, and her lashes fanned down onto her cheeks as she closed her eyes. Shit. He'd hurt her anyway when that was the last thing he wanted to do. She milled around the room as if nothing happened between them, rearranging this and straightening that while he watched her with apprehension. Tension radiated from her. He'd done more than dent her feelings—he'd made her angry. Disgusted that he'd let their physical relationship progress too far, he headed for the stairs.

"Where are you going?" she asked trepidation in her tone.

"To check the locks. I'll see if they need additional reinforcement."

He inspected the locks. They'd hold. At least, he hoped they would. Against a monster like the one that had come after them, he couldn't promise shit. When he returned back downstairs, he scanned the room and wondered how long they'd stay here. He gritted his teeth. Damn. He hated the scrambled emotions running around inside his gut. How could they escape this mess? Obviously, he couldn't handle the beast on his own. Leaving Gina here to battle the unknown would make him vulnerable because he would worry like hell about her. He'd do anything to remove the lines building between her eyebrows and the downturn of that pretty mouth.

"What's the verdict?" she asked, her arms crossed and her face as hard as concrete.

"Locks will hold. At least for now."

She nodded and lapsed into silence.

"If the locks don't prove your friends considered this as a shelter from someone or something, I don't know what does," he said.

Ryan saw the exasperation flow through her pretty face and decided to ignore her indignation. He felt better now they'd barricaded the door. She'd pulled a red button-up sweater over her shirt but she rubbed her arms as if she was still cold.

Concerned, he approached her. "You cold?"

"Nervous."

He walked toward her and cupped her shoulders. She shifted under his fingers, almost as if she wanted to retreat from him. "It'll be all right."

She drew in a shaky breath. "How can you be certain? You've lost a chunk of your memory and now you're stuck in this house with a woman you don't remember and you're holed up in a basement. Not exactly a favorite way to spend a Wednesday afternoon."

He frowned. "It's Wednesday? Damn, I even forgot the day of the week."

The nubby texture of her sweater against his fingers couldn't hide the slender, firm curves of her arms.

"You work out?" he asked.

"Yes."

"I can tell. You have great muscle tone." As soon as he said the words, he wished he hadn't. Images of her thighs, slim and strong, dipped into his mind.

"Ryan? What's wrong?"

A smile flashed quickly over his mouth. "Not a damned thing. I recall something about you."

He released her before he could do something stupid like kiss her again until neither one of them could stand.

"Ryan, tell me." She firmed her lips in a defiant way that now appeared familiar. "What is it?"

Shit, he liked the way she glared at him, as aroused by her irritation as he was by her smile. A desire to tease her demanded attention. But at the core, he wasn't joking. His thoughts were deadly serious.

He didn't back away, enjoying the heat of her nearness. He stuffed his hands in his jeans pockets and shrugged. "I remembered what your thighs look like in shorts." Her cheeks went pink, and he allowed a huge smile to burst over his lips. "Firm. Long. You've got kick-ass legs, Gina."

Her mouth opened and for a second she looked stunned. "Um...thank you."

"You act like you've never been complimented before. Men must come on to you all the time."

Her mouth twisted in deprecation. "Yeah, right. Hardly."

She turned away and sat on the bed.

"With a body like yours, and your face..." His throat tightened as he allowed his mind and soul to take in what he felt. What he believed. "You're the most beautiful woman I've ever seen, sweet colleen."

His Irish endearment hung out there, alive and crackling with energy and purpose. Gina's eyes widened, startled and maybe awed. She didn't have any idea what she did to him.

She started to wander the room with restless energy. "You are full of crap, Irish. You can take the man out of Ireland, apparently, but not the blarney."

He grunted. "I'm not bullshitting you." He heard his accent deepen, a natural thing that he couldn't stop. "I don't lie, Á Stor."

Her eyes widened even more at the additional Gaelic endearment.

Her gaze blazed with roiling emotions. "How do you know? I thought you lost your memory?"

Okay. She was contrary. His observation and gut noticed her tight muscles and tension-filled eyes. Maybe she had claustrophobia. He couldn't think of another reason for her to pace the room like an enslaved animal, her answers snarky, and slightly frantic eyes a sure sign of discomfort.

Correction. He could think of a reason. She hated his guts because he'd kissed her, practically made love to her and then backed away.

You are a fuckin' wanker, Ahern.

Her soft rose scent teased his nose as she walked by. Damn, she smelled of sin wrapped in one delicious package.

Anxiety pinched her features, and he couldn't take it anymore. He sat on the bed and patted the comforter beside him. "Sit down and let's talk." She stopped walking, but the wildness in her eyes didn't leave. When she didn't speak, he tried a new tactic. "Are you claustrophobic?"

She shook her head vehemently then rubbed her arms as a shiver jolted through her frame. "No. I've never...I mean, I've been in basements and elevators and closed places before. It's been a long time since I felt this way. I didn't expect it to still bother me."

Worry made him leave the bed. Again, he found himself in front of her, his hands cupping her shoulders. "Easy. Sit over here and tell me what's wrong."

A flicker of defiant Gina bounced through her eyes. "What's wrong is that we're stuck down here and something seriously creepy wants to eat us. Isn't that enough reason to be nervous?" Her gaze darted to the dresser where he'd placed his weapon. "And all that stands between us is..." She shook her head.

Her delicate frame shivered, anxiety evident in those soft eyes, her easy and fluid grace disrupted. In a few short hours, his mind filled with conflicting emotions about someone he didn't know...but did.

Then it dawned on him what was happening to her—he knew from training on stress situations and the human psyche's reactions. "Did something bad happen to you in an enclosed place?"

Her gaze centered on his, a pleading look that hit him like a sucker punch to the gut.

"You know about it." Her voice went so soft he almost couldn't hear it. "It happened when I was very young. My parents were..." She shook her head. "I don't want to talk about this right now. It'll just make it worse."

"You've told me before?" He allowed his fingers to trace up and down her arms, wanting to reassure her.

She nodded, but didn't speak.

Another shiver coasted through her body. Damn. Taking her arm in a gentle grip, he led her over to a leather recliner and ottoman in one corner. "Sit down and relax. Tell me about your new book. Take your mind off what worries you."

Gina settled into the big chair, and her heartbeat calmed. His strong and invincible presence beside her eased some of her apprehension. The last several minutes had played havoc with her nerves. Being chased into a basement by a monster was bad enough, but having Ryan kiss her, caress her breasts and then say he couldn't become involved with her—well, that was enough to fricassee any woman's wits. Residual annoyance cascaded through her over his rejection.

Ryan's solicitousness comforted and surprised her. Not that he'd been anything but supportive when it came to her past trauma, but he'd never pushed her to explain more than she wanted. For a moment, she'd thought the "new" Ryan might press for too much information and reach into territory she didn't dare resurrect. His uncanny ability to read her emotions hadn't changed—he'd always picked away her outer shell with ease. Maybe her vulnerability to him frightened her as much as the past and the true reason old claustrophobia threatened. She took deep breaths as he walked away.

"I thought I saw a bottle of *uisce beatha* in here." He dug through a cabinet until he located the brown bottle and broke the seal with a twist. "You could use a hit."

His mention of *uisce beatha*, whiskey and the water of life, made her smile. He never just called it whiskey.

He found a small glass and poured a measure of liquor. When he handed it to her, she asked, "You're not having any?"

"I don't drink on the job."

"The job. Is that what this is right now?"

He put the bottle back in the cabinet and closed the door with a firm push. When he turned back, his eyes held confusion. "Beats the shit outta me, *Á Stór*, but I'm pretty sure it's personal too."

Again she felt startled at the endearment, knowing that it meant a lot for a man to call a woman darling. He hadn't used this sweet nothing with her before his amnesia. Why did her call her something so special now?

She took a sip of whiskey and allowed it to heat her insides. Her turn to goad. "Personal in what way?"

He crossed his arms and powerful muscles in his arms rippled. "Don't act like you don't know, Gina. You aren't telling me everything about our relationship, but I do remember caring about you. A helluva lot."

He settled on the ottoman, and his knees almost brushed hers. His statement and his nearness jumpstarted her heart until attraction winged like a swift bird, darting here and there in her body.

"The old Ryan never admitted to caring about me."

He leaned forward, his elbows on his legs, hands clasped between his knees. His attention centered on her. Concern and maybe guilty feelings showed on his face. "Did I show that I cared?"

"You did. In little ways. In big ways too."

His gaze intensified, sliding with unabashed observation over her face. "In what little ways?"

She eased another drop of the water of life down her throat and hoped it would regulate her overwhelmed senses. Senses that fired on impulse, on the crazy sensations he caused inside her. "Too numerous to mention, honestly. Your kindness, your teasing. You did jobs around my house. Helped me build a rock garden outside. You're incredibly clever with your...hands."

Oh, I didn't just say that.

One side of his mouth twitched. Humor danced in his eyes. "How clever?"

She swallowed a larger amount of the amber liquid. "Very. You're mechanically oriented. You can fix cars like nobody's business. You can weld, garden, put shutters on windows...a crazy-making amount of things. Your father was an inventor, so it must be in your genes."

His eyebrows dipped, and he frowned. "I don't remember that. I mean, my father being an inventor."

She sighed. God, she was selfish. "It must be frightening to call to mind some things, but not others."

Ryan shook his head. "I don't have the luxury of feeling sorry for myself. I've got a mission to finish." They lapsed into silence until he asked, "So I'm a handyman as well as a special agent?"

"A regular James Bond."

He snorted. "Yeah, right."

"You're pretty amazing, Ryan Ahern. Don't sell yourself short."

His quizzical expression deepened. "Have I ever been married?"

Another sip of liquor steadied her next answer. "No, but you were deeply in love once."

"Shit," he whispered, appearing sideswiped by the concept. "When?"

Pain centered in her gut as she recalled his tragedy as if it were her own. "Before you came to the United States. Do you remember your parents?"

"Vaguely. My life in Northern Ireland is foggy. Where did I live?"

"Belfast."

"*Beal Feirste,*" he whispered the Gaelic word for the city.

"You grew up there. Your parents owned a bookstore. They made sure you learned Gaelic fluently."

Memories flickered through his face, hard and unforgiving. She saw the pain wrench him. "They were killed. It was a bomb, right?"

She had to breathe slow and deep. "A van parked in front of their store one day. Your girlfriend, Alene, was in the store with them... Are you sure you want to hear more?"

He buried his face in his hands, a soft groan rising from his gut. Oh, good. She'd done it now. The last thing she should do was dredge up horrific memories.

"Finish the story," he said as he lowered his hands. "I don't recall any of it but the emotions. The fuckin' agony."

"We don't have to do this now."

He drew in a ragged breath. "Yeah, we do. Tell me."

"You loved Alene. You were childhood sweethearts, grew up together and planned to marry—"

"After we went to university." He winced. "I can almost see her face." He gulped. "Dark hair, eyes blue. That's all."

Tears rose to her eyes, and she placed the glass on the small table next to the chair. "The bomb was so powerful it destroyed your parents' store and most of the building next to it. Your aunt in Denver took you in after their deaths."

His gaze, planted on his feet, snapped to hers. "Am I Catholic or Protestant?"

"Catholic. You don't practice it traditionally, though."

He nodded, a streak of pure, wounded suffering breaking over his face. "Okay. Enough about my life. Tell me more about you."

Well, that hadn't changed. He could still change subjects with point-blank abruptness.

"What about your family?" he asked. "Where are they?"

"There's nobody but me. My real parents gave me up for adoption. The family that adopted me was...well, let's just say they were dysfunctional."

"In what way?"

Old memories twisted in her gut. "My adoptive father was a drunk, and my adoptive mother so codependent she didn't help matters. When he—"

She didn't think she could say it. Ryan's eyes narrowed and he scooted forward on the ottoman. His legs bracketed hers, and he reached out to gather her hands in the warm fold of his large fingers.

"What did he do?" Ryan's voice turned raw.

Chapter Six

The lump in Gina's throat took her by surprise, but she didn't know if it was her earlier illness or something mental. "I've gotten past all this baggage. Why is it hurting now? Why is it so hard to talk about?"

"Because it feels new. You're in a tough and scary situation. It makes you feel as if you're talking about it for the first time." He shrugged. "In a way, you are."

He was right. "My father abused me."

Ryan's fingers tightened over hers. "Son of a bitch."

"He liked to shove me in a closet and leave me there for hours. My mother tried to stop him, but he wouldn't let her release me from the closet. A few times, she even left the house. She never called the police."

Ryan's lips tightened again, disgust on his handsome face. "He never...he didn't..."

Pure malice sparked in his eyes, and her adoptive father would have felt Ryan's wrath in that moment if he'd been in the room. She knew what he needed to hear, and it was the truth. "No. No, he never sexually abused me."

He dropped his head forward, his eyes closed for a second. "Thank God. How long did you put up with his shit?"

"From the time I was born until I was twelve when he died of liver and heart problems. After that, my mother was useless. Father was a plumber, and Mother socked away money he didn't know about. At least she had the intelligence to do that. We lived off the money, and she did housekeeping jobs. I found a job at sixteen babysitting. It wasn't much, but we made it. I obtained a loan for college and finished a degree

Hideaway

in creative writing. I've worked at two finance companies while writing."

His expression lightened. "And that's where we met? University?"

"Yes." She couldn't help adding, "It was one of the best things that happened to me, meeting you."

He grinned. "I'm glad."

Her heart softened for the tough Irish warrior, her soul wanting his comforting as much as she desired to reassure him. "Neither of us had it easy early on in our lives. But we haven't let it stop us."

"I can feel that."

Feelings. An interesting avenue for a man she'd considered hard, tough and a bit too reserved with his more tender emotions.

His hands caressed hers in gentle motions that sent her heart into staccato rhythm. She fixated on the back of his hand, the square and symmetrical beauty. Long but sturdy, his fingers caressed hers. Her nipples peaked, her pussy clenched and tightened. Moisture gathered in her feminine folds as an ache built. While her fantasies included scenarios where he held her, comforted her, clasped her hands in his, she'd never expected it to happen this way. She'd never anticipated her emotions vibrating with high-voltage excitement mixed with a growing, deepening affection so strong she didn't think she could deny it. Although he'd kissed her and confirmed he didn't want a physical relationship with her, she felt like he'd never touched her before. How could he have such power over her?

"What are you thinking?" he asked.

She allowed a smile to tease her lips. "That sounds like something I should say. I think I like the sensitive Ryan."

"Was I that much of a Neanderthal?"

She shook her head and squeezed his fingers. "No. Not at all. You just didn't show these types of emotions to me often."

An urge to reveal things to him she'd never shown before pushed her to say, "I like this new Ryan. He's tough as nails, but he's different. Softer." Boldness built eagerly inside her. "From the first day you rescued me from that idiot in chemistry class and became my chemistry partner, you've always had my best interests at heart. I can never fault you for that."

He released her hands and eased away, and she wanted his touch back. "Good. I can't imagine feeling about you like this—"

She waited for him to continue and his gaze darted around the room as if he were afraid to lock gazes.

When he didn't finish, she prompted him. "Yes?"

"In the few hours we've been together, I feel like I'm getting to know you again. And I like what I know, what I see very much."

A flush built from her chest through to her face. She'd blushed more the last few hours than any time in her life. No man stirred her, warmed her, drew her closer than Ryan.

Gina touched her hot cheeks with both hands. "Thanks. That means a lot to me."

He winked, and his slow, cocky look made her heart thump a new beat. God, what she wouldn't give to feel his fingers stroking her in forbidden places one more time. Recalling what his fingers had felt like on her nipples sent a renewed flush of heat throughout her body.

He rose slowly and wandered with a more languid pace than he had earlier upstairs. She watched his stride, a walk she knew so well she could pick him out in a crowd.

"I suppose this is where you tell me this conversation is a bit too girly for you," she said when silence continued.

He stopped and turned toward her, his head tilted slightly to the side. He looked open, ready to understand. "Is that what the old Ryan would have said?"

She put her feet on the ottoman and tried to relax. "Yes."

He plunged his fingers through his hair. "You're telling me I've had that extreme a personality change?"

An epiphany came to her. "Maybe not. We all harbor secret sections of our personality we don't show others. Maybe a knock on the head opened parts of you I haven't seen before. You've been well armored for years." Once again, his hands went to his hips. She smiled and gestured to him. "See, that hands on the hips thing."

He lifted his hands and looked at them. "What?"

"It's an action I associate with decisive, unsentimental Ryan. You put your hands on your hips when you're certain about something or worried things are getting too personal."

His smoldering gaze caught hers. "Then I'm not sure I like the old Ryan much."

Clearly disconcerted by her assessments, he navigated the room like a wild creature needing shelter. He glowered, and the change from disarming Ryan to this covert man shook the foundation they'd started to build. "Damn, is it hot in here?" He examined the temperature control. "Seventy-five."

"I'm fine."

She lied, of course. Since he'd arrived at her doorstep she'd alternated between glowing heat caused by his virility, and freezing from fear.

"Humph." He grunted, and then pulled the T-shirt over his head.

She blinked. *Oh my God.* She'd spied his naked torso twice before. Once at a picnic where he'd played volleyball in the summer heat. Another time when she'd stopped by his apartment and found him wearing only jeans.

In both situations she'd almost babbled like an idiot, her conversation meandering, her thoughts turning instantly to sex.

"Something wrong?" he asked.

"Uh, no."

Ryan laid his T-shirt over the back of one of the dinette chairs, walked into the bathroom and shut the door. She closed her eyes and recall flooded her mind. Ryan's broad shoulders, ripped arms and sexy chest would make any woman with half a hormone natter like an idiot. Dark hair fanned over his strong pectorals then down over a muscled stomach to disappear into his jeans. She'd seen good-looking men shirtless many times, but only Ryan made her heart pound.

Why, oh why, did his jeans always fit him to perfection? He wore them low on his hips and she could see his belly button. Unlike the baggy pants popular with many young men, his jeans curved with loving attention over his well-muscled ass and beautifully formed legs. Not beautiful as in womanly. No way. In college, he'd trained for cross-country running, fencing, wrestling and weightlifting. An interesting combination, but one that had kept him in disgustingly wonderful physical condition.

Gina swallowed hard and licked her dry lips. She couldn't—wouldn't—object to this display of sculpted musculature any day of the week.

She heard the water running and imagined him tossing it on his face and allowing it to trickle down his neck and onto his chest. If she didn't stop fantasizing like this, her brain would explode. Nervous and excited in a way that scrambled her senses, she wished she could hit a reset button and restart the day. But what difference would it make if she did? Would she depart the cabin if she knew ahead of time what would happen and leave Ryan to fend for himself? It's not like he needed her help. Did he?

She closed her eyes and allowed her imagination to run rampant. All that wonderful male flesh succumbing to her desires. His hands coasting back to her breasts, his mouth tasting one nipple…his fingers between her legs—

The bathroom door opened and she started from her fantasy. She stood abruptly and wandered the room. He didn't slip back into his shirt. If she didn't think of an intelligent word to say soon, she'd start gabbing like a fool.

"Are you hungry?" she asked, heading for the refrigerator.

"No. You?"

She rummaged in a cabinet for items they'd stuffed inside. Trail mix. Nutrition bars.

"How long do you honestly think we'll be here?" she asked.

"Good question."

When she turned, he stood so near she almost ran into him. Heat spread through her midsection.

Scrumptious didn't begin to explain the incendiary sight in front of her. She felt so many things at once. Breathless. Walking on a tightrope of desire. Teetering on a fragile rope between retreat and needing to explore his body with mouth and fingers.

Big and powerful, Ryan represented primitive in a way that nourished her sexual needs like no other man. Anticipation curled through her belly when his pupils dilated and his lips parted.

She almost backed away, but what sane woman wouldn't want to stay near him a bit longer? "Are you cooled down?"

"No."

Her gaze centered on the middle of his chest, right between those carved pecs. "Oh?"

She sounded breathless and out of her element. Her good friend Ryan sent her into a tizzy, her body melting, her senses reeling.

"I'm hot, colleen. Damned hot," he said.

"Is something wrong?" Concern notched up inside her. "Are you sick?"

"Sick of trying to ignore what's happening between us."

His chest heaved with a deep breath, his eyes intense with emotion, searching for answers she didn't know if she could give.

Gina thought she'd dissolve into a puddle, but she managed to blurt out in defense, "You're one of my best friends. I care about you. There isn't anything going on—"

"Nothing going on? I suppose the way we were getting it on earlier qualifies as nothing?"

What could she say? Disappointment warred with anger. Anger won. "Well, you were the one who stopped kissing me."

His brows lowered as he considered her statement. "You're too special for a man to take advantage of you."

"Now you're treating me like a brainless twit, Ryan. You did notice me responding, right? I knew what I was doing. When you kissed me, were you planning to take advantage of me? Is that what you were feeling?"

"Of course not." He hung his head and wrapped his hands around the back of his neck. A sigh heaved from him. "The last thing in the world I want is to hurt you."

"Then let's agree not to talk about any mushy feelings or physical attraction for now, okay?"

Good. There. That would put this ill-fated lust she had for him in its place, locked away in the fantasyland where it belonged.

"This is a weird situation and we can't let it go to our heads," he said.

She shrugged, keeping her emotions securely reined. "Did you hear me arguing with you when you said it the first time?"

Ryan tipped her chin up with his index finger and his gaze tangled with hers. "I'm not a dumb bastard, Gina. I don't lie, I don't pretend when I have feelings for a woman. At least this new me doesn't."

"Feelings?"

"Yeah. Like I'm aching and about ready to explode."

"You're angry."

"Hell, no." A feral intensity hardened his features. "Yeah, maybe. At myself for starting this whole thing. For coming here and putting you in danger, and for kissing you." A self-assured smile broke over his face. He crossed his arms over his chest. "I've seen the way you look at me. Your eyes are hot." He tapped his forehead. "And I know it up here. My intuition. You want me too."

Frustration arched through her. "And what if I did? You said no to going any further with this, remember?"

"Yeah. It doesn't mean I don't have more questions. What's held us back from each other before?"

Frustrated, she poked his chest with her index finger. "You. Old Ryan was too busy touring the world to places like Iraq and Afghanistan. You were here today, gone tomorrow."

He caught her hand gently and held it to his chest. Her breath caught as his hand completely encompassed hers and kept it pinned against his rock-solid chest. God, why did he have to torture her like this with his virility and concrete strength? More than that, she couldn't resist the old and new Ryan mixed into one scrumptious man.

I'm a goner. A goner.

"That's the only bloody reason why we stayed apart?" he asked, sincere curiosity back in his voice.

Like baby steps, this man's almost childlike wonder at her responses made her want to protect him as much as he'd already protected her.

"Gina?"

She disengaged from his intoxicating touch and pulled her hand back. "No. Alene kept you away too."

This time it was his turn to take a step back. "My dead fiancée?"

"I don't think you've ever gotten over her." Sympathy sent a sharp spike through her. "How could anyone blame you? You loved her more than anyone you've known."

His gaze trapped hers and held it fast. She expected him to speak, but he didn't.

"Besides," she said. "I'm not the type of woman who could tolerate a soldier for a husband. All the traveling you've done and dangerous assignments...well, it wasn't for me when you were in the military, and it isn't for me now."

He walked away, his steps took him from the bed to the dinette set. His hands gripped the back of one green damask-covered chair.

An emotion she didn't expect haunted his face. Regret. His gaze collided with hers long enough to convey genuine hurt. She'd never seen him look so vulnerable, and it touched feminine sensibilities deep inside. Yet as much as her heart wanted to open to his human foibles, she didn't want to take the chance of having her heart chewed up if anything happened to him.

"I asked you once," she said, "why I never saw you date other women."

He continued to grip the chair. "What did I say?"

"That you didn't think it would be fair to either the woman or yourself. With your traveling there's no way you could maintain a romance. No quality time and no quantity."

Displeasure crossed his face. "I said that?"

"Well, you probably didn't use the word romance."

A swift smile flittered over his mouth. "Probably not."

"Your heart is stone when it comes to love."

His fingers gripped the chair back tighter then he released it. "Maybe I was right then."

She didn't want to hear it, but eventually his memory would return. The old Ryan would regret the temporary changes in his personality. He stalked away, and she took a deep breath.

Watching his powerful body move scorched her bone-deep. His body flowed, rippling muscles lengthening, contracting. Gina sighed.

He turned a concerned gaze on her. "You look exhausted. You okay?"

"I'm fine." She lied, of course. Her nerves felt like they might jump out of her skin.

"Get some sleep." When she raised an eyebrow at him, he smiled. "What? You don't want to close your eyes? There's nothing to worry about. I'll keep watch."

"You were always so nice to me, you know that?"

"Why do I get the feeling I wasn't nice enough?"

She shook her head, eager to make sure he understood. "You're always considerate and kind to me. Protective like an older brother. But after this clonk on the head...well, I don't know how to describe it. Your edge is softened."

He winced. "Don't tell anyone. Sounds like it might kill my reputation as a real hard-ass."

She laughed. "You're one kick-butt agent, Ryan. You came in this cabin more like the old Ryan, with few apologies. I like this...combination man."

His expression altered to healthy skepticism. "It feels weird as hell to know you...but not know you."

An ache entered her heart. "I hope the good times aren't erased forever."

He looked solemn. "If they are, there isn't a damn thing we can do about it."

"Then we'd have to start a new slate." She knew she sounded resigned. "I'm not sure I like that."

Hands on hips, his eyes took on the assessing, results-oriented expression she was used to seeing from her warrior.

Her warrior. Yeah, she liked thinking of him as hers for one moment, before she reminded herself that his job would keep it from happening permanently.

"If we start with a clean slate," he said, "we can make new memories and mix them with the old. Isn't that what we're doing now?"

Oh, hell. Her heart couldn't take this. Could he say or do anything else that would diminish her resistance?

No. She was half in love with him, but it had happened over ten long years.

The revelation stunned her.

"Go ahead and sleep. Even for a few minutes. It'll take the edge off," he said.

"What about you?"

"I'll catch a few minutes later. You can be on watch then." He winked.

Her eyes itched and her body ached. Maybe she did need to take a nap. "Okay. Deal."

She returned to the leather chair. She closed her eyes and leaned her head back. As she allowed whiskey to wend through her veins, she savored the silence. For a tiny space, she imagined she was alone in the room and peace reigned. No monsters planned to devour her. No hunky man haunted the room and demanded her attention with his off-the-chart gorgeous body and gallant desire to protect her. Once more, her story formed in her mind. Writing happened naturally, without forcing dialogue, without manufacturing feelings that didn't seem comfortable within the mouths of the characters. Her confidence returned by measures, undaunted by embarrassment for the fear she'd displayed. In a flash of understanding, she had an epiphany that rocked her to the basics.

Amazing it hadn't been clear before.

She'd allowed fears, some real and some imaginary, to clog her creativity. She hadn't been true to herself as a person and expressed what she honestly believed and felt in her writing. If she opened her heart and spilled her truthful feelings on the page, she'd no longer need pretense in her writing, or charade in her real life.

Reality, sparkling clear and honest, waited for her to reveal it on the page. Complete revelation to one of her best friends, the man who had rocked her world over the years, would create the road toward saying what she meant, and meaning what she said.

Chapter Seven

Gina awoke some time later—how long she didn't know. Ryan had snapped on the weather band radio, which could also pick up regular stations, and a tune she'd always loved played. A smile touched her lips. Yes. This was great. Without taking time to think, she sang along with the sensual, slow tune.

"When I thought love was all about pain and jealousy, time made me see, I need to leave the loneliness and emptiness, and find my heart's desire. I feel our love's fire, I know you'll be mine when I find the answer this time." She let the words flow from her as naturally as water down a gentle river. Slow. Lazy. "Caught in eternity, I will find my way and make it through with you. Never will I lose my way or my desire. I will feed our passion's fire. Only when the light of love shines and eternity is ours. Ever will I feed this desire and fire. Only when the light of love shines and eternity is ours."

She stopped singing and opened her eyes. Ryan watched her from his stance near the bed. Arms folded, he stood with feet braced apart. Though his body language spoke of being ready for anything, his face told another story. A gentle smile curved his mouth. The mouth that had warmed hers, loved hers with such wonderful attention.

He returned to the ottoman and sank down as she moved her feet slightly to the side. "You have an amazing voice."

She waved one hand in self-deprecation. "I can barely carry a tune in a bag."

"Stop being modest. Your voice is soft, but it's pretty."

She moved her feet from the ottoman and leaned forward in her chair. She spoke almost into his ear. "I sing okay, but not that well."

Almost nose to nose with him, Gina couldn't miss their strong connection. She allowed what she felt to flow into her body language and her heart.

"Did you sing in a choir in college?" he asked quietly.

"High school only. The basic choir. Mixed choir, I think they called it."

"Mixed?"

"Coed. There was no shame if your voice sucked because no one could hear you if your voice was soft."

"We can't be talking about you."

"Yes we are. Me and a lot of others."

"Uh-huh."

"You don't believe me?"

"I believe you hid in the choir, but you didn't need to." He left the ottoman once more and opened the cabinet to reach for the whiskey bottle. After he added a finger more of whiskey to her glass, he returned the bottle to the counter and went back to his position on the ottoman. With her still sitting forward on the chair, and his position, they faced each other. The intimate distance pleased her, but this time she didn't retreat. If anyone ran away from the high-voltage attraction pinging back and forth between them, he'd have to make the move.

"Are you trying to get me drunk?" she asked.

He looked scandalized. "I've never tried to get a woman drunk."

"Right. Are you just saying that, or you don't truly remember doing it?"

He stared her down. "I've never tried to get a woman drunk to see what she'd do. But now that you mention it, I'd like to see you tipsy once."

"You have. At a party. You were possessive, though. None of the guys there could get near me. Not that I think too many were interested."

His gaze searched hers. "Possessive. Why would I do that?"

She took a deep breath. *Go for it. Lay it out for him. Don't hold anything back.* "For a guy who isn't a male relative or a boyfriend, you sure have a problem with men approaching me."

He sat back somewhat, his spine straightening. A frown ruined the lighthearted expression he'd owned a moment ago. "I can think of only one reason...no, maybe two reasons why I would be possessive of a woman."

She almost held her breath waiting for the answer.

One more time, he sat forward and caught her hands between his. "I feared for your safety. Maybe I got bad vibes from the asshole. Two, I wanted you for myself."

Wanted you for myself.

Oh man, oh man. Did he want me then and I didn't know it?

She smiled weakly. "I guess we'll never know, will we? Not unless your memory returns."

She knew she sounded deadpan, but what else could she say? Silence descended on them until he decided to stand and wander the room in that restless fashion, a man haunted by deep emotion and nonstop energy. She turned away from the question in his eyes and the passionate sense Ryan would take things a step further if she let him.

If she let herself go.

Was there harm in that? At this point, she didn't know. She didn't think she could handle a purely physical encounter. It would damage their friendship when they crossed the line.

"I had an idea for Halloween this year," she said.

His eyebrows went up, an ironic amusement turning into a smile. "Halloween is two months away."

"So? You know me, I love Halloween."

He frowned. "No, I don't know."

In the short time they'd reunited today, she stopped feeling surprise when he stated he didn't recall something. "Like I said, I love Halloween. I enjoy the costumes, the supernatural aspects."

"Do you have a party every year?"

"No. I had one two years ago, but it was a flop. We got two feet of snow and I had to cancel. Very depressing."

He grinned. "Was I invited?"

"You were." She shrugged. "But you were on a mission and couldn't come."

Puzzlement crossed his face for a second. "A military mission."

"Yes."

Silence reined for a few minutes, and she allowed the comfort in quiet to surround her. Despite the circumstances, she considered the basement a security blanket.

"Tell me more about the last ten years. About right after I first met you. Maybe it'll trigger more memories for me."

She hesitated. Perhaps leaving him in the dark worked better. When he didn't know segments of his life, new memories could replace the gap.

"Gina?"

"Okay." She leaned her head back and waited for images. "I told you about the rescue. Where you kept the bully from bothering me." Memories filtered into her head. "I was very impressed with you. Even then you were strong, handsome and capable. You were mature for a guy that age."

"Most college-aged men don't know their head from their ass, I'll admit. But neither do the girls."

She nodded. "I agree."

He crossed his arms and closed his eyes. "What did I do for recreation?"

"Well, I mentioned some of those things before."

He sighed. "Yeah, that's right." He rubbed his eyes. "Damn, I'm tired and I can't afford it. Never mind. Tell me more about your writing."

She relaxed, glad for a break against the intoxicating way he captured her attention. After picking up her glass and cradling it in her hands for a smidgen, she took a slow taste. The drink trickled down her throat with a delicious and pleasant burn.

"I'm working on a manuscript but I'm having trouble with it."

"Back up a bit. Are you published?"

"Yes. I have three books out. They've done well."

"That's great."

"It is. I can't deny it." She told him the trials and tribulations of her current work in progress. "I've been aching to finish *Hideaway*."

"Tell me about it."

She shook her head. "I don't talk much about works in progress. Not to anyone."

"Why?"

"Because it drains the life out of the story before I can put it on paper."

"What kind of books do you write?"

She hesitated, wondering if he would tease her about her genre selection. The old Ryan had supported her wholeheartedly in her career.

"Romance."

His smile wasn't teasing, but curious. "That's great. And revealing."

"Oh? What does it reveal?"

"That you have a warm heart."

She laughed a nervously. "Maybe too mushy."

He wriggled his eyebrows. "How mushy?"

"Well, my books are hot. Erotic, as a matter of fact."

His eyes widened a bit, a soul-stripping, potent gaze that refused to hide his interest. He leaned back against the kitchen counter. "How erotic?"

She threw a sly grin at him. "Steamy, explicit. Nothing left to the imagination."

One corner of his mouth tilted and his eyes went hot with answering exhilaration. "Damn. I never would have guessed."

She smiled. "I get that a lot. I guess people think erotic romance authors wear feather boas and eat chocolates all day. Or live a glamorous life."

"Feather boas and chocolate is a cliché." He winked. "I'd say the glamorous, adventurous life is working for you right now."

She sniffed. "Uh-huh. You call this glamour? I call it screaming terror with the edge barely taken off."

He frowned. "You're right. I wouldn't wish this on you in a million years." Another pause lengthened until he continued. "Did I know before this amnesia that you write erotic romance?"

"Yes."

"What did I think?"

A new fearlessness arose inside her. A wave of heat moved in her belly. Recklessness gathered and refused denial. She wanted to discover everything about the new Ryan, from his favorite food, to his preferred color, to what sounds left his throat when he made love. Pleasure surrounded her. Exploring his essences from top to bottom appealed to her on every level, physically and mentally.

"You thought it was great. But I want to know what you think now," she said.

His eyes shimmered, the primitive connection glowing between them. He wandered to the dining set and propped his ass against the side of the table. "It makes me want to know you, inside and out."

Inside and out.

Whoa.

Rapid-fire sexual attraction simmered, persistent and intoxicating her with promise.

"Any woman who can write about passion like that must have it inside her," he said.

She leaned forward, her drink forgotten. "You don't think she can just make it up out of thin air?"

"She can pretend she's felt it, she can wish she's felt it. But she can't describe sexual passion with quite the accuracy of a woman who's experienced it."

She laughed softly. "What if she has a dildo and fantasizes?"

Ryan's eyebrows went high again. Arousal and surprise covered his features. All of sudden he looked feral, a man on the edge. "Damn it, Á Stor, don't talk to me like that."

"Why not? Does it embarrass you?"

"Shit. No. It makes me want what I can't have." He shifted, and when she dared glance at his cock, it had grown hard and long inside his jeans. "Do you have a dildo?"

Heat filled her face and her midsection in a combination of sultry excitement and awkwardness. Oh, what the hell. "Yes."

"Oh man," he said, his voice a low, husky breath of sound. "You're turning me on."

Satisfaction melted through her like the most fattening, warm chocolate, delicious and forbidden. She put her elbow on her knee and propped her head in her hand.

She tilted her head to one side and thought about his revelation. "I've never heard you say anything like this before. It's...refreshing. Incredible."

"I've never said that to you before?"

"Hell, no." She chuckled.

"Sounds uptight."

She smiled. "I don't think you were uptight. Not about sex, anyway. You never seemed prudish."

"God, I hope not." He waggled his eyebrows.

His antics made her smile. Her grin faded when he hooked his thumbs through his belt loops. His fingers seemed to point downward to his crotch. *Look at me.*

She dared a quick glance.

Oh, no. No, I shouldn't look, or my gaze will stick there and then he'll know how curious I am about the size, the thickness, the length, the hardness of his cock when he's aroused. Yes, when he'd held her tight in his arms, she'd enjoyed a taste of what sexual excitement did to him.

She craved more familiarity. More feeling. More acquaintance with everything their bodies could do together.

Damn it, Gina, you are certifiable.

"What are you thinking? You look scared," he said.

Her breath hitched. "You honestly want to know what I'm wondering?"

"Sure. You can trust me. You can tell me anything."

Oh, she wished she could. "Nothing is too personal?"

"No."

"That's not something I'd expect an alpha male like you to say."

"Alpha male?"

"You know. You've heard of beta and alpha males and females in wolf packs, right?"

"Yeah."

She gave herself permission, in one stunning moment, to do and say what she felt without hesitation. Without censoring the honest woman. She'd needed a time and place where it felt right. Regardless of how their situation finished, no matter how scary the world became, she needed to tell him what she harbored deep within her heart. Screw consequences. Fuck inhibitions.

"You're an alpha male, but you're more. Much more than I gave you credit for."

She stood and approached, dared to leave herself open to the hurt or the ecstasy that might follow. As she came closer to him, she saw the curiosity fill his eyes, along with an undeniable pleasure.

She stopped a foot away. "What do you think of me? Physically?"

Without hesitation or blinking an eye, he said, "You're beautiful."

Her breathing quickened. "You kissed me earlier. Why?"

Ryan shifted nearer, his gaze heating and encompassing her in a growing intimacy she didn't wish to resist. "You know the answer. You felt how much I wanted you."

"Wanted?"

"You're playing with fire."

"Really. How much fire?"

She reached out and touched his chest, placing her hand between his pecs and absorbing his uncompromising heat.

His hand came up and trapped hers against his chest. He took the final step to bring them almost body to body. "This isn't a good idea."

"Who said we have to be wise? Another thing you said earlier keeps popping into my mind." She dared touch his stubble-rough jaw. Pleasure rippled, grew and exploded as she felt his masculinity under her fingers.

His chest heaved. "Damn. This is insane."

Whether he would vocalize it or not, he wanted her physically. Few men had looked at her this way. At least, few she'd noticed. Maybe the difference was she believed the way he looked at her and understood the answering fire in her belly. There were no lies in his eyes, only raw, unfettered passion and caring.

"Because we're in a strange situation, this isn't the best time to let feelings run away with us," he said.

Ryan cupped Gina's face and the warmth of his fingers tingled through her skin and heated the last reserve in her heart.

"Are you telling me you don't feel anything?" she asked. "You wouldn't have kissed me if you didn't."

"It's not that I don't feel." Husky and sincere, his deep voice uttered words she never thought she'd hear coming from him. He released her hand and his touch dropped away from her face. "It's that I feel too damned much."

In this hideaway, this sanctuary against an evil she didn't comprehend, his protection and affection meant more every minute. She simply couldn't allow the fine-edged desire to slip away while she had the chance to express it.

In case they didn't have a tomorrow.

She allowed her fingers to trail with a soft touch over his chest. Heat, hardness, reassurance flexed under her fingers. She'd never felt anything so solid and dependable.

"Why do you want to hold back from me?" she asked, tired of wondering.

Fire ignited in his eyes. Whether he admitted it or not, her proximity affected him. His eyes went hot, his lips parting as he perused her with serious intent. "Because we're in a dangerous situation."

"And you don't think it's safe, mentally or physically, to show what we feel right now?"

"No."

"Because of what?"

His gaze raked her. "Because you could get hurt."

She snorted a soft, unladylike laugh. "Me? What about you?"

Her challenge went unanswered for a mere second. An ardent craving became clear in his eyes. "I can restrain my desires. It's part of the job."

"That doesn't meant you couldn't get hurt. Not if you have feelings for me."

When more meaningful words of affection didn't leave his mouth, pain mixed with shame for letting him see so much.

He clasped her shoulders, and the heat of his touch sent tingles straight through her body. "If you've known me for years, then you understand detachment is part of the job. I had to remain emotionally detached from certain things I did in the military, and this job is no different. You've always known that, right?"

She inhaled deeply and released it slowly. "Yes." She closed her eyes. "It doesn't mean I'm a job."

His fingers tightened on her shoulders, but not enough to hurt. "Damn it, Gina. If you've lived with it this long, what's different about today?"

"Today you kissed me."

The short sentence hung in the air.

She waited for an answer. A sign. An understanding of what he'd do.

He gave it.

He slipped around behind her.

With gentle persistence, he eased her back until their bodies touched. All along her body, her skin prickled with awareness. She drew in another breath and caught the heady aphrodisiac of male, of tantalizing realization. His body, hard and fit, called to hers. His fingers slid down her arms and then his arms encompassed her waist. Rippling with strength, his embrace reassured and fulfilled. With slow, methodical circles, his palms drew patterns over her waist.

Yes. That felt wonderful.

Swift arousal warmed her stomach and pooled low in her groin as his thorough exploration devoured her body inch by inch. Heat moistened her pussy and her clit tingled. She wanted his touch nearer, closer, deeper. She drew in his wonderful scent, a heated masculinity that drove her wild.

His lips nuzzled her ear. "Is this what you wanted then?"

"Yes. God help me. But I do." The words hurt, but once they left her mouth, a languorous ease spilled into her and released years of longing.

He kissed the side of her neck, his lips defining a fine, shivery path over her skin. Spiraling desire coiled deep within and demanded fulfillment. Searching across her belly, he reached under her tops and flattened his hand over her midriff. As the heat of his flesh encountered hers, she let out a small gasp.

"What do you want?" His hot breath puffed against her neck.

Terrified and thrilled, she gasped out, "I don't know."

He burrowed his face in her hair as he moved to the other side of her neck. "Yes, you do. Tell me. What's inside you that craves release."

A tight ache built in her throat. "I…"

"Mmm?" He tasted her neck, his tongue drifting over her skin and flicking her earlobe.

"Oh God."

His soft chuckle came hot and husky. Without a pause, he moved one hand down to undo the button on her jeans. Anticipation welled as she held her breath.

His other hand undid the front clasp of her bra then hesitated at the juncture between her breasts.

"We were here before," he said then kissed her ear.

This time she heard and felt no hesitation on his part. Lingering doubt jumped ship as she allowed wonder, delight and affection to swell within her heart.

Affection?

Who was she kidding?

She couldn't surrender to anything but the utmost.

Love.

Chapter Eight

Speaking the truth would remove the knot in Gina's throat that often rose to choke off her truth. Freedom would own her soul and this man a special place within her heart from now into infinity.

"Should we give in to it?" Ryan's tongue moistened her shoulder as he moved soft material away from her skin. He moaned. "We're insane."

With no regrets, she spoke. "Yes."

"Yes, we're insane, or yes, we should give in to it?"

"Both."

A low, satisfied rumble left his throat. "God, yes."

The sound of her zipper sliding open caught her ears. Down and down he searched and smoothed his touch through her pubic hair. She inhaled sharply.

"All right?" he asked.

She nodded. Her breathing, increasing by the moment, proved excitement. Damn, this was too good. Too amazing. Despite the danger outside, or maybe because of it, her heart raced and they found this piece of heaven.

What they experienced now could disappear after an hour. After several hours if that creature made its way inside. She wanted the ultimate end with Ryan. Now. Right here. Beyond this paradise, she didn't want to think about what came next.

His other hand cupped her breast, moved up the satiny skin to her taut nipple. A gentle brush over her beaded flesh, and she moaned at the exquisite pleasure. He teased, grasping her aroused nipple and strumming. He manipulated the hard buds, pulling, gently twisting, and tormenting her flesh with tugs and brushes. Writhing in his arms, she started to pant.

"Easy," he whispered.

"I can't...you're making me crazy."

"Sweet colleen." Guttural and filled with desire, his accent deepened and heightened her senses like a fierce caress. "Oh, yeah."

Heedlessly, she absorbed sensation and closed her mind to everything but each feverish, seductive movement of his body against hers. Instinct moved her, until her body flowed, enticed by his touch without thought or denial.

Hardening and thickening even more, his cock nudged her butt. He continued to caress her nipples, each tug and pluck sending a new shock of ruthless need straight between the moist folds between her legs. She could hardly stand it, writhing in his arms.

Ryan paused long enough to grasp the waistband of her jeans and bikini panties and shove them down to her knees. Open and vulnerable, she surrendered. He gently intruded on her folds, plying her wet pussy with touches designed to send her into meltdown.

One finger pushed up inside her and she gasped.

"That's it. Jesus, Mary and Joseph, you're so wet," he said into her ear.

He licked her ear, tugged her nipple and gave her aroused clit a flick. The combined touches made her gasp and shiver. It felt so good. He delicately pinched her nipple and it drew into a tighter peak.

Another brush of his thumb over her clit and she moaned. "Ryan, I can't stand this."

He laughed. "How about this?"

Another finger slid into her depths. She sighed with burgeoning pleasure as the pulse in her loins grew by the second. As he stroked her, she shivered and panted. Melting with ecstasy, she clasped her hand over his and held him to her pussy. Her slick opening turned plump with arousal, the scent warm in the air. As he stroked, he discovered her G-spot. Deep within her passage she tingled, ached, dying to discover the threshold that would send her over the edge into a beautiful place. She longed to discover an orgasm more explosive and revealing than any she'd known. Tantalizing friction continued, the steady pressure and caressing bringing moan after ecstatic moan to her lips.

"Oh, Ryan."

"Come on, honey. Tell me what you want."

Instead, she pulled away from his embrace and turned to him.

Stark with passion, his gaze danced over her. "What's wrong?"

She smiled tenderly. "Nothing. Everything is right."

The puzzled, troubled expression chasing over his features disappeared when she leaned down and undid her athletic shoes and tossed them away along with her socks. She made quick work of her jeans and flung them onto the bed. With an upward yank, she removed her tops and bra and discarded them with a flick of her wrist. They landed on the floor. Naked and flushed, she watched as his gaze devoured. Searing hunger flashed in his eyes, a flicker she wanted to fan into a blaze.

There was no turning back.

She understood when they crossed from merely best friends to man and woman on a hunt to discover the furthest limits of physical love. That time was now.

Gina absorbed once again the planes, the angles, the sheer power within his torso. With voracious attention, she explored his chest. She closed her eyes as she swept her fingers over the crisp hair and hard pecs. Feathery arousal tickled her lower belly as she enjoyed the sensation. With scorching intensity, he gazed into her eyes and drew her toward the fiery promise she'd wanted deep within her soul. Her heart ached, her mind spun, so many words she needed to express. He gathered her in his arms before she could speak.

He lowered his head and his lips touched hers, hot silk and clinging. He brushed his tongue over her lower lip then dipped inside. Dizzy with desire, she plunged into the kiss. Her arms went around his neck and clung. With steady strokes, his tongue tangled, twisted with hers. Ravenous for his taste, wanting to plunge into this experience until she forgot everything but their physical bodies, she kissed him back with fervent passion.

He broke away long enough to bend down to her breasts. As his mouth closed over one nipple, she gasped with the sweet pleasure. Her nipple tingled under the persistent brush of his rough-soft tongue. Her pussy clenched and released, wanting his heat and hardness thrusting hot and thick into her center. Gina panted as the concentrated desire sparked a fire so intense she gasped and writhed under the pressure. He sucked greedily, his lips distending her nipple, then soothing it with long sweeps of his tongue. Moving back and forth between her breasts, he licked, savored. With sensual acquaintance, Ryan tested the tight buds with tiny touches and long, firm suckling. She moaned continuously, no longer able to hold back stunning desire. Whimpering, she plunged her fingers into his hair and tightened on the smooth strands.

Ryan glided down, lowering to his knees until he nuzzled her pubic hair with his nose. She gasped in excitement. He looked up. In his eyes, she saw answers, a mesmerizing attention that burned into her memory, never to leave. She quivered as he urged her to part her legs.

"Let me taste," he said huskily. As he stared at her pussy, he licked his lips. "Damn, honey. You are so ready to be fucked."

Delight sent a quiver through her. "Ryan. You are a very bad boy."

Rather than answer her tiny admonition, he leaned forward and buried his nose in her pussy hair. "Jesus, you smell good."

Her face flamed. Fire burned in his gaze, turning blue eyes into a blaze of rushing desire. He didn't wait—he buried his mouth in her pussy, his tongue brushing through her engorged pussy lips. Exquisite tension broke inside and to her amazement, a tiny, bursting, sweet orgasm shot through her clit.

"Oh." She sighed and whimpered at the surprise pleasure.

Ryan laughed softly, the rough, masculine sound filtering through the fog in her senses. He continued, thrusting his tongue inside her, then drawing the soft and rough texture of his tongue over her clit. She writhed, and he grasped her butt cheeks and held on. Licking, feasting, he took her higher. She spread her legs wider to give him greater access. Again, he stabbed his tongue between her pussy lips and the sensation of hot tongue buried in her vagina made her squirm and gasp. He palmed her ass then released her to reach up and clasp her breasts. She felt the long stroke of his tongue just as he pinched her nipples. With each tweak of her throbbing nipples, she felt an equal tug low in her belly.

"Oh. Oh God, please don't stop," she said, the ache in her pussy heightening.

His skillful tongue savored with warm, tender licks along the fold of each labia, reaching deep to flick softly, slowly, with infinite care. Arousal screamed through her, gathering quickly and without restraint under his mouth. She panted, the fire building between her legs almost too much to bear. He stopped. Gina moaned in frustration.

"What are you doing to me?" she asked as she looked down at him.

A wolfish grin touched his mouth. "Getting you ready. I may not remember much of the last ten years. But I know that

I've wanted to fuck you for a very long time. I don't want to rush this."

He tweaked her nipples again and she gasped her pleasure. Desperate for completion, she trembled. He'd wanted to take her for a long time?

Walloped by the stunning information, she said, "You mean we could have been doing this ages ago?"

A wide grin parted his lips, his teeth white and his eyes sparkling with thoroughly wicked intent. "Yeah. If I hadn't been so fucking stubborn. God, I shouldn't have pushed you away. I shouldn't have put barriers between us."

She pushed her fingers into his hair. "That's all right." She grinned wickedly. "I have you right where I want you now. On your knees. My sex slave."

He laughed. "Is that what I am, now? Are you sure about that?"

Without waiting for her answer, he grasped her ass, squeezed and buried his tongue between her legs. He concentrated on her clit, fluttering his tongue over it until she thought she'd howl to the moon. She sobbed for breath, her hips wriggling in his grip, her clit throbbing for fulfillment, wanting it, dying for it, ready to beg and say she'd do anything. With each relentless flick of his tongue, she went higher.

She whimpered. "Oh God. I can't. I can't."

"Mmm. Yes, you can." He put two long fingers to her slippery, soft entrance and slipped deep up inside. "Give in to it. Take it."

She moaned at the exquisite delight as his fingers speared straight up into her swollen, hungry core. He withdrew them and she moaned again. He plunged them deep and she gasped. His tongue slipped over her clit as his fingers started a steady, unstoppable fuck, sliding in and out of her dripping-wet passage. With a driving rhythm, he ate her pussy and thrust his fingers. Wildness, happiness and a dynamic need to take what he offered drove her to the top, held her on a fine edge of a knife until she lost it. Ecstasy slammed her. Gina yelped. Her vaginal walls gripped his fingers in tight pulsations as he continued to smooth his fingers in and out. His tongue kept up its relentless licking over her clit. Clamping and releasing, her muscles rippled and contracted in spectacular waves of dazzling pleasure. He slipped his fingers from her and stopped tonguing her pussy. Shaking as the storm eased, she clasped his shoulders and gasped out her breaths.

A satisfied male smile curved his mouth. She could almost hear his thoughts. Good. No more waiting. Not this time. Time had become a luxury.

He stood quickly, got rid of his boots, shucked his jeans. She could see the rigid line of a very thick, very long cock pushing at the material of his black briefs. Her mouth literally watered. Gina almost reached out to touch him. He stripped the briefs down, and seconds later revealed the cock she'd fantasized about for years. She knew her eyes rounded with awe. She'd never been into measuring a man's cock, but Ryan's penis was big, gorgeous, greedy male. With a jerking motion, his cock twitched higher. Gina dared look at him. Lust mingled with indisputable tenderness in his eyes. He gathered her into his arms, and the sensation of his hard, hot body along hers made her close her eyes and sigh in ecstasy.

"We need protection," he said quietly, "because if we take this further, I want to be deep inside you when you come."

His words, punctuated by a kiss, fired her libido into hyperdrive.

She opened her eyes and hurried to put him at ease. "I'm on the patch. And I'm healthy."

His fingers traced over the patch on her hip. He nodded. "The SIA tests us, and I'm totally healthy. I've never made love without a condom before." He smiled. "God, being inside you bareback..."

She trusted him. An ache of love speared her heart. And she wanted to feel his naked cock deep within her. Wanted to feel his semen filling her. She'd never experienced cravings as powerful before.

Ryan grinned cockily. "Turn around, honey."

He urged her toward the kitchen counter.

"What are we doing?" she asked.

"Like you want it. Like I want it. Fast."

Fast. Ferocious excitement took hold, her heart slamming faster, her belly trembling, her breathing increasing.

He urged her to lean over the counter just at the right level. She opened her legs wide as he reached around to clasp one breast. He took hold of her nipple, twisted, and rolled the tight flesh. A moan escaped her. Another groan came on its heels as his broad cock head touched the heated, wet folds. He thrust, burrowing slow but relentlessly.

"Ryan. Oh God."

"So tight." He moaned, as he forced deeper.

She shuddered and her back arched. She'd never had a cock this big inside her, and as each thick, long inch worked down, down deep, she groaned with the delicious sensation of being spread wide. Finally, he could enter no further. His length packed her to overflowing. Her pussy gushed liquid over his cock, easing his penetration as he drew back the slightest bit then pressed forward. Gina whimpered at the exquisite sensation as his naked flesh caressed her deep inside. Panting, she felt her vaginal walls spreading wider, allowing his cock to plow her straight to the womb. Each slight movement he made sent wildfire splinters of heat darting into her exquisitely responsive channel. She fell into the physical realm with a deepness that assured unremitting bliss. Her heart pounded, her limbs shook.

Stuffed until the root of his cock touched her pussy lips, she squirmed. "Ryan, oh my God. You feel so good."

"Mmm." He lay across her back and kissed her neck.

"Please. Do something...I'm...I can't stand this."

"All right?" His voice, husky with Irish tones, whispered into her ear. "Am I hurting you?"

"No. I'm just aching. I want..."

"Tell me."

"You're so big. So *hard*."

His soft chuckle brushed her ears. "Yeah?"

"Yes."

"Does that please you?"

The power of him driven into her body like a thick spike made her want to scream with pleasure and frustration. "Yes, yes. Do something."

"At your command."

He drew back slowly until only about an inch of him stayed inside her. The slick ease of his passage soothed and drove her mad at the same time. In he moved, taking her by small degrees, and his hardness spread her, the friction incredible. No other moment in her life felt so good or so right.

She twisted in his grip as he flicked and teased her nipples and finally bottomed out inside her once more. Beginning a new stroke, he increased the twisting, plucking of her nipples. Spasms within her pussy tightened and released on his cock. He started a motion, a ruthless caressing inside her tight passage. He barely moved, his cock sliding slickly within her well-lubricated pussy.

"Oh," she breathed out in ecstasy. His strokes tormented as he continued the incremental push and pull that rubbed a spot deep inside. She'd never felt anything like it. "Oh my God."

He wouldn't speed up, wouldn't thrust harder. Stroke, pull back slightly. Stroke with ruthless power. His hips pulsated against hers, his loins tucked tight up to the wet labia that encased him. She spread her legs wider, wanting him closer yet. She felt the brush of his pubic hair against her pussy and the strength of his thighs brushing hers. She quivered under the most sensual assault she could have imagined, her mind a fog of staggering paradise. His hands wandered over her shoulders, her back and then to her hips where he held her in place.

Her pussy walls gushed cream and grew wetter as he drew back and then thrust hard. She moaned in pleasure. He thrust again. And again. He shortened his strokes, moving his hips closer until each plunge was a digging, driving force.

"Oh, shit." Her voice went high.

She'd never been fucked out of her mind like this before. She wanted an orgasm so badly she could almost taste it, and yet she never wanted their dance to end.

Pleasure coiled in her belly, and she couldn't stop moans from escaping. He thrust harder between her thighs, claiming her. He sank into her repeatedly, the driving fuck sending her into the stratosphere. Pleasure stirred, tingled in her depths and she demanded, panting out her words of excruciating ecstasy until her voice went rusty. The beautiful pleasure was too much, too powerful. Every slick plunge inside drew her higher toward the most inconceivable beauty.

"Ryan." She moaned, unable to stop the sweet pulsating that grew and dominated until she became nothing but matter, but the stars and heavens.

Here, beyond the thunder and lightning that had dominated her world not long ago, beyond the fear, she dissolved into nothing more than physical being.

Grunting now with each reaming thrust, he growled out his demand. "Come." He gasped, he urged her onward. His fingers tightened mercilessly on her hips. "Ah, colleen, come on, darlin'."

Panting nonstop she writhed. Impaled on his hot, thick cock until her world revolved around nothing but his body inside hers.

One last hard thrust, and she detonated. She shrieked, her wail of mind-melting delight high-pitched and true. Gina shivered in his embrace as waves of hot pleasure melted in her core. Her breath panted from between parted lips as ecstasy ebbed. Then she realized he was still hard inside her.

He slowly slid from her body and turned her around. He cuddled her close.

Eyes melting, his nostrils flaring with each deep breath, he said huskily, "I want to see you come. You know what it felt like when you climaxed? Sweet, hot. You trembled around me."

The low intensity of his deep voice vibrated nerve endings she didn't know she had, and his amazing sexual prowess inflamed more long-buried desires.

The glow in his eyes melted her heart. "Ryan…"

What could she say? He'd robbed her of breath, of enough thoughts to make a coherent sentence.

He brushed his index finger over her moist lips. "Don't say a thing. Just feel what we've got. Right here. Right now."

He led her to the bed and eased her onto the coverlet. Though the room was cool, and her skin prickled with momentary goose bumps, anticipation drew her body into an eager frenzy. Her heart pounded with renewed excitement, and she felt hot cream slicken her pussy and moisten her thighs as her body reacted to the thought of more sex.

As he lowered his body over hers, she cupped his face and gazed into the depths of his eyes. "If we make it out of here—"

He kissed her. Soft, chaste, yet promising much more, his taste tender and giving. "We'll make it out of here." He gently pulled her hand down until her fingers encircled his hard shaft. "Do what you want with me."

When had a man ever asked for her this? None. Not until now.

She understood what she wanted and experienced it in the earnest reaches of her heart. With a grin, she pushed him onto his back. He grunted and smiled back.

Leave it up to a guy to communicate his more animal excitement with unusual noises. Sprawled on his back, naked and vulnerable, Ryan represented delicious, dangerous man. He stretched his arms above his head, and she watched his biceps ripple. Her heartbeat quickened, her mouth literally watered. He spread his legs and gave her full view. Long-limbed, he stretched out on the bed, a feast for her devouring. His hair was tousled, his jaw stubbled, the extreme desire in his eyes a fuel for her trembling hunger. His broad chest and muscled stomach were perfect, a banquet for the eyes. His cock stood straight up from a nest of black hair, a testament to his arousal.

Strong legs tempted her touch as she brushed her fingertips over his thighs and down to his calves. Ryan's muscles shuddered under her onslaught. He drew in a hissing breath. Awareness heightened for Gina as she enjoyed his reactions. Licking her lips, she leaned over and took his mouth. His hands clamped on to her waist and drew her on top of him. Chest hair tickled and aroused her nipples. She wriggled against his cock, then released his mouth long enough to sit upright. His cock was a long, hard bar along her soft tissues. With a movement she knew instinctively, she rubbed her moist labia and clit along his cock with excruciating slowness. She ran her palms over his chest, her fingernails gently teasing his nipples.

He sucked in another breath. "Ah, hell. Gina."

"Yes?" she asked with a wicked grin.

"You're killin' me." His voice thickened, went deeper with passion.

"Is that a good thing?"

"The best damned thing that's ever happened to me."

Her inner diva caught fire, loving the hooded look in his eyes, the spellbound attention. She winked.

"If you don't fuck me soon, I'm going to lose my mind." The deep purr in his tone sent shivers of fine-edged excitement across her skin and between her legs. She ached to move the few extra inches it would take to slide him home. Nestling him within her body and taking them to new ecstasy wouldn't take long.

"Are you punishing me?" Ryan smoothed his fingers over her hips. "Getting me back for forgetting our ten years together?"

Without warning, his words caused tears to fill her eyes. She felt the burn, the terrible realization that she might cry like a baby any second. She heaved a deep breath and hoped the tears wouldn't pop over her lids.

"Don't be silly. You didn't forget me for long," she said in a strangled voice. "Besides, this is about now. About what we've built together."

There, she'd admitted they had developed a relationship — a close friendship at the very least.

With a touch that branded her heart, he brushed his fingers over her jawline. Liquid soft, his eyes reflected a sweet gentleness, a defenseless light. It staggered her, took her breath and stole her soul.

"I can't believe I forgot you for even one second. Remind me again," he said softly.

Tears escaped, and this time she didn't attempt to hold them at bay. She heaved a shuddering breath.

He frowned and reached up to brush them away. "Whoa. Why are you crying?"

She took the plunge, shoving aside fear. "Because I've never been this happy before."

His frown dissolved into the cocky Ryan smile she understood so well. "You're driven in here by a monster from another dimension, a good friend doesn't remember your name, and now you're locked in the basement and not sure when you'll escape, and you've never been happier?"

She leaned forward until her lips brushed his. "Yes."

"Then show me."

She kissed him with furious need, driving her tongue between his lips and tasting him with deep strokes. After feasting on his kisses, she drifted down his neck, up to his ears, lingering long enough for his breath to catch and solid moans to escape him. She licked a path over his collarbone, down to one nipple. She nipped. He laughed. She drew her fingers up to his other pectoral and pinched his nipple while taking a long, sweet pull on the other nipple with her lips. Fire and craving melted her as she savored the hardened beads under her fingertips and lips. His breathing came harder, his continual moans of pleasure firing her arousal to new heights.

Her hunger reignited like a fireball. Passion drew her into a no-mind state where thoughts drifted away and only his body moving and gliding, their skin touching meant anything. Her mind filled with his essence, what made him Ryan through and through. For his strength, generosity and protection, for his gentleness and so many things, she'd give him her body. Her heart.

She grinned wryly and leaned forward, her intent clear. "What have we got here?"

"Ah, Jesus, Mary and Joseph." His accent thickened into a heavier brogue. "Please."

"Please what?"

She skated down his body and explored his muscled stomach with pure excitement. When she reached his cock, it stood proud, long and thick. Her fingers glided over hard flesh, encompassing his strength. She glanced up and his breath caught as she stroked from root to tip. With one touch she smoothed pre-cum over his cock head, then polished down in one movement. He groaned and his hips twitched. Oh, yes. She liked having this power. Had she ever felt this strong before? This aware of her womanhood? No. Her past boyfriends hadn't given of themselves, unequivocally and without inhibition like Ryan did. She saw it in his eyes, and the passion-strained tightness of is lips. His breathing quickened as she cradled his cock lovingly, navigating his burgeoning shaft as it thickened and pulsed under her touch. Every inhibition eroded as she lavished his flesh with stroke after stroke. Unafraid, she caught his gaze with hers and held it. His eyelids dipped as his bold attention enslaved her senses. The mingling of his musk with her liquid excitement combined into a heady chemistry. More heat trickled from between her legs and her core ached with scalding requirement for conclusion. She knew she'd never discover satisfaction until she could enjoy his thrust spearing her once more. His hands moved over her shoulders, her sides urgently as if he couldn't get enough of her.

"Please what?" she asked. She allowed her tongue to lap over his cock tip and tasted a pearl of his life-giving force. "Mmm."

He drew in a quick breath. She spied his rapt attention. His eyes narrowed and he licked his lips. With a low, hungry lust in his voice, he said, "Suck me. Lick it."

Fire burned in her belly at his rough demand. She loved the freedom, the wildness and joy washing every bad memory away. Only now remained.

"Damn it, Gina. Put me out of my misery."

She laughed softly and took his entire cock into her mouth. His breath hissed inward on a groan. As she licked and sucked, his breathing grew harder, his moans excited.

"Fuck me." He couldn't mask the boldness, the untamed quality within his harsh words.

He'd taken her where she'd never been a few minutes ago, when his cock had slammed into her center. She vowed he would feel the same out-of-this-world, heart-shaking sensations.

Gina was flooded with a dauntless desire to possess part of him within her forever. She released his cock. It might be the wrong time to say this, it might be *completely* wrong. She didn't care.

His smoky eyes met hers. Within his gaze, she saw passion and a tortured, wrenching acknowledgment. "I know. I know what you're feeling, colleen."

And she realized he did understand. A profound link formed between them years ago, and their experiences today assured the connection stayed strong. Tears mixed with her melting desire to show him how much she wanted and cared for him.

She poised her wet, aching pussy above his cock. "What do you need?"

A disarming smile boldly curved his mouth. "Everything you can give."

She reached down and cradled his cock in one hand. She tightened her grip around him as she rotated the wet tip along her sensitive pussy lips.

His nostrils flared, and his hands reached up to grip her waist. Hard and sure, his fingers kept her in place. Gliding her slick flesh over his, she eased down.

"Oh," she said as his bluntness parted her.

"What's wrong?"

She wriggled on his cock, less than an inch of his solidness buried within. She shook her head. "I'm tight."

"Yeah, you are." A satisfied grin crossed his face. "Hot, wet and tight. And it feels fuckin' wonderful."

She smiled and pushed down. Rising then falling, she worked his shaft with steady rhythm. Two inches of wide, thick cock speared inside with steady plunges as she moved her hips, gyrated to a beat only she knew. His hands on her hips helped her with the flow. Gina closed her eyes, and swiveled her hips. Shimmering waves of pleasure tingled and built. She concentrated on the sensation, centering on the heat, the broadness of his cock, until his inches thrust to the womb.

"Oh, yeah." He breathed the syllables, raw and rough.

Feeling devilishly wanton and free, she allowed her hands to slide from her hips, over her belly, up to her rib cage and on to her breasts. She cupped her breasts, and his hands covered hers. Gently, he massaged, keeping her fingers under his so they both manipulated her nipples. Writhing into the scalding arousal, she pumped her hips. He bent his knees, planted his feet on the bed and thrust upward. Again and again he thrust, she counterthrust, and their scorching connection blitzed her with pleasure. Pulsating and tingling, she ached to come. Ragged breaths left her throat, and the words left her without inhibitions.

"Ryan. Please. Please."

With heart-shaking beauty, the escalating inferno exploded inside her. She flushed, burned, as savage orgasm shook her to the core. She cried out as the whirlpool of pleasure raged through her.

Ryan's body went into a frenzy. His mind was blank, filled only with the extreme pleasure watching her climax created for him. God, she was beautiful. Fucking sexy as she bounced on him, and he thrust his hips, pounding into her as hard as he could. Her cheeks flushed, her eyes closed, her lips parted. Pleasure washed over her face as she climaxed, her wet heat rippling over his cock. He pushed up, thrusting, fucking, taking everything she wanted to give and sending it back. She released her breasts and his fingers returned to her nipples to pluck and strum. Her nipples felt like hot little pebbles under his fingertips. Pinching gently, he drew them into tight points. Up and down she rode him with an abandon and eagerness that blew his mind and sent it to the four winds. The sensation of her enclosing and caressing him melted him into a fireball. He wanted her to come again and again. So he assured it, continuing deep, rhythmic thrusts.

Her eyes widened as astonished pleasure pulled her over a new precipice. "Ryan!"

Her head fell back, and as she screamed his name and ecstasy convulsed her body again, he lost it. Thrusting wildly, he grunted, panted, found the animal inside him and rode it. He growled as pressure drew his balls tight and released. He let loose a wild, animalistic cry as he spilled inside her and shook with orgasmic pleasure.

As their bodies came down from the bliss, he drew her on top of him and cradled her close. His hands charted her back and down to her ass as he caressed her. He savored their beating hearts, their slowing breaths. Light perspiration dampened her skin.

She sighed, and the sound held pure bliss. Happiness blindsided him at the same time concern hit him like a roundhouse kick. While he didn't regret their physical relationship, he worried big time what she expected now.

He knew he didn't do significant relationships. While they'd discussed earlier why they hadn't gotten together and his girlfriend who'd died in Ireland, he hoped their physical connection didn't make things awkward. For the moment, her hand caressing his chest and her trim thigh lying over his leg enriched the fading glow. Yeah, he'd admit it. This woman made his heart tumble, his body implode with incinerating sensations. As a rule, he didn't think he spent much time analyzing his feelings. Right now he felt out of control, tittering on the brink of so many emotions he couldn't identify them.

When she propped up on one elbow and looked down on him, he smiled. "Hey."

"Hey." Her soft tone and the melting look in her eyes warned him.

Oh, boy. That look was rife with emotions, with feelings he didn't know if he could return. Not while they battled a strange creature and unknown realms. Not when he should spend time determining their escape plan or next move. Her mouth, moist and red from kissing, beckoned him into wanting another bout of body wrestling. His cock twitched.

God, he was fucking pathetic.

He winced as a pain darted through his temples. Shit, he was thinking too hard. He closed his eyes and rubbed his temples.

"Ryan?" Her question held strong concern. "Are you okay?"

He smiled faintly and opened his eyes. He returned to embracing her. "After-sex headache, I guess."

She frowned. "I've never heard of people getting a headache after sex. I thought that was reserved for people who didn't want to have sex."

Ryan chuckled. "Well, it's true. Happens sometimes when sex gets particularly…vigorous."

She blushed, and he laughed again.

"Don't laugh. I'm not an innocent. I just hadn't heard of–"

He plunged his fingers into the hair at the back of her neck and tugged her into a tongue-thrusting, deep kiss. When he pulled back, the flush in her face broadened rather than retreating. God, he loved the sparkling life in her eyes, the way her parted lips begged for another kiss. Plunging into another soul-stealing romp wasn't wise with a beast stalking them.

Soon after, they closed their eyes and fell into a light doze.

Chapter Nine

Gina awoke from her half state of sexual daze and sleep. Lying on her left side with Ryan spooned behind her and cradling her in his arms, she knew total comfort, security and bliss. She drew in the spicy, sweet-salty musk of their sexual acts. What happened between them arose in her mind with stunning clarity. The passion, the heat their attraction created. She'd climaxed with wrenching force, and she'd never imagined anything this beautiful could happen to her. Writer or not, creative or not, she'd never quite expected this. Never believed a unifying moment between her and Ryan could bring them to a time where quiet and contentment surrounded them.

Glorying in what she'd experienced in Ryan's arms, she felt as gooey as a scrumptious dessert. He'd tweaked an enticing and evasive part of her heart, her physical hungers and brought them to fruition. She knew more lay within her, ready to splinter apart in a climax.

Affection, delight and growing tenderness blossomed inside as she savored what she'd shared with Ryan. God, it had really happened. She'd loved and been loved by him, no longer thwarted by fear that once made her sluggish and cowardly with her emotions, no longer agitated by a want she couldn't have. She'd taken him, and him her. No denying the way he'd excavated her desires and fed them to her in glorious, unfettered passion. Realization of a long-desired dream made her joyful in a way she'd evoke for the rest of her life.

Hard, powerful arms braced her back against a steely body. She sighed and enjoyed the strength of his biceps and forearms, the press of his stalwart chest against her back, the solid, ridged belly, the aggressive pillar of his cock against her ass cheeks. Another forbidden delight tingled in her belly and sent a trickle of wet heat between her legs. She wanted him in places she'd only imagined before in the farthest, darkest reaches of her mind.

She reveled in sensual comfort. As she shifted in his embrace, her skin heating, Ryan's hands skated over her highly sensitized skin. His legs tangled with hers, and hard thighs, rough with hair, brushed against her legs with exciting promise. She inhaled deeply and allowed her mind to drift. If the storm continued to rage outside, she couldn't hear it. A glance at the clock by the bed would tell her the time, but she didn't want to look. What mattered was the sweet languorous place where only the two of them existed.

Put this in a romance novel.

Yeah, she just might. If she could recreate the feelings, the textures, the sounds. It hardly seemed possible to record anything this magnificent on paper.

Warmth spread from her stomach outward as her body ignited under his touch. One hand cradled her rib cage and tilted her farther back into his arms. He skimmed his other palm over her hip, kneading with gentle attention then moving back far enough to coast lightly over her ass. He palmed her skin and lingered over the indentation between her butt and the back of her leg. It should have tickled, but instead the sensation warmed her skin. She quivered delicately, astonished by the frantic return of desire welling inside her. Moaning, she closed her eyes and took pleasure in the gathering flame within her belly and the instant arousal.

She gasped as he twisted her nipple with tender attention between finger and thumb. Delving into wet heat, he traced her folds. Each torturous touch made her shiver with delight. Without rush, he showed her a new world of excitement. Never before had a man taken such care, displayed such patience. His fingers teased her nipples, shifting back and forth between her breasts to cup, squeeze. He held one breast captive while his other hand traced the hairs over her mound, tugging and testing, then slipping down to part her. Every brush of his fingers so close to her clit made her writhe and gasp. She almost begged, the sensual misery acute. His tongue traced her ear, his breath hot. She shivered as incendiary needs rioted within her body and demanded fulfillment. Fragile sanity hung in the balance, her breath ragged as she reached down and followed his path over her mons.

"Show me," he whispered into her ear.

He took her hand and pressed it into her folds. She gasped softly as she touched her wetness and his fingers guided hers directly over her clit.

"That's it," he said.

He encouraged her fingers into an up-and-down, circular motion over her clit. Keeping the pressure light, he assisted her. She'd never pleasured herself in front of a man, but this excited her with a heady rush.

Ryan drew his hand away, but only long enough to nudge her thigh up and slip his thick, smooth cock between her legs and across the wet surface of her pussy. She gasped in delight. His cock pushed high until the tip brushed over her clit, so long and hard and demanding attention.

She clamped her thighs on him, he gasped and oaths escaped him. "Fuck. Hell."

She laughed softly. "Like that?"

His breath rasped in her ear, his voice now guttural and deep with harsh desire. "I'd like this even better."

His hips flexed back as he lifted her thigh again. With one determined thrust, he speared through her hot, wet opening and deep inside. She gasped and moaned as his heavy cock buried so high up inside she swore he touched her cervix. His arms snaked around her tight. One hand grasped her nipple, strummed and swirled. She arched against him, twisting her hips. He slid from her body, drawing back almost entirely.

With a raw snarl of primal male desire, he thrust hard. She cried out as he speared deep and hard.

Tumbling into a mindless physical state, and knowing only his possession, she sobbed out a shaky gasp. His hips stirred until his quickening strokes pushed high and fast. Urgent strokes pushed her into an exquisite glory. Bold and brazen, his fingers dived between her legs and found her clit, starting a teasing tempo. The magnificence of their joining tumbled her into a ceaseless, glorious hunt for ecstasy.

She grasped wherever she could touch him, her hands finding his powerful thighs and holding on. She panted, her body on fire as his hungry conquest took her on a journey so fired with passion and glory she knew it would imprint on her mind for eternity. Something stoked brighter within as his fast thrusts caressed her hot channel. The tempo increased until his thrusts plowed her. Lost in the rhythmic tempo and his fervent plunges, she craved each movement as he filled her. His brutish length plowed hard, the abandon of his animal reaction firing burning need inside her. Her vagina clasped tight and released over his thrusting cock. He growled and jammed hard into her. She splintered apart, her pussy tightening and releasing in waves of rapture so intense she screamed.

Ryan wanted her writhing, her wordless gasping to continue. He bucked, his hips pumping, digging, rooting for the heart of her. Her hot, wet, slick grasp around his cock drew him into copulation frenzy.

His mind flew away on the utter wildness, the soul-stealing sensation of thrusting his swollen, taut cock as hard into her as he could manage. He power-housed into her, relentless in his search for her pleasure and his.

"Fuck," he growled as he drove harder, thrusting with a crazy cadence that threatened to stop his heart.

Again, her breathing accelerated and pleas broke from her lips. "Oh God. Oh God."

Then, as he felt climax taking him on a final journey, he slipped his fingers over her clit and rubbed. She trembled anew as he stroked her flesh. She shrieked, her pussy clasping him in a tight fist as she contracted in waves of orgasm. He thrust his cock through her climax, hoping to prolong her pleasure. As her panting slowed, he eased from her and turned her over on her back.

Ryan leaned over her, his hips lowering between her thighs as he thrust once more into her. She moaned softly, loving the sensation as she planted her feet on the bed and pushed up to assist his entry. His groin pressed against her pubic bone and his balls rode the crease in her ass. Feeling more than stretched and plenty full, her pussy ached, eager for more. She encircled his neck with her arms, and he buried his face in her neck. Untamed, primed for more excitement, her body electrified.

She grunted at the sensation of thickness stabbing deep inside, then he withdrew, and thrust, withdrew and thrust until his hips pistoned, his groin grinding against her pussy. She clawed at his back, her world the fierce sound of grunting, moaning, panting. His hands levered under her ass, grasped her butt cheeks and he pounded into her mercilessly. His fingers tightened on her ass as he ground into her with staggering intensity. The bed creaked, the frame rattling as they settled into forceful cadence.

She screamed, her pussy trembling over his cock and sending his own climax shooting to the top. Growls escaped him as the pinnacle hit him hard. Climax slammed him in wave after wave of shooting pleasure. He shivered with each pulse from his cock, each satisfying sensation of rushing semen exiting his cock and into her hot depths. He shivered and relaxed.

* * * * *

Niggling doubt moved insidiously into Gina's mind as she worked up a lather of soap in the shower. Had she made a mistake making love to Ryan?

Although his lovemaking had been tender and fierce, she possessed doubts. As she washed her hair, she burned to ask him questions. Although she'd always believed she'd been honest with him, she recognized now that her integrity hung in a balance. If she confessed what she felt in her heart—

What did she feel anyway?

Concern. Friendship. Passion.

If she took the next step, she knew her heart might crumble from rejection. Big time. Therein lay the problem. Her feelings lay on the surface, too sensitive, too on the edge. With everything that happened, she couldn't rely on sensible thinking to put emotions into coherent phrases. Better if she kept quiet and once they got out of this situation, she would rethink what occurred between them.

She left the bathroom redressed. Her heart pounded a little in anticipation as she observed Ryan's naked form sprawled on the bed where she'd left him. With his fingers laced behind his head, his biceps bulged with delicious muscles. His legs spread out in a hedonistic fashion that made her lick her lips in approval.

Before she could speak, he cracked a cocky grin and sprang off the bed. He prowled toward her, all lean muscle and undomesticated male animal.

Without a word, he drew her into his arms and lowered his mouth to hers. Instant and intoxicating, his lips shaped and molded hers with blatant sexual hunger. Warmth heated her from the inside out, and amazingly, arousal tickled her. She dove into his kiss, rubbing her breasts against his chest, and nestling her hips close to his. Luxuriating in the moment, she accepted the deep thrusts of his tongue. Her stomach clenched as she remembered how his cock had tunneled in and out of her. God, this man would drive her nuts yet.

When he released her, a grin blossomed on his face. "Damn, that was nice."

He strode toward the bathroom, and she didn't hesitate to enjoy the view of his broad, muscled shoulders and back and—oh, yes—how could any woman ignore that tight, round backside?

He turned around. "If you hear anything trying to break down the door up there, let me know."

"Sure."

When he retreated and closed the door, she sighed and closed her eyes. The man was sex walking. How could she guarantee when they survived this if her heart would be intact?

When he came out of the bathroom a few minutes later, he'd dressed. Damned shame concealing any portion of a body like that. Oh, well. Ryan couldn't run around naked all day. Unfortunately.

"Something wrong?" he asked.

"No." She sat in the chair again and this time put her feet up on the ottoman. She sank into the comfortable leather.

As before, he sat on the side of the ottoman so she couldn't avoid his blazing, direct gaze. He propped his forearms on his thighs and laced his hands together.

"Are we okay?" he asked.

The worry in his eyes surprised her. Could his interest be more than just sex? Of course it was. She'd felt his emotion, his desire both physically and mentally to become one with her. At the very least, he cared deeply for her.

"Of course." She took a chance and reached out to ruffle his unruly toss of hair. "What happened between us was the most beautiful thing I've ever experienced. It's never been like that for me."

"Never?"

"Never. You lit me on fire. I thought I would die it was so good." She kept her heart in her eyes, allowed him to see it.

A gratified smile passed over his face. "That's good." He slipped his hands over her thigh. "I didn't know it could be that exciting."

"You're kidding. A man like you must—"

"What?"

"Have many satisfied lovers."

He grunted. "Well, thank you. But I haven't slept with that many women."

"You remember?"

"Not exact numbers. I just know it hasn't been many."

They went silent for a moment, and then she saw him look over at the unusual closet set into the east side of the basement wall. She'd caught him glancing at it more than once, but this time it was obvious.

Recognition built in his face, then that wince that signaled pain in his temples again. "Ryan? What's up?"

He stood and headed for the doorway. "I'm not sure. Maybe nothing."

"Are you in pain?"

He rubbed his forehead then shook his head. "It's all right. It's already fading. I was thinking too damned hard." He growled out his next words. "Shit, I hate this. Every time I try to remember something there's this fucking wall that comes up then the burn in my temples."

Concerned, she frowned. "That worries me."

He shook his head slowly. "It's all right. I'll be fine. But thanks for caring."

"Of course I do."

He shrugged. "Anyway, I was looking at this doorway." He moved toward the elaborately carved wood door. "It's like the front doors on this cabin."

She glanced at the strange design. "It's beautiful. A bit strange, but it has that sort of Greek or Roman frieze appearance. I think it's elegant."

He perused the design centered in the middle of the door, and a memory flashed into his head like lightning. "Damn."

"What is it?"

He swallowed hard. Sure, he'd wanted his memory back, but this piece of remembrance battered at his psyche and threatened to remove the peace he'd found in her arms not long ago.

"Ryan?"

"This design is Mithras as the Romans saw it."

Obviously perplexed, she groaned. Little lines formed between her eyebrows. "Mithras. Why does that sound familiar?"

"It was a religion some Romans followed before it was superseded by Christianity. Many of the rituals performed in the religion are similar to Christianity, but with a completely different take on creation of the earth. The religion originated in Persia and took its name from the Indian and Persian god Mithras."

Interest flared in her eyes, and she drew closer to the door. "Tell me more."

Did he honestly want to? When she heard what he knew, what he understood about this religion and what might lie somewhere within this house, she might not want to know more. She might be scared as shitless as he was starting to feel.

"Mithras spread throughout the Mediterranean and northern Europe. It's tied up in astrology and astralism. By the time Romans became involved in the religion, it was different from the original incarnation."

"When did it flourish?"

"The high point was around the third century AD."

She moved even closer to the door. "Who is Mithras exactly?"

He crossed his arms and closed his eyes, accessing the information from the foggy memories and incompleteness he still felt. When pain didn't spear his temples, he opened his eyes. "Mithras was a god and appeared as light from the sky. He was given life by a rock—"

"By a rock?"

"Yeah, I know it sounds weird. Mithras was birthed on the banks of a river under a sacred tree. Shepherds witnessed his birth. He was armed with a knife, a torch and a cap on his head. They gave him shelter, offered him gifts and worshipped him. He started a series of deeds designed to fight evil in the cosmos. He challenged the sun, but when the Sun was defeated, the Sun struck up an alliance with Mithras. That's why you'll see Roman carvings of Mithras with a radiant crown."

"And there's probably more to the story than that."

"The bull story. Want to hear it?"

"Go on."

"Mithras captured a bull and took it to his cave. There were obstacles set in his path. The bull escaped, but the Sun sent an order to Mithras by a messenger, the Raven, to kill the bull. Mithras went after the bull and was helped by his dog."

She grinned. "His dog?"

A returning smile touched his mouth. "Yeah. Cozy, eh? Anyway, Mithras grabbed the bull and plunged a knife into its side. From the side of the bull came plants to inhabit the earth. From its spine was wheat, and from its blood the vine. Ahriman, god of evil, hated this sign of life and sent the scorpion and the snake to fight the spread of life. He failed, and the bull's seed created every species of animal. Mithras and the Sun had a feast. Mithras climbed into the heavens by way of the Sun's chariot and looks after the faithful from there."

"You're right. It does have connections to Christianity. You can see it in the story."

He liked seeing the way her lips parted in excitement and her eyes widened a bit. She looked sexy as hell this way and it drove him nuts.

"Why do I sense there's even more to this than you're telling me?"

Damn it, count on her to see every angle. "The cult chose dark places to worship such as caverns and natural or artificial caves."

"Why?"

"The caves or underground shrines symbolized the cosmos. Objects placed inside were symbolic of cosmic elements and regions of the sky."

She nodded. "An allegory."

"Exactly."

"What else?"

He shifted on his feet. "For them earth symbolized matter which made up the cosmos. The structure alludes to stages made by the soul into the world beyond."

"Fascinating." Her voice, liquid soft, purred against his ears.

"Because the soul went through stages, a devotee to the religion went through seven grades in order to achieve redemption. Raven, Occult, Soldier, Lion, Persian, Runner of the Sun, and Father. There were also seven doors, seven planetary spheres, seven days of the week and seven metals. The Moon was silver and assigned the first door, Mercury was iron and had the second door. Venus was tin and had the third door. The Sun had gold and was the fourth, Mars was alloy and the fifth door. Jupiter was bronze and the sixth door and Saturn was lead with the seventh door. The signs of the zodiac were also associated with the planets." He took a breath. "There's more if you want to hear it."

"Sure. This is really interesting."

"The soul passes through the seven planets and frees itself from astral influences associated with each of the planets. These influences were acquired when the soul passed down to earth. On the way back up to heaven, it leaves behind elements. It's a purification process. The rites of the initiate symbolize that journey. Initiates wore animal masks to show what stage they were."

"Did they have animal sacrifice?"

"Good guess. The sacrifices were dignified by cosmic and universal salvation."

He saw deep thought in her eyes as she absorbed the implications.

He pointed to the door. "This is called the Tauroctonia. It's a sacred image."

"Like Taurus in astrology."

"Exactly." He traced the image with his fingers. "The young god plunges a knife into the bull. The dog and snake lick its blood. The scorpion is trying to reach the bull's seed. Killing the bull is creation of the universe."

She moved closer to the doorway. "What's this other carving beneath? It's almost…macabre."

He couldn't deny that. The symbol had brought back one disturbing element of his memory he didn't think he wanted back. He traced the lion's body. "The lion is Zurvan. Man and beast." His fingers touched the creature with the head of a lion and a body wound 'round with the coils of a snake. "Zurvan shows Time with its ability to devour. The wings show the speed of Time. The gaping jaws show Time's voracity. Time is the maker and destroyer of all things. My guess is there's more symbolism somewhere in this house."

"Why? You don't think my friends are worshippers of Mithras, do you?" She gave him an indulgent smile.

"No." He rubbed at his forehead.

She smoothed her hand over his shoulder and biceps, and his body quickened and heated at her touch. Shit, even with a headache renewing in his skull, she gave him a hard-on.

"Why don't you sit down?" she asked.

"I'm fine."

"You'd say that even if you weren't. You're stubborn that way. One of these days it'll get you killed."

She sounded bitter, and it touched a hard place inside him. He felt the obstruction melting. Okay, so she knew him too well.

He touched her hair, a caressing motion he couldn't stop. Then his hand dropped to his side. "I'm sorry. I'll try and take better care of myself." He cleared his throat. "I don't have time to feel bad."

She pulled at the neck of her sweater as if it choked or irritated her. "No, I'm sorry. I shouldn't have snapped at you." She took a deep breath then shifted gears. "Why do you think there should be more symbols around the house?"

He paused and realized he didn't have a firm answer. He scratched his head. "I don't know."

Her brow knitted. "Ryan, don't hold back on me now."

"I remembered this lion creature and the history behind the Mithras religion. The rest of why it's important isn't clear."

She narrowed her eyes, and the dubious light there said she didn't quite believe him.

"Damn it," he said. "My shit is roasted if I can't think why this door is important."

"You think the door has something to do with your case? How could it? Wouldn't Marcus have told you?"

"Not if what I discovered out there in the woods isn't what any of us expected."

"The monster was anticipated, right?"

He nodded. "Yeah. But maybe not in the form we thought."

He saw the moment recognition hit her. She put her hand to her mouth and stifled a gasp. Her eyes went round. "Oh." She uncovered her mouth. "Zurvan. Are you telling me in that covert way of yours that the monster chasing you is this Zurvan thing? That's insanity."

"Is it?"

"Yes. It's crazy."

"We're not in the sane world you knew before today, Gina. This is a whole new ballgame."

He inhaled deeply. Gina's delicate scent, as illusive in definition as his memory, sidetracked him. *The woman is delicious. A fucking hazard to my equilibrium. I can't think about what I need to do with her around.*

"When I woke up this morning the world was simple. Eat breakfast, sit my butt in a chair, fire up the laptop, and there's my novella. That stinking novella that doesn't want to go where I want it to go. It was killing me. Now you're telling me some ancient creepy deity from history is stalking us? I'm all for imagination. I use it in my job, so I won't knock it. But if you're saying that thing that crashed into the house upstairs is this evil incarnate beast from a religion thousands of years old, I say you're nuts."

She walked into the kitchen and started fumbling with the dishpan on one side of the sink, then dug around in the cabinets below. He watched in silent amusement when she tipped far too much dish soap into the dishpan to wash one glass. She cursed. Rather than answering her last question, he kept his mouth shut.

What could he say? Her disbelief came clear. "Then what do you think is out there?"

She turned toward him, plastic gloves dripping water. "Earlier you said Marcus told you not to reveal the monster's identity. It was classified. So why would you suddenly tell me now?"

She swung back to the sink with an almost angry jerk.

Yeah, well, he'd jumped straight into this mess, he'd have to get himself out. He strolled toward the kitchen. "When I first looked at this door, it didn't mean anything to me. Not until the beast broke in. Then it came clear. Marcus explained about the beast, but I couldn't remember seeing it. Now I know what the hell was chasing me through the woods."

She rinsed the glass, put it into the drainer, removed the gloves and placed them neatly on the side of the drainer. She turned to face him. "But why did you come here? Sanctuary?"

Confess. Tell her why you came here.

He moved nearer to her, proceeding across the room with purpose. He knew she felt the heat between them, the sexual spark that hovered just out of reach. When he stood near enough to capture her scent, he braced his hands on either side of her so she couldn't escape.

Gina thought she'd never breathe again. The fire, the sultry burn deep in his gaze, the way he caged her so that she wouldn't leave made her heart race. A low, steady ignition swirled within her belly. She forgot her curiosity about the beast and drowned in the essence of man.

"I ran through the forest as if the devil was on my heels. And maybe he was. In Mithras legend, Ahriman is the god of evil, and he sent the beast into our dimension. Ahriman and the beast Zurvan are from a real place, Gina."

She'd heard his legend with a full ear, yet she couldn't admit it. Because if she believed in this Mithras religion and its trappings, she'd feel as if she'd lost her mind.

She gazed up into his crystalline eyes, and her resistance started to fade. "That's not possible."

"The Shadow Realm is a dimension. You've heard of string theory, right?"

"A little."

"The SIA discovered a hell of a long time ago that this theory is right. Long before scientists on the outside world said it might have validation. String theory says there are other dimensions. The Shadow Realm is real and it has many nasty creatures in it. Some of them have been making their way over here for centuries and causing havoc. Zurvan is one of them."

She shook her head, unable to believe. "So somehow this house and the Shadow Realm are connected."

"Bingo."

Gina stared at Ryan in disbelief. Intuition flashed through her mind. "This doorway…is that why you were on your way to the cabin?"

"I'm pretty sure it is."

"That explains the coincidence of you coming to the cabin to escape the creature. It wasn't coincidence after all."

"I have small flashes of running through the forest as fast as I could. Zurvan was chasing me, and I knew hauling ass was the only way I'd survive." He drove his fingers through his hair. "No matter what happened I had to make it this cabin and to you."

Get to you.

His words hovered in her psyche like a mantra, warming her soul. "You were worried about me?"

"Damned worried. Still am."

"Why? You said we're safe in here."

Confusion, anxiety, maybe self-reproach flitted through his eyes. She'd never seen him this uncertain before. It startled her, but it also brought her closer to the incredibly human side of Ryan she'd watched in action today. Only a few hours transpired since he collapsed at her doorstep, yet it felt like days. So much happened in so short a time. Seeing him exposed, even for a millisecond, threw her off guard and resurrected everything protective inside her. She hated his uncertainty because it highlighted her insecurities as well.

"There's a danger out there I've never encountered before, Gina. That's why I'm worried. You can't shoot Zurvan. There are other things you have to do."

"Such as?"

"That's the bitch of it." He made a slicing motion with one hand, frustration clear in his impatience. "I can't remember. I needed to reach this cabin, to this door." He gestured toward the Mithras door. "That's why when I came in the house, I was compelled to look around for a door with this symbol of Mithras on it. I wasn't sure why. When I didn't see the doorway...shit, I figured I was screwed. Then I saw this door and a ton came crystal clear."

She didn't like his concern-laced tone. "Tell me more. What are we dealing with here?"

He backed away from her. He cupped the back of his neck with both hands and kneaded the muscles. "The Shadow Realm is a complicated place."

"I gathered that."

He laughed, but there was no humor in the sound. "I don't know everything about the Shadow Realm. What I recall is disjointed."

She walked across the room and retreated to the chair. She looped her legs over one arm of the chair so that she faced him. "I'm listening."

He went to the single barstool near the kitchen counter and sat down. His gaze held hers with probing intensity. Awareness tingled through her and robbed Gina of complete confidence. His attention fixated on her like a brand, hot and intimidating. Almost as if he touched her in private places she didn't wish to reveal. Even in the face of danger, she couldn't deny her attraction for him. She waited patiently, though, for him to continue.

"I just remembered another thing about you." He swiveled the barstool so it faced her. "I should have guessed."

Puzzled, she frowned. "What?"

"Damn, I can't believe I didn't figure it out before."

She held her right hand up in a fist and shook it at him in mock threat. "Tell me what the hell you're talking about, Ryan Ahern, or I'll hurt you."

He winked. "Ooo. I'm scared. Hurt me. Hurt me good."

A tiny snort of laughter escaped. "You know I can."

His eyes sparked a kindred flame of laughter and sexual heat that combined into a lethal combo. He took a deep breath and looked away first.

She gasped. "You never look away first."

His eyebrows knitted. "Now it's my turn to ask what the hell you're talking about."

"Our stare-down challenges. You don't recall that?"

"No."

"I always looked away first until this time. You have incredible staying power." The last couple of words slipped from her before she could rephrase them. "Ummm…"

"I know what you mean." His smirk said he did, but that he'd joke with her anyway.

Innuendo hung thick in the air between them. She swallowed hard. "Anyway…"

"Anyway, there are beings that live in the Shadow Realm that are from our nightmares."

"Monsters?" she asked, dubious.

"You could say that. The SIA figures we've only run into a few of them."

She wrinkled up her nose. "You mean, like the Loch Ness monster?"

He smiled and nodded. "Yep."

She groaned. "You're yanking my chain."

"No, I'm not."

Still unable to believe, she squirmed until her head nestled in one corner of the chair. Sure, she believed in the paranormal, but she also had one foot in the practical arena. "Most of the things we think are paranormal are explainable."

"True. But not everything. We mentioned Bigfoot before. They do exist, but not on this dimension."

"Then how do we know about them if they aren't on this dimension?"

"Because sometimes they cross from the Shadow Realm to this dimension. One that occasionally crosses over into ours. Intersects and sometimes purposely intrudes. Loch Ness monster, Bigfoot, banshees, you name it. They aren't originally from our plane."

She shook her head and folded her arms, trying to obtain a grip on what he told her. "Aliens?"

"No. So far, the SIA maintains that aliens probably exist, but they haven't visited us. String theory tells us there may be many different dimensions other than our own."

"And the SIA has contact with every one of them?"

"All they know about is the Shadow Realm."

Skepticism and a growing sense of awe kept her from believing everything he said.

"You don't believe me," he said a second later.

Gina shrugged and unfolded her arms. She held her hands up in a helpless gesture. "Did you believe this the first time you heard it?"

He smiled in apparent chagrin. "No. But I've seen evidence."

"You've seen Bigfoot carcasses? Nessie?"

"I've looked at photographs taken by other SIA agents that are verified as authentic."

"Are some of the photographs other people have taken of these creatures real?"

"Some of them, but not many."

While disbelief continued to hover around her psyche, fascination started to overtake it. "Tell me more. Are ghosts from the Shadow Realm?"

"No. Ghosts are entirely different. Even the SIA isn't certain about them. It's something we investigate, but only when the so-called ghosts become a hazard to human life. And most ghosts aren't like that."

Tension crept along her shoulders, and she rotated her head to loosen muscles. "How did the SIA find out about the Shadow Realm?"

"The highest levels keep that under wraps. As an agent, even I'm not let in on every secret."

"This is wild," she said in wonder. "Absolutely wild."

A sparkle lit his eyes. "It excites you. I can see it."

She grinned. "Well…yes." She scowled as a more grave consideration took over. "Will you get into trouble telling me about the Shadow Realm?"

"I don't know. That's why the SIA will want to send in a replacement for me. Without all my memories, I could be a danger to this case."

Logic told her this made sense, but she hated the idea he might be reprimanded. To avoid thinking about it, she quizzed him.

"What other beings inhabit the Shadow Realm?"

"Weredemons. Those are weird as shit. Then there are creatures we used to think belonged to ancient mythology from Greek and Roman times."

"Like Medusa?" She shuddered.

"You got it."

"What else?"

He looked thoughtful. "Manes. The Romans thought they were spirits of the dead who they could stave off with prayer. They inhabited the houses of married couples."

She screwed her face up. "Why married couples?"

"Beats the hell out of me." He quirked one eyebrow. "Now you know why so many married couples fight. The Manes are causing it."

She laughed. "Right."

"The Romans had plenty of rituals to drive off Manes. They did special chants they said nine times that used black beans, striking of bells and pure spring water. If they ignored doing the rituals, they had troubles. We think maybe the Manes are the ones that cause poltergeist activity."

"But I heard some parapsychologists thought poltergeist activity is caused by adolescents. Psychokinetic powers?"

"That's what parapsychologists outside the SIA think."

Gina tried to wrap her mind around what she'd heard. "I'm not sure I can take all this in at once."

"Let it soak in gradually. That's what I did. Not every agent knows the entire picture of the Shadow Realm."

"I'd think the SIA would want agents to know everything in the Shadow Realm. What if they run up against a creature they don't understand?"

"They don't know everything because if any one agent knew all the secrets, it could be dangerous."

The light bulb came on. "Ah, I see. Keep the information a bit fractured."

"Yep."

"If the agent was captured by some enemy, that agent couldn't give away every secret through torture."

He smiled. "Damn, woman, you are sharp."

A warm glow stole into her heart. "You used to say that to me before. Before you joined the SIA. You haven't said it much lately."

His brow wrinkled with a perplexed expression. "Oh, yeah? I don't..."

"You don't remember saying that to me?"

"No."

"It's okay. At least some things are coming back to you." In her eagerness, she repositioned in the chair, swinging her feet to the floor and leaning forward with her forearms on her thighs. "Don't stop now. This is interesting. Someone must know everything within the organization."

He shifted on the stool, his own intrigue with telling her these tales obvious. "The only person who knows absolutely everything is our librarian."

"Librarian," she said deadpan.

One corner of his mouth quirked. "She oversees every record we have on the Shadow Realm and its creatures and beings. Her name is Dorcas Shannigan."

She visualized a dried-up old woman with a gray bun on her head and a cranky, tight-lipped expression.

"Dorky," he said, "is her nickname. No one sees her, but she's a frequent voice over the intercom at meetings supplying other agents and officials of SIA with information. She knows so much about the Shadow Realm and our world that some people call her the oracle. She's the keeper of the flame, I guess you could say. The head of SIA doesn't know everything she does about the supernatural world, the natural world and the Shadow Realm."

Interest stirred deeply inside her. "That's incredible. But why doesn't anyone ever see her and why would SIA entrust her with all the information on the Shadow Realm and not the head of SIA?"

"Beats the hell out of me. That's one of those intangibles no one explains to the agents."

She sighed. "Well, no government agency is perfect."

New thoughts flooded her, but one in particular gripped Gina's attention more than others. "The public doesn't know the truth because it would change everything and freak people out."

"Yep."

His one-word answer made her press for more answers. "Would it be a sort of H. G. Wells' *War of the Worlds*' scenario if people knew?"

His crooked smile, so damned sexy and endearing, made her stomach tingle. "Yes."

"So...why are you? I mean, telling me about this Shadow Realm."

"If there's one thing I do recall, it's your stubbornness."

She grimaced. "People tell me I'm a little too obstinate. Especially you."

His voice softened. "It would kill me if something happened to you and it was because I didn't supply you with the ammunition you needed to survive."

Tears burned Gina's eyes, and she quickly held them back. Could she confess what she felt? She hesitated only for a moment then a dam broke. "I was ten years younger when I met you, and I felt..."

"Yeah?"

"I was flattered and amazed you would want to stand up for me. Everyone in college knew me because of my stunts."

"Stunts?"

"Most of my life I've been a risk taker."

"Taking risks isn't always bad. I've obviously done that in my life too."

"True. But my friends say I go too far." Her throat went tight, and she wished she understood why right here, right now, this subject should choke her up.

He stood and walked toward her. When he sank down on the ottoman to watch her, his proximity sent wild thrills through her stomach. Her nipples tightened in an instant. Her heart started a new, frantic response.

"What kinds of risks?" he asked quietly.

She closed her eyes to avoid his probing assessment. "I've tried about everything. Hang gliding, water-skiing, regular skiing on some extreme slopes. I love to ski." She smiled, but kept her eyes closed. "I hunger for winter so I can hurry to the slopes and experience the cold, and slicing and gliding through the snow." She opened her eyes. "When a lot of kids in college were dying to take a cruise, I wanted to take an African safari."

"Did you make it?"

"Not yet. But I'll get there."

"What else have you done? What aren't you telling me?"

She heaved a deep breath and let it out slowly. "Bungee jumping."

He chuckled. "Have I ever done that?"

"No. Not that I know of."

"What else? Other than being adventurous, I don't see the problem here."

"I've done spelunking, backpacking into a Central American jungle and climbed a mountain in Canada."

His eyes widened gradually. "Anything else breakneck?"

"When I was in college I went out with this boy who had stolen a car. I didn't know it wasn't his. Unfortunately, I was in the car when the cops found out he'd stolen the car."

"Shit."

"That's about the size of it."

"Were you arrested too?"

She nodded, surprised when old shame arose and took over. "Luckily the police were sharp and they realized after talking to me that I didn't have anything to do with the car theft."

"Good thing. That wasn't your fault. What does it have to do with taking risks?"

"I already had the reputation at school for taking chances. I shoplifted once and got a juvenile record for that. I did it just for the thrill, thinking I couldn't be caught. I was wrong. Guys assumed that meant I would put out too. That was the only reason they paid any attention to me—they thought they'd get sex. They didn't."

He watched her with hooded eyes, his expression restrained. He left the ottoman and walked around the room in a restless fashion. Finally, he stopped prowling. With his feet planted square in the middle of the room, hands on his hips and gaze nailed to the floor, he seemed stalwart and unbreakable.

He asked, "Did you start being more of a risk taker after your father locked you in the closet?"

She couldn't speak for a second, her mind refusing to supply the answer. "I guess it was after he locked me in the closet." Anger sliced through her like deadly splinters, nausea churning in her stomach. "How could I have missed recognizing that about myself?"

Ryan's eyes were sharp and assessing but overlaid by gentleness that eased some of her fury. He slid his fingers down over her cheek in a tender touch she imagined he meant to reassure. "Everyone has baggage they don't notice until it smacks them across the face one day. Sometimes they have to be hit more than once to see it."

His words fired her disquiet and removed the undeniable pleasure his touch provided. "I couldn't just be a thrill-seeker like you because I like it? Why is it okay for you to risk life and limb and not me?"

His face hardened. Unyielding, his gaze demanded her attention. "Because it's my job. Not because of some deep-seated need to forget pain."

Tears blurred her vision. "Are you sure, Ryan? Really certain? What if you have a death wish because your parents and your fiancée were killed? Because deep inside there's a little part of you that died with them that day?"

His gaze widened. "Jesus. No."

She stood and marched away to stand in the middle of the room to gaze at a blank wall, her heart squeezing and tears spilling over her cheeks.

Chapter Ten
∞

Gina inhaled deeply and wiped the tears from her cheeks. She turned back to Ryan. "There's something else bothering you. Spill it."

He stood and approached her, his steps slow. Surprise glittered in his eyes. "How did you know?"

"I'm proficient at knowing what people will say before they say it. In your case, you planned to say the Shadow Realm is on the other side of that door."

One side of his mouth quirked up. "That's very good. But was that deduction, or were you reading my mind?"

"Does it matter? Maybe it was a combination of the two. Don't turn all logical on me and ask how I got the answer. That's how I used to fail math."

He laughed. "Your teachers thought you weren't doing the work."

"Right. I was doing the work, but with my intuition, not with a logical, flowchart mind."

"I'll bet you frequently tell people what they are going to say."

"I've done it too many times to mention."

"Pretending not to know when you do...damned frustrating."

She thrust the truth into the open air. "Yes."

"Because it's rude to finish other people's sentences."

"Exactly."

Making love had changed everything and nothing. She'd expected him to close off, to do a stereotypical male detachment once sex finished. Instead, to her alarm and delight, he'd spoken his truth and helped empower her.

She inhaled and it set off a bout of dry coughing. She covered her mouth with her hand and tried to hold it back.

"You okay?" he asked.

"Yes. I've had laryngitis lately. Just managed to get rid of it, but today it's back to being a bit scratchy."

His lips twitched in amusement. "You did some screamin' there. I imagine that didn't help."

She flushed and almost smacked him on the arm. "So?"

"There's more to the throat situation than out-of-this-world sex. I have a theory about your throat problems. Did you ever wonder if the laryngitis came when you were under tremendous stress?"

She inhaled slowly and deeply. Of course. The revelation hit like a sledgehammer. "Damn. That should have been a no-brainer."

He shrugged. "Why?"

"In psychology they call it somatoform disorders. But in the metaphysical world it's just what you said." She rubbed her throat. "But you know what? My throat has cleared up almost completely since you came to my door. What does that tell you?"

He winked. "You're speaking your truth?"

She nodded. "Maybe for the first time in a long time."

A comfortable pause came between them, a small increment unfilled by tension, innuendo or thrum of desire.

She took a deep breath. "I believe in extraordinary senses and abilities. You blurt out to people that you have this sixth sense and they think you're blitzed. That you often finish people's sentences before they speak because you know what they'll say ahead of time."

Seriousness left his eyes as a smart-aleck grin touched his mouth. "Own up to it."

Startled, she frowned. "What?"

"You said 'you' as if you were talking about someone else. I've seen you struggle with it for years. I never considered what you could do supernatural." Husky and soft, his voice deepened to that crazy-making Irish accent. "It's a very natural part of you that you shouldn't hold back." He smiled. "I'm glad I remembered that." He didn't move away, but he hooked his fingers in the loops on his jeans. "You have a logjam in there, a need that wants to break free. It wants to run manic through the house, shouting in joy whenever you finish a project. It wants to create stories as passionately as we fucked. But it's like your telepathy. You want to hide it. Why? What happened that made you decide to stifle who you are?"

She put her hands in her pockets. He'd shocked her with his obvious understanding of what made her tick and her procrastinations designed to drive away fear. Trepidation assured she hid more and wrote less. His accepting gaze and calmness unleashed her desire to explain.

"I've reached that positive manic state in creativity before, where sanity stands on edge, where a link between darkness and light grows a bridge, and I stay only in the light." She smiled.

"Does it scare you?"

She nodded vigorously. "Absolutely." She gestured with one hand. "Most of the world out there doesn't think what I do is worthy, doesn't understand it, finds it mysterious and too strange."

"And the manic state, when it's good and positive...people would still say it's an obsession?"

She sighed in relief. He did understand—more than she'd given him credit. "Yes."

He reached out, clasped her shoulders and brought her flush against him. "When you're creating stories about love and sex, you're fulfilled and happy."

"Over the top."

A spark of light entered his expressive blue eyes. Golden and rich, inspiring and giving. "Then you must do it first thing in the morning, without eating, without starting the laundry, sweeping your porch, any of that shit. Turn off the ringer on your phone." He winked. "Let it rip, baby, and don't let anybody stand in your way. Especially not yourself."

"That sounds so easy."

"Sure, creating can be hard work part of the time, but the rest of the time it's easy. You have to take the good with the bad. Some days you'll feel like retreating. Don't. Some days other people will want you to give up. Don't. Do you want that muse back? Do you want it to course through your veins and make you so excited you can't wait to rise in the morning and start? Do you want to make writing the most important thing in your life again?"

Most important thing? Once again, she couldn't say the words that ached to leave her throat.

I love you, Ryan. I think I've always loved you. You are the most important thing in my life. Then comes creating.

Gina turned her gaze to the floor, as he had earlier.

He lifted her chin with one index finger. "Don't be ashamed of passion. About wanting something that much."

Ah, he thinks he knows what I'm feeling.

"So how does a guy who isn't a writer know about this creative process?" she asked in defense.

He chuckled. "It applies to anything in life a person wants to do, not just writing."

She nodded, understanding entirely for the first time. "Makes sense."

"Same thing goes with your interest in the supernatural. There's no need to hide it. People have to take the real you the way you are."

She tried to wrap the concept around her mind. "My ego is talking. I've always wanted to know more about the universe. More about the stranger things that reside out there in the world." She swallowed hard. "And my creativity has...well, as I told you before, it's losing its steam. Its power."

He looked thoughtful. "When we were on that bed together, *we* created something damned strong. We reaffirmed life and gave it meaning." He leaned in and kissed her, his lips soft with promise. "Remember that energy, that heat every morning before you write. Feel it in every part of your body. Those erotic love scenes will be hot."

She couldn't help it—her smile grew wider. "I've never heard a man talk about creativity and sex at one time. You're amazing, Ryan Ahern."

"Flattery will get you everywhere." He nuzzled her cheek, his breath hot and exciting. "I want to be inside you. Around you. With you."

"Oh, Ryan."

He gazed at her, holding her with the intensity in his eyes. Incredibly captivating, his eyes held everything she needed. She could see them together from this day forward, exploring the numerous qualities they'd discovered in each other today, and learning new things from each other tomorrow.

He leaned in and kissed her neck, breathed the next words into her ear. "You're aroused. Excited by what you feel when you're with me. Just as excited as I am when you're near me, when you touch me."

He pulled back long enough to look deep into her eyes. She shivered when she saw the untamed intent inside him.

His words continued to flow. "There's something electric when we're together. It's always been there, hasn't it?"

"Yes." God, she had to admit it. Couldn't help it.

He kissed her forehead, her cheeks, all the while murmuring. "I was a fucking fool to ignore it for so long, Gina. Even if I never get back all my memories, I know I want to explore what we have. This damned adventure proved that to me. When I was racing through those woods, there was one thing on my mind besides reaching this cabin and safety. Reaching you. Keeping you safe." He pressed impassioned kisses to her throat. "I would do anything, risk anything for you." He cupped her face in his hands and trapped her with his gaze. "I'd die for you."

Happiness ripped Gina apart from the inside. She'd fantasized about this moment, dreamed about it, craved it for years. Now that it was here, she wavered between fear the feelings would disappear like smoke in the wind and the realization of a wonderful fantasy.

"Ryan. You...I..."

"Yeah?" He smiled crookedly. "Don't worry. This time I can finish the sentence for you. You want me. I know you do."

She inhaled deeply, her face still trapped between his cupping hands. As tears spilled over and rolled down her cheeks, she welcomed this wild ecstasy enveloping and taking over her world. "Yes. Damn it, you've made me admit it. I want you."

With a groan, he took her mouth, his arms anchoring her to him with a strength she didn't wish to escape. Excitement and happiness, sexual and deep, pulled her closer into his arms.

Then she felt his cock pressing her belly, hard, hot and ready. Violent desire slammed her. With hunger, she slipped her arms around his shoulders and pulled him down for a deep, feral kiss. His tongue warred with hers instantly, an animalistic moan leaving his chest.

His kisses grew almost frantic, and she fed passion back to him as her hands searched his shoulders, his neck, the silky thick texture of his hair. Heat mixed with compassion, with a desire to provide everything he wanted and take all she could. His hands went under her sweater and made short work of her bra clasp. It snicked open and bared her breasts. He cupped her breasts, and as he teased her with swift passes of his thumbs over sensitive nipples, she moaned with pleasure. Impatient, she reached for his belt buckle and made short work of his button and zipper. She shoved down his jeans and they dropped to his knees, then she pulled his shorts down. All the while, he tweaked, caressed, teased her nipples into taut, needy points. Repeatedly his tongue thrust into her mouth. The sensual pleasure of his tongue rubbing over hers made soft moans leave her lips. Ryan grunted and shivered when she palmed his cock.

Her body craved, ignited, knew intuitively what they both needed in this tiny space in time. A warm ache built between her legs. The heat trickled, arousal sweet and needy. Before he could do it, she pulled out of his arms, yanked off her shoes, socks pants and underpants. For one second she hesitated. What she saw in his eyes removed any doubt. Heated, uncompromising desire filled his gaze.

"Don't hold back with me," he said.

"Never again."

Swiftly, he urged her into his arms, lifted her against one wall. Her legs came up around his waist and his cock touched the wet heat of her pussy. *Oh, yeah. Oh, oh, yeah. I want this. Gotta have it. Must have it.*

"Yes," she whispered. "Yes."

He thrust hard and deep, pressing until his thickness impaled her to the root. He rotated his hips, caught between her legs in a grip that didn't give him much movement. As he twisted his hips with a little thrust, she gasped and moaned. The sensation of his cock stretching, moving and thrusting the slightest bit inside her receptive pussy set her on fire. He circled his hips and pressed firm until her clit started to throb. She whimpered and writhed, pleasured and shocked by the stunning awareness of rock-hard cock spreading her wide and deep.

"All right?" he asked.

"More than all right."

A rough sound of desperation left his throat. Ryan's lack of inhibition, the out-of-control sexuality in his sounds, his expression, actions, ripped the keg open and ignited a firestorm. His hands cupped her ass, fingers digging into flesh. Her pussy rippled, clenched over his cock. He groaned and pulled back, then slammed forward. Started a relentless rhythm of hard cock into pussy. She wriggled her hips and tried to bring them closer. Every slamming thrust brought a groan of pleasure to her throat.

"That's it," he said with a gasp. "Don't hold back."

"Oh!" One hard thrust startled another amazed sound from her. "Oh!"

With groans of pleasure, he thrust with ruthless plunges straight to the heart of her. Her head fell back against the wall. She writhed as the hard bar of heat impaled her, over and over, relentless with each hammering stroke. She felt her pussy opening wider, growing wetter, aching with the never-ending beat.

Mindless with pleasure, she chanted. "Yes, oh, yes."

Her breath went choppy, her heartbeat frantic. A wave arose, heady and excruciatingly beautiful. Tingling heat, amazing in pleasure, rippled and grew inside her vagina. Feeling coalesced and expanded, her body and mind in harmony, at one with his and inside the act. Turned on by his astonishing strength as he held her up against the wall, she panted for breath.

She'd had clitoral orgasms before, the tight little bursts of extreme pleasure. This was so different she was floored. A tiny part of her latched on to that illusive sensation, felt it, knew it and allowed it to grow.

Ripples grew inside her pussy, deep where he pressed, then retreated, rubbing, thrusting, caressing. As she lost every sense of time and fell into the bliss, he jackhammered inside her. His guttural moans, the scent of arousal, their heated skin melded in her mind into one beautiful, overwhelming flash.

The exhilaration within her expanded like a supernova and ruptured into sweet, mind-blowing tremors. She was caught up in the universe and joining ecstasy-filled insanity she never wished to end. She cried out in harsh enjoyment.

"Christ, yes!" His shout sounded almost painful.

She savored the way his body shook, and each pulse of his cock drew repeated groans from within him.

When he stopped shivering in her arms, he lifted her slowly off his cock.

He grinned as she slid down his body. "That was the best fucking sex I've ever had in my life."

She giggled and kissed his chin. "The best fucking sex, eh?"

His voice sounded hoarse. "Yeah."

They cleaned up again, but this time didn't take full showers. When she walked past him as she left the bathroom, he drew her close for a warm, deep kiss.

Her heart fluttered with a singular happiness she couldn't recall feeling at any other time in her life. "This is crazy. I should be scared out of my mind about what's going to happen with this Zurvan creature. All I can think about is being with you."

His right eyebrow quirked up. "You could always take a few moments and write. Great sex can make people creative."

He released her, and they went back to a small silence that felt comfortable, yet charged with the emotions they generated between them moments ago.

He wandered to the kitchen counter and braced his hands upon it. Before he could speak, a loud pounding pummeled the door above.

Chapter Eleven

Gina started, her heart tripping over itself. Ryan jerked around and looked up at the doorway. Loud and mind-bending, the noise hurt her ears, and she automatically put her hands over her ears.

"Shit!" Ryan yelled above the racket. "That's what we've been waiting for!"

She lowered her hands to hear him. "For what?"

"Zurvan!"

"You still think—"

"Yes!"

He grabbed the backpack he'd placed on the floor earlier, while she snagged her small purse and looped it over her head. He clutched her by the arm and raced for the door with the symbol of Mithras carved into it. Incessant thudding continued on the doorway above.

"What are you doing?" she asked.

"We need to get the hell out of this room, and into that one!" He gestured at the Mithras door. "Now!"

Surprise slammed her. "I figured it was a closet!"

"Nope!"

He dropped the backpack nearby. He took a couple of short steps backwards from the Mithras door. With a charge, he let out a cry and put his weight into a door kick. Wood cracked, creaked and the door flew inward.

Gina's heartbeat tripped over and stuttered. She glanced quickly back at the door at the top of the stairs.

To her astonishment, the metal started to bow inward, then suck back the other direction. "Oh my God!"

He eyed the contorting door. "Shit!" He grabbed his backpack and her arm in the same instant. "Let's go!"

As a horrendous roaring, like that of a lion, penetrated the walls, she didn't need another incentive to get the hell out of Dodge.

"Zurvan." Ryan's voice roughened as he tugged her into the dark passageway. "Son of a bitch!"

He flicked on the flashlight and they ran as they followed the wide illumination offered by the Halogen.

The light showed a rough-hewn floor paved with large flagstone. She guessed the width of the tunnel to be maybe ten feet across, with the ceiling no taller. The walls were plain, the ceiling undecorated.

"Where are we going?" she asked as breaths panted through her lips.

"Anywhere."

Ruthlessly, he pulled her along. Keeping pace with his long legs proved a tremendous challenge. Light from the flashlight bounced along the interior near the floor like ball lightning. They ran onward, and she listened for the sound of Zurvan behind them, but heard nothing.

As the tunnel turned and twisted, she wondered if they'd left the sanctuary only to be lost in a worse place.

Her mouth felt as dry as sandpaper, her heart thumping frantically, her side aching, but she kept on running, running until the yards of tunnel made her dizzy.

"Why is this thing after us?" She gasped the question.

"Who cares?" His answer echoed off the walls. "We're not sticking around to ask it."

Her writer's imagination constructed horrifying scenarios in short order. The tunnel collapsing. The tunnel filling with water from the rains. Zurvan catching up with them. She shook her head and banished imagined terrors. No time for situations that hadn't occurred. Staying alive mattered.

Suddenly her right foot snagged on a loose flagstone. Her body jolted, her right knee sliced with pain. With a startled gasp, she pitched forward. Her hand ripped from Ryan's grasp.

"Damn it!" She grunted as she fell flat on her stomach and the wind whooshed out of her.

Ryan bent over her as he placed the flashlight on the floor. "Fuck! Are you all right?"

She opened her mouth and gaped like a fish, unable to answer him.

"Gina?"

He dropped to his knees just as she managed a word. "Ouch."

"Are you hurt?"

"No. Just embarrassed," she managed to gasp.

"No time for embarrassment."

Her right knee hurt, a surging pain that almost caused her to cry out. Her rib cage ached. His arm slipped around her back as she sat up, one hand tilting her chin up.

Concern deepened his eyes in the dim light. "Are you sure you're not hurt?"

As they rose together, a guttural roar sounded through the passageways. "Oh, no."

"Come on." He lifted her up, grabbed the flashlight, and they continued their rapid pace. He took her hand in an almost painful grip.

Her knee and ribs protested their pace, but she held back her pain and kept moving. Pain receded in the stark fear that ripped into her like a knife. Panic ached in her throat, hanging up on a scream. She must have made a noise, because Ryan slowed just enough to glance back at her. Two emotions raged through his face. Determination and the solid presence of a warrior.

Flash-fire terror eased as she recognized one undeniable fact. She had unshakable faith in him. Whatever happened, he would get them out of this hellhole.

Ryan saw the fear etched on Gina's face, as well as lingering pain. She'd lied about her injuries, but they needed to locate an exit from this place and couldn't slow down. Tightening his grip on her fingers, he hauled her along as quickly as they dared. Frustration drove him onward. He wished to fuck he could recall more about this assignment. Marcus had told him what he knew, but Marcus also didn't know the pieces that Ryan managed to forget back there in the woods. Whatever fucking purgatory Zurvan came from, whatever dimension, Ryan needed more information. He knew one thing—making it out of there in one piece would prove to be a bitch.

Ryan drew in quick breaths, pacing his steps. Taking in his surroundings on automatic pilot, he noticed nuances he hadn't before. Dark and oppressive, the atmosphere could dampen any soul. Nothing in his life prepared him for the bombardment of odd feelings. As if all the ages resided in these tunnels, in the niches decorated with wild symbols of snake, scorpion, bull and Mithras.

"I don't hear anything behind us," she said, her breaths catching on each word.

"We have to keep moving." He squeezed her hand in reassurance.

"How do we know when to stop?"

"When it feels right."

He didn't understand how he knew this, other than the intuition he'd developed in the military. Danger heightened his senses, spurred him onward. His body and mind had kicked into battlefield readiness the moment that steel door in the basement had started bowing in and out as if it was fuckin' breathing. Adrenaline streaked through his veins and powered his endurance. His biggest worry was keeping Gina safe, and it fueled his energy the way nothing else could.

Up ahead he noticed a light, and it slowed his speed.

"What is it?" she asked.

"Light. See the luminescence?"

She came alongside him as he stopped, her breath coming fast and hard. He couldn't see her fear, but he felt it down in his sinews. She battled with the dread and wanted solace, but he knew there would be none until they left this labyrinth.

She wriggled her hand a bit and he realized he was holding it too hard. He released her and crept forward. She followed.

"Stay close to me," he said, keeping his eyes on the strange light.

Her hand touched his back and stayed, as if some touch reassured her. Truth be told, it made him feel better too.

"It looks like light from underwater creatures," she said.

He didn't answer, his sense keenly focused on watching for danger. As they rounded one corner, he never expected what they saw next.

"Jesus," Ryan whispered. "Would you look at that?"

They stepped into the threshold of a sanctuary to Mithras. The incandescent glow emanating from the walls, ceiling and floor meant he didn't need the flashlight. He turned it off to save battery life. Like a cave, the room felt forbidding and yet less scary than the closed-in tunnels. Unlike the tunnels, this room had a twelve-foot barrel vault ceiling. He guessed the room was about fifty feet across. Walls were lined with brickwork, except for the areas that sported marble niches. Some of the niches held symbols from astrology, others snakes, scorpions and the dreaded Zurvan. Marble benches, pitted with age, lined the walls on two sides. At the far side of the room, a statue of Mithras with his flowing cape. Ryan took in the decorations depicted in ochre and green paint on the arch above the statue. Mithras was shown touching the heavens and the symbols of the zodiac above. Ten smaller scenes were depicted above the central one, arranged in two vertical strips of five showing the mythical deeds of Mithras.

"Look at this." Ryan pointed to the scenes. "Jupiter hurls a thunderbolt at a snake. This second scene shows Mithras being born from the rock and holding the knife and torch."

"Where is the light coming from?" Gina moved away from him and pivoted as she looked around the room.

"I don't know. But it reminds me of something I read about Mithras being the god of light and therefore he banished darkness." He shook his head. "I don't know. It doesn't matter. We need to keep moving."

"You're sure you don't know how to kill this thing?"

"I'm buggered if I know."

She smiled, and a short laugh left her lips. "I haven't heard you say that in a long time."

"If I knew how to kill it, we wouldn't be in this tunnel right now."

For one second her apple green eyes sparkled. Danger receded in his mind. Again, he touched her lips with a soft kiss. Anything deeper would make him forget why they were there and what they needed to do.

His senses prickled with growing danger. "Come on. Let's get moving."

* * * * *

Gina gasped in awe and a creepy appreciation as they encountered another chamber after what seemed a solid hour of walking. Along the endless path, they'd paused and witnessed deep niches and catacombs as offshoots from the main tunnel. Gloom settled over her. They might not find their way out of this huge maze. Ryan didn't speak about it, and neither did she.

"Look." She grasped his forearm.

He halted and turned his flashlight into the chamber. The entrance revealed a dazzling array of white stuccoes. Griffins and sea monsters contributed to a fantastical world. Cupids and maenads wove through an endless geometrical tapestry of roundels and quadrants across the ceiling. On the back wall, two huge red centaurs fought with black panthers.

"What is this place?" She stepped forward, for once back to her energetic and risk-taker personality.

He followed, shining the flashlight at an angle so she could see. "We can't afford to explore."

She turned toward him. "We haven't heard any sign of Zurvan in a long time. Where are we going anyway, Ryan? I don't think either one of us have a clue."

He drew in a deep breath. "I have an idea."

She cocked her head to one side. "You didn't say anything before."

"Because I didn't want to frighten you." He took her arm and guided her with him back into the tunnel.

"I don't scare easily."

"Obviously."

"Damn it, Ryan, don't return to your protective mode."

He stared at her in the half-light illuminating only a small world around them to fight back deepest blackness. They might be the only two people left in the world. A shiver coasted up her spine. A wave of heat followed, but this time it wasn't sexual attraction. She actually felt ill.

He drew her closer, his arm going around her. "When we find our way out of here, I'll fuck you until you can't stand."

She let out a startled laugh. "And what does that have to do with stopping to smell the roses?"

"Nothing. But you're making me insane, Gina."

She slid her hands up until they cupped over the hard planes of his chest. "And when I piss you off you want to...fuck me?"

"Yes," he said with a soft growl.

He tightened his embrace and dove into a kiss. As his tongue stroked hers, she fell into a different world from this damp, claustrophobic realm of mystery and strange beasts. She was back in that bed with Ryan, taking his body into hers. They'd fucked like mad things, like beasts unable to stop copulating. She'd never come so many times in her life. Never known an attachment as strong and staggering as what she had with Ryan.

He broke away. "Let's go."

The next chamber they came upon fifteen minutes later had a fluorescent glow spilling from the wide threshold.

She squinted, wishing for sunglasses. "This is incredible."

Ryan read the Latin above the doorway and translated. "The Necropolises on the Via Ostiense." He peered at the fading letters carved into white marble. "That can't be right."

"What's wrong?"

He gazed down at her. "The Necropolises on the Via Ostiense are near Rome, Italy."

Baffled, she didn't speak for a good thirty seconds. She peeked into the illuminated doorway. She wrinkled her nose. "Tombs?"

"Yeah."

Gina abruptly felt as if she'd slipped into a lost world. The answer seemed more than simple and deeply terrifying. "Are we in the Shadow Realm?"

"My guess is we're in part of it. The transition of death to life. Dorky explained it to me once. The Shadow Realm is approached from the death end and into the life, unlike our world which approaches things from life and finishes with death."

Taking in what he said, she soaked in the idea before she spoke. "Fascinating, if a bit confusing."

He grinned. "Think of it this way. We're dealing with things that shouldn't work in the current laws of physics...unless you believe in other dimensions."

"I think I do now. You're saying this Via...Via..."

"Ostiense."

"Right. Ostiense...is a replica of the same place in Italy? An alternate yet somehow duplicate world?"

"Possibly."

"And there are doppelgangers of us all running around in the Shadow Realm."

"Possibly."

She playfully swatted him on the arm. "Stop saying that."

"Like I said before, there's also a lot I don't know."

She stuffed her fingers in her hair in frustration. "This is too much. If I went back into our world and told people this was happening..."

She didn't finish.

Ryan acknowledged her fears. "People would say you're barking mad."

Her laugh came out short and sharp. "Yes."

He turned more toward the glowing entryway. "It was either come in here or face Zurvan."

"I know you're right. It's just that I'm confused and scared."

Remorse rose high in his expressive eyes. "I won't let anything happen to you." He moved into the room ahead of her and switched off his flashlight. "You know that old Irish saying?"

"How could I forget? Every time in the last ten years when I told you I was worried or afraid, you always said the same thing."

"God invented whiskey so the Irish wouldn't take over the world."

"Yes." She couldn't help the small laugh that left her throat. "And I always asked you what that had to do with being afraid."

"Nothing. But it makes you laugh."

She put her hand over her mouth and muffled the next giggle. "Damned if you aren't right, Irish."

He reached out, his hand beckoning her to cross the foot separating them. "Glad you finally realize that."

"Don't push it."

Without hesitation, she stepped toward him and placed her cold fingers into his amazingly warm hand. His hand was big enough it almost encompassed hers. Strong and yet moderated not to hurt her, he tugged her toward him until they touched chest to chest and hip to hip. She looked up at him and wondered how blue eyes, as tumultuous as a mountain stream, could ever be cold. No, the melting warmth she saw there ignited a fire inside her she couldn't resist.

She reached up to touch his stubble-rough face. Her emotions bounced again, and she couldn't recall her moods vacillating this often before. Ryan did this, and no other man could equal him in her heart. "What would I do if you weren't here?"

"You'd find a way. You can stand up to anything. You're strong and capable."

"Thank you, but I've never dealt with a world like this before."

"As my father used to say, it's a bleedin' challenge, but we get through it."

She squeezed his hand. "You've remembered more."

He grinned cautiously, doubt in his eyes. "Damned little. Enough to get my ass into hot water."

He released her hand and drew her into a close hug. She burrowed into his embrace with a sigh and pressed her cheek to his shoulder. "God, this feels good. Just hold me for a minute."

"Anything you want." He kissed her forehead and breathed deep.

Gina tilted her head up to see him, and the heavy-lidded, sultry promise in his eyes captured her like a snared butterfly. His head dipped and within seconds, his penetrating kiss sent her into a maelstrom of returning desire. Sliding her hands around his waist and then palming his broad back, she fell into his uncompromising demands. He possessed her heart and soul, body and life. She would have it no other way. His mouth skated over hers with deliberate, intense passion until she whimpered. With cherishing licks, he deepened the kiss until his tongue plunged deep and thrust with carnal rhythm.

The kiss went on and on until she finally pulled back to catch her breath. "Maybe we should take inventory of this place we're almost standing in."

His chest heaved up and down, his eyes bright from the passionate abandon they'd shared seconds ago.

As she stepped into the luminescent area, she looked up for the source of the light but found none. A jumble of niches, sarcophagi and chests lined the room, which was at least fifty feet across and as much in length.

"The niches look like..." She laughed. "Like little bake ovens."

An incredulous grin transformed the harsher lines in his face. He laughed and shook his head. Something heated and interested flared in his eyes and exploded a million sparklers in her stomach. God, when he looked at her like that, she could easily forget Zurvan chased them, and their lives dangled in the balance. Life seemed pretty damned good, no matter what.

Yeah, if you get out of this place in one piece, don't ever forget it.

"Congratulations," he said. "That was either the most ungirly thing I've heard a woman say, or the most girly. I'm not sure."

She broke into a wide grin. "Thanks. I think."

As they walked with deliberate slowness through the intricate and labyrinthine sequence of funerary structures, she shivered. Dampness, cool and moldy, touched her nostrils. One thing made her stop.

He turned back to her. "What's wrong?"

"I expected this place to feel different."

"Different how?"

"It doesn't feel evil." She walked onward, fascinated. "I expected to feel creeped out when we first stepped in here. Disturbed."

"This place is damned strange."

"Did you expect to see this when we first came into these tunnels?"

"No. If Dorky told me about this, I've forgotten some of it."

"I don't mind saying I'm still confused as hell," she said as she stopped by one sarcophagus.

"About what?"

"Did the Romans know about the Shadow Realm?"

"I know what you're thinking."

"You do?"

"Romans copied what they knew about the Shadow Realm. At least that's what they thought. That they honored the Shadow Realm by emulating some of it. But what if the Shadow Realm copied them?"

"Dorky told you that?"

"No. I theorized it myself."

"Well, that would explain why this stuff looks Roman."

They went silent once more as exploration and fascination absorbed them.

Ryan stopped at one tomb to read. "This one lists family names, ages and professions. It has an invocation to the Manes to protect them after their death."

"I can't believe I forgot that you took Latin in high school."

He winked. "Maybe that's why the SIA hired me."

She sniffed. "Hmm. Or they hired you because you're tough, physically fit, and your military training was superb."

Hot need entered his eyes as he stood near her. He slipped his arm around her waist and brought her near. Feeling protected and cherished, she inhaled his masculine scent and savored the power in his embrace.

"Are you trying to drive me nuts?" he asked softly as he looked down at her.

She turned so she could press both hands against his chest. "Why would I do that?"

"I don't know. Mystery of woman." His lips touched her forehead with another lingering kiss. "Do you know, Gina, I'd do anything for you? I'd fuckin' cut my heart out if you asked me to."

It wasn't a declaration of love, but coming from Ryan, the often stern and sometimes undemonstrative, it might as well have been.

One of his eyebrows lifted when she didn't respond.

Finally, she did speak. "Sorry. You stunned me. I'm flattered."

Clear disappointment flickered in his eyes. "That's all?"

"You're wonderful, smart as hell, handsome, and the best friend I've ever had, Ryan."

"Friend?"

She pulled his head down for a lingering, loving kiss that turned ultra-hot within seconds. "Does that taste like just friends to you?"

"No way."

"And if I wanted to be just friends with you, do you think I would have slept with you?"

He shook his head. "No."

"It's settled then."

He cupped the back of her head and pressed an exquisite kiss to the sensitive flesh beneath her right ear. "Ah, colleen, it's far from settled. When we escape here, we're holing up for as many days as we can both take."

"Then what?" she asked breathlessly as he nuzzled her ear.

His voice went rough with seductive, male urgency. "We're going to fuck for days."

As his roughly masculine statement soaked into her, she quivered as a fine thread of desire spun like a top inside her stomach. Pleasure made her sigh and close her eyes. "And maybe you're trying to distract me. Keep me from thinking about Zurvan and how we're finding a way out of this place. I'm assuming somewhere in here there's a direct connection to the actual Shadow Realm."

He gazed down at her grimly. "Yeah. I think that's why Dorky said to keep going to the right. Tunnels to the left lead directly to the Shadow Realm."

Annoyance filled her for this mysterious woman. "Why would she leave you in the dark about which way to go? Why would she use riddles?"

He shifted the backpack to his right shoulder. "Good question. I think I asked her that. She said something esoteric like, 'humans need to learn through example or the lesson doesn't stick'."

"Humph."

His sardonic twist of the mouth said he appreciated her humor. "Let's get on with this. We need to go through this area and see what's next."

She paid attention to details around her, distracted by Ryan's presence but once more in equilibrium.

The sizable burial area in this room featured tombs from various periods.

"Livia Nebris, daughter of Tibrius," Ryan said as they stopped at one tomb. Floral motifs and pretty festoons covered the walls near the woman's niche. Delicate figures seemed to float among plant motifs. Griffins and winged horses, an eagle, and other hard to make out decorations formed a pattern of story, of life.

As they finished out their exploration of the one area, they headed out one end and into another long tunnel. Her aching knee and ribs dogged her, but she persevered. Occasionally, a weird lethargy gripped her, as well as a wave of heat that made her feel unstable. She caught Ryan's assessing stare more than once, but didn't give in to a desire to lean on his strength. He held her hand the entire way, and his touch brought comfort. She didn't dare think what it would be like if she'd been there alone. She knew she had the strength to fight anything that came her way, but his knowledge of the situation and his physical protection gave her added confidence. If the malevolent creature had come before Ryan had arrived, she couldn't say for certain what she would have done.

Ryan examined his watch. "We've been running two hours."

"We haven't heard Zurvan for at least an hour."

"We need to find a place to rest."

She let out a slow breath. "That would be great."

In the minimal flashlight glow, she saw vulnerability within his eyes once more. Slicing guilt arrowed deep into his expression and struck her in the heart. She ached with a need to reassure him. Instantly, before she could reach out and touch him, hardness masked the one millimeter of uncertainty.

"You know," she said, "I used to get bored easily, and part of me thinks that's why I felt like I needed action all the time. Loud noise and running from place to place appealed to me because it wasn't ordinary. I'm surprised I accomplished any writing."

A smile eased over his mouth, his eyes lighting. "I'm not surprised. You're obviously a tough woman. Soft shell on the outside, strength and purpose on the inside. And if you love writing and it's your career, you find time for it, right?"

She smiled back. "Yes. You know what, I think I'll slow down on the adventures. More time for writing, and less time risking my neck."

He cleared his throat. "If it's what you want. But don't stop having fun. Keep on doing the things you love if you love them. It's only a problem if you're running from your feelings."

Her heart contracted, her eyes tearing up for what seemed the hundredth time today. "How did you get so damned smart, Irish?"

"Probably about the time I met you." He grinned wickedly.

"Which time? Years ago, or just today."

He thought for a moment. "Both times."

Ryan's answer, soft and with a warmth she experienced in a joyful rush, gave her new hope. They would make it out of here.

"Had enough excitement for today?" he asked.

"Right now, I'd take ordinary and boring." She blinked rapidly.

"Hey, it's all right. Don't cry."

She shook her head. "My eyes itch. There's something down here that bothers them. Dust maybe."

He brushed his thumb over her chin, his smile rueful. "Yeah, you have a few smudges of dirt on you."

They wandered forward in silence, with the sound of dripping water, their feet treading cool earth and sometimes cobblestone to let them know they were alive.

She sneezed, and the sound echoed. They stopped and listened, and she knew they waited for evidence of Zurvan's pursuit.

"I feel like I'm passing through centuries," she said almost in a whisper.

Without saying a word, he tugged her along until their pace returned to a steady, almost trotting attempt to cover more ground. A few more minutes and they turned a bend to encounter a huge, arching doorway up ahead.

Hope rose inside her. "God, I hope this is a way out."

They stood in front of the door, and his gaze scanned the dark door with its weathered face. She started to speak when the door made a loud cracking noise.

Chapter Twelve

"Get back!" Ryan shoved Gina behind him.

She grasped his shoulder and peered over. "What is it?"

"Beats the shit out of me."

Seconds later the door opened a crack and a bright light flashed into their eyes. Instinct sent her reeling back a couple of steps.

"Damn it," Ryan said, braced for anything.

He kept his body between her and the door, weapon leveled in front of him.

As the door swung open, he stepped back and so did she. The light, at once blinding and almost painful, cut down suddenly to a soft, manageable glow.

"Son of a bitch," Ryan said.

She put her hand on his shoulder, grip concerned and seeking reassurance. He didn't dare take his attention away from the door. Nine feet wide and twenty feet high, the arched doorway seemed almost new, as if someone had recently carved the intricate swirling design of Mithras, the stars, the bull and the other trappings of the religion.

He peered through the doorway. Nothing stirred, no creatures or other danger appeared to lurk.

Still, he wouldn't take chances with Gina's life. "Stay here."

She grabbed his arm as he started forward. "Don't."

He didn't look back. "Gina, I've got to."

She released his arm, and he walked inside. Keeping his weapon at the ready, he surveyed his surroundings. This tomb, unlike the others they'd walked through, was built on an enormous scale. At first the place reminded him of Via Salaria in Rome, a mausoleum for Lucilius Peto, a wealthy military tribune and prefect of the smiths and the cavalry. As an Etruscan burial mound, it was somehow filled with as much life as it was death. Inside this tomb wasn't exactly as he expected. In the Etruscan tomb a long corridor had led down to a catacomb with double rows of cavities for graves. This area held four niches along the walls for adult-sized bodies. He imagined the bodies once there wrapped in shrouds.

When he didn't see any immediate danger, he edged out of the doorway and waved her inside. "It's okay. Just stay close."

She nodded.

"Tomba Rotunda," he said as he continued to scan the place.

"What?"

"A rotunda tomb like one I remember from Rome. It belonged to a wealthy Etruscan."

"When were you in Rome?" Doubt gave a lilt of sarcasm to her tone.

"I don't know."

She said nothing for a few seconds, then, "Without that strange glow in here, it would be weird. Oppressive."

She sighed, and he turned to look at her. Exhaustion drew her mouth down into a frown. He relaxed the tension in his shoulders and put the weapon back in his back waistband. He walked toward her.

"You okay?" he asked as concern lanced through him.

"I'm fine." A quirky smile passed over her lips. "I'm tough, Ryan."

"I know you are. But being tough also means knowing when you should slow down and refuel."

He thought about how she'd huddled in his arms after they'd barricaded in the basement and the lights had gone off. Holding her warm and safe in his arms felt instinctual, but he bet a hundred bucks she found it embarrassing. Many women did when they turned to a man for comfort, for a sense of safety.

"I'm not questioning your abilities. You're strong as hell. But I also have endurance training you don't. Just take it easy on yourself, okay?"

She closed her eyes, put her hands on the back of her neck and rubbed. "I can get through this."

He clasped her shoulders and rubbed them. "'Course you can."

Though they'd pushed onward for a long time, he figured this place would be good as any. He had a feeling the strange light that illuminated this structure would keep evil at bay for long enough for them to rest.

"Why don't you sit down somewhere and close your eyes. Rest," he said.

Her hands dropped to her sides. "Rest? Shouldn't we keep moving?"

He put the pack down and rifled through it. After retrieving a protein bar, he tossed it to her. "Eat this. It'll keep your strength up."

"Thanks." She opened the bar and took a delicate bite of the corner. Her nose wrinkled. "Tastes like cardboard."

He grabbed one, ripped open the package. He chomped down on the protein bar and chewed. "Mine isn't too bad. Peanut butter."

She grinned around a bite as she chewed. "Mine is oat wheat. No wonder it tastes too good for me."

She wandered about the chamber, her stride undeterred by fatigue, and he wondered if maybe he had underestimated her endurance.

"The ancient ashes of our past," she said. "I still don't understand how these Roman ruins are here in the United States."

He followed along behind her as she gazed at the walls, decorated with various creatures from lions, to bulls, to wood nymphs. "We're not in Kansas anymore, Dorothy."

"Cute." She took another bite of protein bar.

"This is the Shadow Realm. Don't think of it as being in the United States. We've walked into a threshold, a portal to this world."

She stopped treading the room, her expression dubious. "I'm sure some archaeologists would turn over in their graves if they could hear you say that."

"Think about it. Shakespeare said there were more things in heaven and earth, and damned if he wasn't double right."

She rubbed the back of her neck again, and his worry for her grew. Yeah, she was tough. Yeah, she could take care of herself. But damned if that all didn't matter when it came to his desire to keep her safe. He needed reassurance.

"Here." He put out his hand when she crumpled the protein wrapper. "I'll put it in the backpack. We don't need to leave Zurvan a trail of breadcrumbs. Besides, who knows what other Shadow Realm creatures might take offense to our litter."

She handed him the wrapper. "Maybe Zurvan has given up."

He went back to the pack and stuffed it inside one pocket of the pack. "If we're lucky."

For a second her slender-boned body and delicate features registered stark fear. "You said other Shadow Realm creatures. Do you expect us to see some?"

"You never know." He shrugged it off. "Don't worry about it before you see one. You'll waste energy."

She wandered back toward him, her uptight stance and the way her eyes scanned the room told him she'd tensed up. "What else do you know about your mission?"

"Other than running through the forest and this terrible pain crashing into my side and my head...nothing."

He came up behind her and clasped the delicate bones of her shoulders. Tough as old boot leather, his aunt used to say, but as breakable as a shoestring. With care he worked her muscles.

She shivered and moaned under his fingers. "Maybe you should do this for a living instead of chasing monsters."

"That doesn't sound like a half bad idea right now."

Silence stretched around them for quite some time, and he realized none of the sounds they made echoed in this place. Very strange. He continued kneading her shoulders, urging her to relax. He felt it working as she leaned into him. Finally, he ended the rubdown and curved his arms around her waist. He needed the comfort of holding her while this weird world revolved around them and they stumbled through the unknown minute by minute and hour by hour. She snuggled into his embrace, and he kissed her head.

"Mmm," she said softly. "I feel so...so languid."

He grinned. "That's good. Maybe you should sleep."

"What? And miss all the running and screaming and monsters? Surely, you jest. This is going to make a good book someday."

"You think?"

"Are you kidding?" She turned in his arms and looked up at him. "Of course, I might have to change the names to protect the innocent."

"Huh." He grunted. "There is no innocence here."

The jovial light in her eyes extinguished, replace by genuine apprehension. "I don't know if I can sleep, but I'm so dead right now I'm a walking zombie."

"Over here." He slipped his arm around her waist and urged her toward one wall. "Lean up against here and close your eyes."

"What about you?"

"I'll keep watch."

She settled onto the floor, a shiver rolling through her frame.

"Cold?" he asked.

She rubbed her arms. "Yes."

A memory flashed through his head. "Dorky told me the illuminated rooms are colder. The light is for protection." Understanding hovered on the perimeter of his mind. "Zurvan also doesn't like cold. This room is a good ten degrees colder than the other ones we've been in. Damn, we should have brought you a coat."

"What about you? All you have is a T-shirt."

"I'll be fine."

Skepticism lined her face. "Maybe Zurvan will stay the hell out of here, then?"

"I hope so."

As another shiver passed through her frame, he changed plans. He sat on the floor next to her with his back propped against the wall. He left the weapon on the floor next to him.

"Sit with your back against my chest," he said.

When he spread his legs so she could sit between them, she didn't hesitate to climb between them and cuddle. As she nestled back into his arms, Ryan encircled her. He enjoyed her soft, warm body against him, and the unmistakable rose scent that drifted up toward him from her shiny hair.

He inhaled deeply. "Damn, you smell good."

"Do I really? After all that running amok—"

He laughed. "If anyone smells bad, it's me."

She sniffed. "Yes."

"Hey." He nudged aside her hair and kissed her ear. "That deserves some punishment."

"Save your punishment for later when I have more energy and can enjoy it."

Laughter barked out of him, and suddenly he couldn't control it. He didn't give a shit whether Zurvan or other demented creatures from this underground world heard. Full guttural amusement exploded from him. He shook with it and wanted to howl like a beast.

She laughed too, her sound more a giggle than anything. "Stop that."

"You're laughing too."

"Only because you are."

If she'd been turned around to face him, he would have kissed her. Instead he gathered her closer in his arms. As his laughter died down, he savored the way she fit in his arms, the way her body nestled as if she belonged there. He breathed in and her scent soothed him, her warmth comforted. They went quiet, and in the total silence he found a peace he never expected.

"If Zurvan came right now, I'd still be the happiest son of a bitch in the world."

"Why?" she asked, her voice a thin thread of sound.

"Because you're here."

He felt her shiver, and he rubbed his hands up and down her arms a minute. Then he heard the sniff and her wobbly sigh.

"Hey, what's wrong?" He kissed her ear.

"I was thinking the same thing. If Zurvan came, and I died, I'd be here with you and that's all that matters."

He could tell she cried—the shaky voice told him. "I'll get you out of here. I promise."

She nodded, and then relaxed back into his arms. Quiet enveloped them, and fatigue liquidated his muscles and put lead weights on his eyelids. He succumbed to bone-melting rest when she eased into the jellylike relaxation signaling sleep.

* * * * *

Ryan's dream unfolded in colors and sounds so vivid, he couldn't ascertain realty or if he'd wandered in his sleep to a weird realm. He stood in another tall tomb, this one almost two stories tall. Warm copper light illuminated it from an unknown source. Niches stacked one upon another. Urns with ashes once stood in the niches, but most of the niches now lay empty. A warning in Latin flowed into his mind. *"Ne tangito, o mortalis, revere Mane deos."*

He shivered at the meaning. *Do not touch, oh mortal, respect the Manes.* He didn't know where the warning originated, but his gut urged him to follow it.

A shadow approached from his right side. Sibilant whispers echoed around the room. His stomach clenched. Danger lurked. He tried to see the shadow, but it flitted away as soon as he turned his head toward it. He continued around in a circle, on guard. From all around him came a growling, a low-grade rumbling that he remembered from somewhere in his deepest memories. Was this Zurvan? His temples started a nasty throb, and he put his hands to his head and winced.

With a start he awakened. His arms had tightened around Gina as they'd slept. His temples hurt, but not as bad as they did in the dream.

Anger with himself for falling asleep made him grit his teeth. He scanned the room for any sign of threat. The illumination had died down to a softer glow, and edges of the room once completely lit up faded into shadow. Apprehension assailed him from all sides. Evil awaited them the longer they stayed there, and Ryan's protective instincts reared up. He must get her out. Doubts eroded his confidence. With loss of memory and the uncertainty of how or when they could leave this tangled place, he wondered if they would die, forever searching for escape. He inhaled deeply to quell rising fear. Bullshit. He couldn't think like this. He couldn't allow this place to win. The idea of Gina losing her life because of his failure on this mission wrenched his gut and fired his determination. No. He would lead her to safety.

"Gina." He kept his voice low. "Wake up." When she didn't move, he squeezed her gently and leaned down to whisper in her ear. "Wake up. We need to leave."

When she still didn't move, renewed fear stabbed his gut. He brushed aside her hair and searched for the pulse in her neck.

When he found a steady, strong pulse, he sighed in profound relief and whispered to whichever gods listened, "Thank you. Thank you. Just let me get her out of here safely."

He kissed the side of her forehead and felt extraordinary heat. Oh, damn it. He placed his palm over her forehead. She was burning up. What the hell had happened? Had the infection she'd experienced with the laryngitis worsened? He looked at his watch and realized they'd slept over four hours. Damn it all to hell. She'd lain here in this cold room with only his arms for support and warmth. She needed a bed and medical attention.

"Shit. Shit."

He eased her away from him then rearranged her in his arms so she lay over his right arm and legs, her butt nestled in his lap. She whimpered.

"Wake up, Gina." He heard the urgency in his own voice. Nothing mattered but seeing her pretty eyes looking at him. "Please wake up, honey."

Her eyelids flickered, and her eyes opened. Her gaze didn't focus. "Irish."

"In the flesh, colleen. How do you feel? You've got a fever."

Her normally smooth brow wrinkled, and her gaze cleared. "I feel...achy. What's happened?"

He kissed her forehead. "You scared the hell out of me, that's what happened. I think that laryngitis you had earlier has come back with a vengeance."

"My voice is fine."

He cupped her face, hoping his palm was cooler. "Yeah, but it's turned into something else. You're sick. Come on, we have to find a way out of here. You need medical attention."

As he had earlier, she glanced at her watch. Her eyes widened. "Four hours?"

"Yeah. I had the same reaction."

She shivered.

"Are you cold now?" he asked.

She rubbed her arms. "Yes."

When he put his hand on her forehead, he still registered a fever. "Yep, you're sick, all right."

Instead of releasing her to stand up, as he'd planned a second ago, he drew her close into his arms and pressed her head against his chest. He rubbed his hands over her arms and back.

"Oh, that feels good," she said, her voice almost sleepy.

He tilted her chin up. "Don't go to sleep."

She smiled. "Are you kidding? This feels too good with you holding me."

He wanted to return her smile, but fright ate at his gut. "Do you think you can stand up?"

"Of course." She sounded indignant, and he figured that was a good sign. At least she had coherence and spunk.

He eased her back and stood at the same time as she did. Ryan kept his arm around her waist.

She moved away, but he watched her closely. "I'm okay. You can stop watching me as if I'm going to flop over. I'm good."

Gina didn't want Ryan to fuss over her, because if he did, she knew he'd hover or expect to carry her. While the thought of him carrying her held pleasant connotations, they couldn't afford the slowdown. A shiver ran through her and then a heat wave. She sucked in a large breath to stabilize her breathing. She couldn't let how she felt block their escape. They headed toward the next wall opening. He turned back toward her and rifled through the backpack.

He removed a half empty bottle of water. "Have a few sips. Not too much at first."

"Yes, doctor."

"Shit, if you're talking back, you must be okay."

"Must be." She decided to believe it. Parched, she forced only small sips then handed it back to him. When he drank a little she said, "You'll catch what I have."

"I've kissed the hell out of you more than once in several hours. If I'm going to catch what you have, I think the damage is done."

She sighed. "You're right."

She scrubbed her fingers through her hair. Weariness staggered her, and for a minute she didn't know if she could take another step. Her eyes felt scratchy, her body ached, her throat tight. She leaned one hand against the cold wall.

As her eyes flickered closed, she felt his strong hand cup her face. "Hey, are you all right?"

"I'm fine." She dared to open her eyes. "I think."

"You think."

"I have to be. We need to keep moving."

Ryan planted a light, tender kiss to her forehead. "You tell me if you start to feel faint."

"Okay. But I've never fainted once in my life, Ryan Ahern."

He chuckled. "Good. Then don't start now."

"What do we do next?"

"Move to the next room."

"It's darker in there."

He clicked on the flashlight. "Let me go first."

He moved in front of her and stepped through the darkened threshold.

Shaky, but determined, Gina followed. They stepped into a long hallway lined with brick. A glow lit up the other end of the hallway. Another room, another light. When would this end?

Before Ryan could make a move toward this new room, a voice echoed from within.

"Enter," an airy, feminine voice said from the open doorway.

The voice sounded so soft, so gentle and without malice, that Gina couldn't see a reason to hesitate. She stepped forward into the golden light.

"Wait," Ryan said as he grasped her upper arm. "I'll go first."

As he stepped in front of her, she smiled at his protectiveness. "You make me feel too girly sometimes with your desire to protect me."

He frowned. "Is that a bad thing?"

She sighed and let the truth out. "No. I don't think so. Your concern warms a part of my soul I didn't know I possessed."

Something changed in his eyes—she knew it the moment she saw it. Deep understanding, appreciation and maybe love. Now she knew without much doubt that whatever they faced next, she could handle.

His hand went up to cup her face, his thumb caressing as he leaned close. Even on the verge of discovering more of this strange new world, she felt stirrings of arousal heat her belly.

His warm breath brushed across her lips as he said huskily, "You're the best thing that's ever happened to me, Gina."

Her heart pounded, her breath coming harder. Whether her senses boiled because of the danger or his stirring proximity and words, she couldn't say. Maybe both. Before she could answer, he leaned in and captured her lips.

Gentle and cautious, his kiss gave her strength. Tremors fired to life in her stomach and quivered over her entire body. He pulled back and released her.

"Come on, colleen. Let's go."

As he stepped into the unknown, she took the leap of faith and followed.

Ryan tensed. Gina's words before they'd entered had rattled him. While he appreciated companionship and comfort, he knew what he felt for Gina went way beyond pleasant. They'd crossed into feverish, over-the-top emotion. She didn't know how she made him feel—not really. At this point, it would mean breaking down and crying like a baby or keeping emotions tucked close to his vest. He couldn't afford the first one, and they didn't have time for the second.

The golden light went from blinding to a subdued glow. Unlike the other rooms they'd passed through in this cold subterranean way, this room held the brightness of new stucco, fresh-looking mosaics and frescos.

The being in the middle of the room reminded him of every description he'd heard of an angel. With long, snow-white straight hair flowing over her bare shoulders, an alabaster pale face. She wore a satiny white garment attached by sparkling clear stone broaches. It draped along her thin body and reminded him of a statue he'd seen once of Athena. From her ears dangled matching chandelier-type earrings. The woman didn't speak. Narrow and pale, her face had a strange ethereal beauty that defied normal standards of beauty.

But one detail stood out beyond the others.

She had white wings.

Her wings flexed, went out in full spread of several feet then folded back behind her again.

"Please come forward," the woman said. Her tone pulsed with warmth that calmed him. Her voice held a strange accent, not quite Queen's English, not quite American. He'd never heard anything like it before.

"Who are you?" he asked, half expecting to feel alarm, as if he should stay on guard.

She stopped several feet away from him. "I'm sorry. It's taking a few moments for me to adjust to your language. Here we speak what you refer to as Latin."

He nodded, surprised at how comfortable he felt under her intense stare.

"You have..." Gina started to say.

"Wings." The woman nodded. "I'm Nidia of the Marcanas of the belowworld, the realm you now occupy."

Marcanas. He'd never heard of it.

"Pleased to meet you Nidia," Gina said amiably.

To his surprise, Gina didn't seem to find the situation half as unnerving as he did. Or maybe she hid it well. He kept his weapon in hand, but the winged woman didn't appear to care.

The winged woman glanced at Ryan. "If you wish to clean up, we can wash your garments, you can come back in here and sleep undisturbed for a few hours. No one will bother you. It's imperative you rest before you attempt to leave."

"I'm not going anywhere without an explanation of where we are and what's happening," Ryan said.

"We will speak of this later," Nidia said. "You are cold and tired and you need sleep."

Ryan slipped his arm around Gina and drew her close. His instincts said he could trust the ethereal-looking woman, but he didn't want to let his guard down yet.

"You are a careful man." Nidia smiled. "That is a very good thing. But you have nothing to fear from me and my kind. Our goal is to protect human life. We are a part of you and you are a part of us, even though our realms exist on two different dimensions."

Ryan kept his expression cool and straight. "How do I know we're safe?"

"Zurvan cannot reach you here. Not in this room."

"There were other rooms." Gina took a tentative step out from under his arm. "Bright ones like these. We were safe there too."

Nidia smiled. "Yes. Very perceptive."

"You started to say who you are." Gina glanced around the room. "I mean, who your people are."

Nidia stayed as calm and bright as the moment they'd walked in to the room. "It is not for you to know everything about us. We are the Marcanas. A race long connected with humans in your dimension."

Gina's cheeks pinked, and she looked a bit embarrassed. "You look like an angel."

Nidia's warm laugh filled the room. "In your realm, that is what people think we are."

"Jesus," Ryan said without thinking. "Angels?"

Nidia nodded. "There are many truths and myths about us. We've crossed over into your realm many times to help humans in need. Just as there are monsters that have crossed over from our realm to harm humankind."

"Zurvan," Gina said.

"Zurvan crossed into your dimension more than once many thousands of years ago and that's when the Mithras religion flourished. Humans at that time couldn't understand Zurvan any other way than to think him a god. There are many understandings and representations of the eternal light, the all-knowing and -loving which created every realm and dimension. But Zurvan is not a part of that god. He tricked humans into thinking that he is more that what he is."

"Sounds reasonable to me," Ryan said, a bit tongue-in-cheek.

She waved one hand. "Enough for now. You are tired and hungry. I heard you coming, but couldn't cross over into the other rooms to help you reach safety. It was up to you to find your way here."

Ryan frowned. "An angel who couldn't help us."

Nidia didn't look fazed by his criticism. "This is why your SIA was formed, to try and understand our realm and protect humans against its evil forces."

"How do you know about us? How do you know about the SIA?" Gina asked.

The angelic woman smiled. "I have my ways. Just as I know about the SIA, I know your names. Gina and Ryan."

Ryan's concerns went on full alert. He stepped forward. "What we don't know is how to get out of here in one piece."

Nidia peered at him as if he was a bug under a microscope. "You have many secrets of your own, Mr. Ahern. I can sense them just from here. Telling you too much would create confusion and wouldn't help your cause."

Ryan's skepticism refused to dissolve. He planted his hands on his hips. "And what do you think my cause is?"

"To leave here alive."

"Ryan has amnesia," Gina said. "But he's regaining his memories. If he knows about the Shadow Realm already, there isn't any harm in telling us everything, is there?"

Nidia walked around the room with light steps, as if she weighed no more than the air around her. "I doubt Mr. Ahern knows everything about us. You are from the Special Investigations Agency. They sent you here to either destroy Zurvan, or send him back to this dimension. As you know, the SIA is the only group in your dimension that understands a little of the realms here...the aboveworld and the belowworld of the Shadow Realm. Yet they have much to learn."

"Aboveworld and belowworld," Gina said.

"The Shadow Realm is comprised of two worlds...one is below ground, where you are now. The other is the realm of lightness, of the fairies and elves." Nidia walked toward a doorway at the south end of the room. "Come with me to the next room. To the nympheum."

Ryan stayed close to Gina as they followed the woman. He put the safety on his weapon and slipped the gun into the back waistband of his jeans.

The space they entered held a multitude of wonders. Frescos and mosaics beneath their feet showed elements of water. Scattered with furniture, the room had old-world elegance.

"This looks like a room in Pompeii or Herculaneum," Ryan said.

Gina stood next to him, her gaze coasting over the room, wide with wonder. "It does. And it's beautiful."

Nidia tilted her head to the side, and her silvery hair slid over her right shoulder in a silky wave. "Where do you think Pompeii first devised the idea?"

As he took in the intimate room, he recalled more. Ryan felt his mind opening to knowledge, but whether he'd known it in the past or somehow clairvoyantly understood, he couldn't say for certain.

He circled the room, taking in his surroundings with fascination. The carvings and paintings surrounding them stirred his voice into action. "Homer said the daughters of Zeus are beautiful maidens found in glades and clearings where they hunt and dance. They live in caves where water flows. They interpret the messages from water."

Ryan recalled another tidbit. "A nympheum in Roman times was a place dedicated to the cult and veneration of nymphs. Nereids, Naiads, Oceanids. They embrace all manifestation of water. They are young and graceful." He felt a strange pull toward Nidia, and he walked toward her. A niggling panic threatened, one he couldn't control as he came closer to the tall figure before him. "They live in peaceful valleys, near riverbanks and brooks, in magical solitude. They're alluring and bewitching and anyone who sees them is seduced. Anyone who glimpses a nymph is rendered insane. Are you a nymph, Nidia?"

Nidia threw her head back and laughed, the sound sweet and not the least menacing. "If I was, you would be babbling and mad, don't you think?"

"Only if the legends are true. After what I've seen, I could believe it."

"The legend, in this case, isn't true. I am not a nymph. As I said, I am Marcanas. We have lived in this realm forever. Our origins are somewhat obscure even to us. Please, sit down."

Nidia gestured to a cushioned bench near one wall. A long table graced the area in front of it. Two comfortable-looking chairs sat across from the bench.

Before he could ask another question, Nidia clapped her hands and a man walked through an open door with a tray. "This tea does not taste like anything you've had before, but it is perfectly safe. It should give you energy and help heal imbalances in your system from your long hours of walking."

Ryan kept an eye on the toga-clad man, a huge redhead way over six feet tall and with the build of a wrestler. The man kept his huge white wings tucked securely behind him. The man didn't look at any of them and retreated from the room the instant he put the tray of glasses and small brown wafers on the table between them.

"Eat," Nidia said. "I'll tell you more."

Gina reached for a wafer, and he almost grabbed her hand. Gina tasted the food slowly, and a second later a surprised sensation came over her face.

"What is it?" he asked, worried.

She smiled and continued to chew. "It tastes like Scottish shortbread." She raised one eyebrow and glanced at Nidia. "Is it?"

Nidia poured a clear liquid into two large milky white glasses. "Similar, but with more nutritional benefits." She handed a glass to Gina and one to Ryan. "Tea."

Assured that Nidia meant them no immediate harm, Ryan chugged down an entire glass. Delicious, cold liquid gave him a sharp headache for a second, but he didn't care. Gina drank more carefully.

They ate in silence until Ryan couldn't take the suspense. "Since I can't remember everything the SIA told me about the Shadow Realm, could you fill me in?"

Nidia's smile was all-knowing. "I think that would overwhelm you at this point. It's better you leave this place. You've accomplished what you set out to do, Mr. Ahern."

Ryan took another sip of tea. "I did?"

"You brought Zurvan here. It escaped from the dungeon we'd placed it in six months ago after a rampage into your dimension."

"My God," Gina said.

Ryan's mind wrapped around the idea reluctantly. "How do you know what my mission was?"

"We have a contact within the SIA. We receive information that way, just as we provide information to the SIA through the same channel," Nidia said.

Nidia didn't partake of nourishment, but she sat back and watched them with a happy glow in her eyes.

His mistrust started to dissolve. "Who is the contact?"

"The person's identity must remain a secret for their safety. There are forces within our dimension that would harm them."

Hideaway

He nodded, choosing to believe Nidia. "Where do we go from here? You said I completed my mission. Have you recaptured Zurvan?"

"Not quite. But it shouldn't be long. We know where the creature is and will harness him as soon as possible."

"Then my mission isn't complete. First, I get Gina out of here safely, then I need to finish securing Zurvan."

Chapter Thirteen

"No, Ryan." The words left Gina's throat without a thought. "I'm not leaving here without you."

He glared at her, his dark brows drawing down. "Yeah, you will. I won't allow anything else to happen to you. This is my job, not yours."

Gina bristled, but decided ignoring his mandate for the moment might work.

"Tell us more about the dimension. What is it, exactly?" Gina took a sip of the unusual tea and the feverish exhaustion she'd experienced earlier started to ebb.

Nidia folded her hands in her lap. "All civilizations have explorers, and many of them found us. Some survived when they traversed the mazes as you did. Some lost their way and never returned to your dimension. You've heard of people who disappeared never to find their way home. In your world, you assume serial killers snatched these people. There are many openings to our world. The door in your friends' cabin is one of these doors."

"You know which door we entered?" Ryan's voice held disbelief.

"Of course." Nidia didn't seem the least surprised by his question. "Your friends, Gina, are agents for the SIA, just like Ryan. They have safeguarded the doorway, just as others have before them."

Gina had an epiphany. "That's why you headed for the cabin. You figured Zurvan might use the Mithras door to return to the Shadow Realm. If I was in the cabin at the time, I could be hurt or worse."

He shook his head, a distant look filling his eyes. "My partner was with me. We'd chased down Zurvan for several days. We'd made it into the woods when Zurvan attacked from behind. The son of a bitch killed my partner. I fought him off and then realized the bullets I used weren't doing a damned thing. My particle sword was also lost in the fight, and I had to run."

Pain flickered over his face, and he buried his face in his hands. A shivering sigh shook his body. "Fuck me. I failed my partner. I fucking failed him."

Gina's heart broke for him, her throat tight. She slipped her hand over his back. "I know you, Ryan, even when you don't know yourself. You fought Zurvan the best you could. Remember, you were unconscious at my door. You fought hard." Curiosity made her pause. "By the way, what is a particle sword?"

He lifted his head and stared at the women. "Something you don't want to mess with."

Frustration ate away at Gina. "Ryan, now is not the time to keep me in the dark."

Her throat tightened and then a cough burst from her. She threw her hand over her mouth as a dull ache entered her throat.

Ryan slipped his arm around her shoulders and held her close. "Damn it! She needs to get topside. She's sick."

"I'm okay," Gina said, her voice raspy.

Nidia's brow knitted. "You felt better after the tea, didn't you?"

"Yes," Gina said.

"Then perhaps all she needs is a little sleep before she tries to leave," Nidia said as she poured more tea for Gina.

"If we can't leave immediately, I want you to lie down and rest," Ryan said.

Despite his genuine concern, she wanted to smack him. Once again, she scooted out from under his embrace. "I'm not leaving here until I hear the whole story. Now." She inhaled deeply and pushed away tiredness. She kept her gaze trained away from Ryan, certain disapproval would show in his face. "Nidia, what else can you tell me about this world I've fallen into?"

"It's a dimension too amazing for most." Nidia stood and wandered to a mural featuring an aroused Pan taking a human female from behind. She traced one finger over Pan's back. "Our world is far too complicated for most humans to understand and filled with things you can't imagine."

"Oh, I don't know," Gina said as she leaned back against the couch. "I can imagine an awful lot."

When Nidia turned around, her pretty mouth turned up at the corners and amusement lightened her already remarkable eyes. "Is that so?"

"She's a writer," Ryan said.

Nidia clasped her hands in front of her. "That certainly would explain the imagination. The Marcanas applaud human creativity. As you can see from our murals, art is important to us. Yet there are many things here that would repulse the more puritanical elements in your society."

Gina smiled and stood. "There's nothing puritanical about me."

Nidia's brow went up. "Your writing?"

"Erotic romance," Ryan said with genuine appreciation.

"Ah, I see." Nidia tilted her head to the side. "You are a very brave one."

Gina didn't feel brave. "There's one thing I didn't envision when we came down here. I didn't realize such a pretty place could exist when we were running from Zurvan." She wobbled a tiny bit and Ryan sprang to his feet and steadied her with an arm around her waist. "Does this dimension have sunlight and rain and...I don't know. Anything beyond this underground area?"

"Oh, yes." Nidia came back toward them, her grace and patience evident. "In the aboveworld the ground looks as it did during the time of the Romans in your past." She gestured back at the table. "Please, finish eating. You'll need your strength."

While Gina's fascination with this place heightened, so did the knowledge she couldn't push too much harder. She slipped from Ryan's attentive grip and back to the couch.

After they'd eaten their fill, Nidia's wings rustled and caught Gina's attention. Light shimmered from the gossamer wings, the sparkle and beauty so captivating that Gina didn't hear what Ryan said.

"You all right?" he asked, his fingers brushing over her shoulder.

Gina jerked to attention, her back ramrod straight. "What?"

"You had a fever earlier. You shouldn't push it." His gaze pinpointed Nidia. "Is there somewhere Gina can lie down?"

"Certainly. Follow me to the other chambers."

Gina followed Nidia through the door and into another room. Gina sensed things spiraling out of her control, and she didn't care for the sensation. She pulled her arm from Ryan's grasp and folded her arms. "What if I don't want to leave?"

"What?" he said.

"Like I mentioned before, if you're staying here and fighting Zurvan, so am I."

"I don't think so."

"Hear me out. You don't think with all we've been through I'll leave you to fight this creature by yourself."

Nidia held up one pale hand. "Relax first. There is time to concern yourself with this later."

Ryan squeezed her shoulders. "Please take her advice."

Gina relented under the pressure. "All right. Only for a little while. The sooner we trap Zurvan, the sooner we leave."

As they followed Nidia through one short hallway, then another, weariness spread through Gina. Okay, she'd admit it now, she felt tired as hell.

Nidia opened the dark wooden double doors in front of them and they swung wide on quiet hinges. After several twists and turns through a maze of corridors lined with closed doors, they came to another set of dark wooden doors.

They stepped into a cozier version of the rooms they'd left moments ago. A large chest of drawers that looked like an orphan from a Queen Anne collection graced one corner. A mirror sparkled above it, the dark wooden frame screamed old traditions, and a wardrobe sat in one corner nearby a large roll-top desk. A gossamer pale blue canopy draped a large king-sized bed on a wood frame. Pretty murals of Etruscan splendor graced the walls.

Gina looked up at the ceiling and smiled. "My, my."

Ryan followed suit with a "Wow".

The painted ceiling depicted a sexual scene that made Gina's jaw drop. One woman found pleasure in a ménage with two men.

Nidia frowned when she noticed their attention riveted on the ceiling painting. "Is something wrong?"

Gina couldn't wipe the grin off her face. Apparently, this dimension was as horny as the Romans used to be. "No. Nothing is wrong."

"If you need anything, you know where to find me," Nidia said as she left them at the door.

As the wide double doors closed, Gina sighed. Ryan sidled up to her, his gaze apprehensive. "You all right?"

She smoothed her hands over his chest, and his hands clasped her shoulders. "Yes. I'm great now that I'm safe here with you."

Hideaway

"You aren't fighting Zurvan with me."

Weary of the conversation, she decided to deny the controversy for the moment. "Let's sleep on it. That bed looks delicious."

His lips quirked, and laughter glinted in his eyes. "Yeah. And the view looking up at the ceiling isn't bad either."

* * * * *

Exhausted, they slept for several hours, and when Gina awoke, she burrowed closer into Ryan's arms. They'd stripped naked. Even though Gina at first felt self-conscious that someone might walk into the room at any time, the door had a lock and they used it. Dog-tired, they'd curled up in each other's arms. Rested and feeling better than when they'd walked in this room for the first time, she savored the sensation of powerful arms around her. Ryan felt so wonderful against her. So capable of taking on anything. She knew, through their adventure together, that Ryan's love meant everything to her. Wondering if he'd feel the same, if he'd want to stay together after this strange situation…well, that worried her more than she wanted to admit.

A wave of heat went over her that had nothing to do with sexual interest. It felt sickly. Uneven. Shivering, she huddled closer to him. Even with the warmth of blankets over them, cold seeped like slow-moving ice into her blood.

"Mmmm." His murmur brushed her forehead, his warm breath turning up the pilot light on the slow sensual burn in her stomach. "Is that a beautiful woman in my arms, or a nymph?"

"Definitely a nymph."

He kissed her forehead. "You're too damned modest, colleen."

"What I am is starving." She shifted in his arms so she could look up at him. "And cold."

He rubbed her arms and kissed her long and deep. His tongue caressing hers sent brand-new spirals of want into her bloodstream. Yet the unsettled feeling wouldn't leave.

"Let's dress and find something to eat," he said when he pulled back.

She didn't cherish the idea of dressing in her old clothes. When they climbed out of bed, they discovered their laundered garments folded neatly on a chair seat.

Ryan lifted his underwear and jeans off the pile. "Whoa."

Feeling unsteady on her feet, she reached for her clothes and ignored the feeling. "Whoa is right. They slipped in here without us knowing."

"I'm not sure I like that."

"I think Nidia is fine. I didn't feel like she wanted to harm us in any way."

"You're right. But I'm not comfortable with the arrangement. It still feels like something is lurking around the corner."

Okay, so maybe that weird sensation in the pit of her stomach had as much to do with security worries as illness. She hoped so and concentrated on breathing deeply and dressing.

After they'd finished putting on their clothes, he reached for the weapon under his pillow and stuffed it in the back of his jeans again. "Let's see if we can find Nidia."

They left the room in short order. As they traversed the passageways, apprehension eased into her gut yet again.

"Do you remember how we got here?" she asked.

"Yep."

"Good, because—" Strange noises ushered from the hallway behind her. "What's that?"

She turned to look at the same time he did, and froze in fear. Two dark figures, faces hidden under crimson cloaks, stood but twenty feet away. As she gazed into the blackness where their faces should have been, an inexplicable dread filled her center and tightened her throat. She gasped for a breath, her heart slamming in her chest. She understood their evil without anyone explaining, in the deepest, most sensitive regions of her soul.

Ryan grabbed her arms and pushed her behind him. Over his shoulder, she observed the figures. With their arms folded, and a brown rope tied about their waists, they appeared as monks or perhaps double grim reapers. One held a scythe, the dull pewter-colored metal glinting dully. Cold then heat rolled through her body in a fierce wave.

"Great. What the fuck is this?" Ryan said so softly she barely heard him.

Before she could respond, the two reaper-like creatures leaped forward as if someone had launched the beings from a springboard. Ryan leveled his weapon on the creatures. Gunfire split the air in the small hallway. The reapers fell back, their cloaks waving in a nonexistent breeze.

"Run!" Ryan cried out.

She turned to run, but made a half-dozen steps when a creature from her nightmares appeared at the other end of the hall.

From seeing the carving on the doors and in these tombs, she expected Zurvan to be more elegant, more a caricature of a god. Standing about twelve feet high at the shoulder, the gunmetal-gray scaly creature possessed a long neck. A knife-sharp bony ridge curved along the top of its skull. She gasped as the creature opened its mouth and out came a long forked tongue. It stood on four legs, its body almost skinny. She couldn't see a tail, but she guessed it probably had one.

"Jesus. It's fuckin' Nessie," Ryan said behind her.

Zurvan didn't look like the carvings at all, if indeed this was Zurvan.

She turned swiftly. Ryan held his gun at the ready, but he turned toward the two reapers and something far nastier behind them. A lion's head tacked on a body with wings, and that body wrapped around with coils of a snake.

Okay, now she'd seen Zurvan.

I'm in a nightmare. I'm still sleeping, and I'll wake up soon.

The reapers advanced.

Suddenly Ryan started speaking. "Time's voracity, the movement of stars and heavenly bodies, the sun, the winds tracing their path. Send us, oh Mithras, a guardian. We ask you for wisdom, might and victory, health and healing. May we traverse through this world absolute masters, crushing evil beneath our feet."

"What's that?" she asked breathlessly.

"A chant...a curse I learned at the SIA."

Everything happened so fast. Behind them came a screech, a furious cry high-pitched enough to hurt her ears. Which way to turn?

Seconds later, she fell to the ground under a heavy weight. Pain rocketed through her head, arms and stomach on impact. She struggled under the suffocating weight, gasped for air. Fear sliced deep as a knife into her soul. *No. No.* She had too much to live for, too much writing to do.

She loved Ryan with a fierce intensity and wanted to spend the rest of her life with him.

Noise clashed around her. Ryan's shout of anger echoed, then a roar. She tried to move under the heavy weight pressing on her back but it wouldn't budge. A hissing and a growl came from the bizarre Nessie creature, and Gina looked up through blurry eyes. The reptilian creature lumbered their direction. Terror spiked inside her.

She wanted to call out to Ryan but the weight compressed her ribs. She tried to take a breath and couldn't. She heard shouting and managed to open her eyes and tilt her head so she could see some of what happened. Several male figures, their wings spread in full, flew behind the serpent creature.

They hovered like angels, their faces beautiful, carved and furious. Maybe avenging angels would save her and Ryan.

Everything went dark.

Chapter Fourteen

Ryan started, his eyes popping open. A slow ache rolled through his body and he moaned as he shifted on cool fabric. Feeling one hundred percent awake, he tried to recall what happened after the cloaked figures and Zurvan had attacked. The serpent creature had charged at the same time as the lion-headed Zurvan. Before he could move to protect Gina, the lizard creature had plowed him over, his head had cracked against solid stone, and that's all he recalled. He squinted in the bright light, the illumination dimming to a softer glow as his eyes adjusted. His head ached like a son of a bitch, but he could think.

One thought instantly penetrated his rattled brain. *Gina.*

"Gina?" His question came out hoarse.

No answer.

Again, he looked around. Instead of crumbling mosaics and fading artwork, the walls held beautiful full blues, reds and a variety of other colors in murals that appeared as if they'd been painted yesterday. He was back in the bedroom where he'd slept with Gina safe in his arms.

He sat up and realized he was stark naked and without a sheet. "Fuck me."

"Perhaps we should leave that to Gina," the soft voice said from somewhere in the room.

The woman stood at the open mouth of a wooden doorway, her smile gentle. She didn't look like she cared one way or the other if he was as naked as the day he was born.

Nidia.

Relief filled him.

He slid out of the bed and tested his legs as Nidia walked forward. Her gaze didn't waver, her expression imperturbable. When his feet touched the granite stone flooring, the smooth texture felt cool but not as icy as he expected.

"What happened?" he asked. "Where's Gina?"

"Do not fear for her safety. She is very well."

While he wanted to believe Nidia, his alarm for Gina bubbled to the surface. He swallowed hard. "If anything has happened to her—"

"She is safe and you will see her shortly."

He took a deep breath and pushed back his fears. "We were on our way back to you when those creatures came after us. I thought this was a safe zone."

"Nothing is one hundred percent safe. Unfortunately, Zurvan cracked our protection shields and came after you. But the serpent, Bantium, saved you from certain death."

He shook his head as a harsh anxiety rolled in his stomach. "What the hell is a Bantium?"

"A friend who protects the inner sanctum of our dimension."

"How the hell did we make out of the situation alive? I don't remember much."

"Several of my compatriots came to your rescue. With the help of Bantium, they drove off Zurvan."

"Damn it. Why didn't they recapture it?"

"Their first priority was saving you."

He shook his head. "Fine, then take me to Gina."

She laid a thin, pale hand on his shoulder. "Don't despair. She's quite all right."

Anxiety tightened his throat. "Where is she? Why isn't she here with me?"

"Because we are treating her."

"What's wrong with her?"

"She was battered by the attack. As for you, the head injury you suffered before you came to this realm finally took its toll and you needed different treatment."

"How long was I out?"

"A day."

He drew in a deep breath. "Shit."

He put his hands on his hips, and he saw Nidia's gaze drop to his cock for a moment. Maybe his nakedness affected her a little. He saw his clothes piled on the chair and went to grab them.

As he swiftly worked on donning his clothes, he said, "Take me to her."

"She's resting and recovering from sickness."

He slipped his T-shirt over his head as impatience filled him. He couldn't seem to control the anger rising inside him. "I said, take me to her."

"You're angry and worried. There is no reason for either. She needs another day's rest. Her body is fighting realm sickness."

"What the hell is that?"

"A fever contracted by most people who venture into this dimension the first time. Some people equate it with high-altitude sickness. Her system was weakened somewhat when she entered—no doubt that's why she's suffering now."

Self-recrimination rolled through his mind. *Damn.* "I shouldn't have brought her in here."

"Did you have a choice?" She smiled, and her eyes warmed. "You couldn't have helped it. You are a strong man, Ryan Ahern. But you're only human."

He paused, mind spinning for answers. Could he have done anything differently?

"Zurvan was after you and coming into this dimension in the first place was your only choice," she said as her wings stretched out behind her then folded back into place.

"Other than trying to escape the SIA's plans to cook his ass, why would Zurvan come after me?"

"For the very reason that you understand what it is. Most humans don't know Zurvan exists, therefore they are no threat."

"Shit. That means I did put Gina in jeopardy when I went to the cabin."

She sighed. "Unknowingly. You had amnesia and your mind was jumbled, you did the only instinctual thing. You worried that because Zurvan was in the area, that Gina would be hurt if Zurvan decided to use the portal to this realm located in the cabin. So your only thought was to keep her safe. Without you by her side, she might not be alive now."

He scrubbed his hands over his beard-stubbled jaw. "Yeah, I've protected her, all right." Self-recrimination battered at his confidence in a way it hadn't since he'd immigrated to the United States.

Nidia's lips turned up in a smile. "You're feeling a bit sorry for yourself, aren't you? It's understandable. But you don't have time for it, and I'll tell you why. The Realm Guardians are evil beings and they want nothing more than to disrupt our world and yours. You see, I don't think Zurvan actually escaped this dimension. I think the Realm Guardians let him into your world on purpose, as they have many times to confuse and harm humans as best they can. It isn't just this realm they want to destroy. They want to harm your world as well."

"Who are these fucking Realm Guardians for real? You haven't told me that much about them."

"Just know this. They serve Zurvan and are the worst of the evil here, and when they are full force, they are almost invincible. The Marcanas have fought them for hundreds of years." She frowned, but she kept her gaze pinned to his. "There is an individual who once belonged to our world who has the power to defend anyone against the Realm Guardians. But she isn't here anymore."

"Where did she go?"

"I can't tell you that."

Anger surged once more. He wanted to wring the total truth out of her. "Before I passed out, I saw winged men behind the serpent. Who are they?"

"Other Marcanas of the soldier caste. They battle evils within our belowworld, but we're up against a difficult fight with Realm Guardians and Zurvan."

He sighed. "You're saying we've stepped right into a centuries-old war?"

Nidia's gaze didn't waver when she looked him in the eye. "In a sense, yes."

He pondered her statement and the ease with which she admitted the situation. He stalked around the room a few moments. Finally, he stopped. "Why didn't you tell us before?"

"I planned to."

"No, I don't think you did. You figured we'd be out of here, and you wouldn't have to explain."

For the first time since he'd met her, Nidia looked uncomfortable. "Perhaps I made a mistake. I should have told you the full extent of what we face in this realm."

More concerned than ever for Gina, he decided to wait for more explanations. "Take me to Gina."

"You need rest. You don't have the realm sickness, but your body is still weary. You're recovering as she is."

"I don't care. I need to see her."

She nodded and sighed. "Very well. She was right."

"Who was right about what?"

Nidia's lips parted, then she pressed them together and her expression darkened. "Our contact on the other side. She said people from your dimension are stubborn."

While she might seem wise, he now realized Nidia didn't have all the answers. "I see. Well, your contact is right. We are obstinate as hell. It's what keeps us alive."

She smiled. "Apparently." Her voice, now softer and kinder, whispered over his senses. "Come. I'll take you to Gina."

* * * * *

Gina wanted to open her eyes, but they felt heavy. Her eyelids, her arms, her legs. Nothing would move. Under her body, she felt the most exquisite luxurious cushioning. A lightweight covering kept her cozy. She sighed, wanting nothing more than to return to sleep.

A woman's beautiful voice, warm and gentle, followed. Nidia. "Give her more time to recover. You both had quite a battle with Zurvan."

"Yeah. It lasted all of two seconds." Ryan's voice held distrust. "She has a fever." His voice rose, and Gina heard panic and anger mixed. "She's still unconscious."

Confusion battled with Gina's desire to waken fully, and she tried again to open her eyes but to no avail.

"With the potion we gave her, she will recover nicely. She must not exert herself for a few hours yet. You both need time."

"There isn't anything wrong with me."

"Transition from the Shadow Realm back to your dimension isn't like—what is it called in your dimension?—driving through a fast-food restaurant."

If she'd had the energy, Gina would have laughed at the woman's sense of humor.

"Gina needs medical attention back in *my* dimension." Ryan's voice sounded closer.

"She has a mild infection caused by a rude introduction to bacteria in the Shadow Realm. Her body is not used to it, but she's strong, and she will recover nicely."

This statement wrested Gina from her stupor. She shifted and struggled to open her eyes.

"She's waking up," Ryan said, sounding relieved.

"You will distract her from healing if you stay too long. She needs solid sleep."

Distract her from healing? Maybe, if he turned that all-out sexy smile on her. She wanted to see him so much.

Gina peeled her eyes open slowly, and when she spied Ryan standing beside her soft cocoon, she grinned.

His expression held a seriousness that scared her. Her gaze flicked around the room. This room held murals, drapes, many of the things the other room possessed. This one, though, also sported a pink bed much like the blue bed where she'd slumbered with Ryan.

He sat on the side of the bed and put his hand on her forehead. "Hey. How are you feeling?"

She returned his smile, scanning his face for signs of wear and tear. Other than a shallow cut above his right eyebrow, he remained the most gorgeous man she'd ever seen.

Profound happiness filled her heart. "I'm fine. I think. I heard your conversation with Nidia." She struggled to sit up so she could peer around the room.

He clasped her shoulders and gently urged her back. "Whoa. Don't sit up yet."

She sank back into fluffy pillows—her body ached anyway, and dizziness threatened. Comfort enveloped her as the soft, warm coverings drifted over her naked form.

She gasped and held the coverings up to her neck. "I'm naked."

He threw her a quirky, mischievous grin. "Yeah, I noticed."

He gathered her right hand in both of his and the heat of his big palms and fingers soaked into flesh.

Remnants of fear flickered in his eyes. "You scared the shit out of me."

"Why?"

"Why? Because after I woke up, I thought something horrible happened to you."

"I feel safe." She acknowledged the sentiment without hesitation. "Are we? Safe, I mean?"

He nodded. "Yeah, I think we are."

She detected wariness in his eyes, but didn't know the source. Maybe he was cautiously optimistic.

"Where are we?" she asked as she scanned the room.

"Back at the safe zone. We're still in the Shadow Realm."

The large room held a strange glow similar to the catacomb they'd slept in earlier. Unlike the roughness of the catacombs, the murals, pillars and finished walls appeared new. The room was a comfortable temperature. When she turned her head to both sides, she noted bed stands in a white, marble-like substance that gleamed. One bed stand held a basin, a pewter goblet and a matching pitcher.

She lifted her left hand to touch her hair. "I feel clean. Did they bathe me?"

He nodded. "Yeah, they did."

He gathered her hand in both of his and pressed her fingers to his lips. After the gentle kiss, he closed his eyes and sighed. "I was so damned scared. I didn't want to leave you."

Awe held her speechless. He did care about her, his wobbly smile and the sheen in his eyes testimony to his feelings. He blinked rapidly, and she knew—much more and he'd cry.

She reached up with her other hand and drew her fingers down the side of his stubbled cheek. "You're wonderful, you know that? Stop looking at me as if I'm on my deathbed. I'm feeling better just since I woke up. No more dizziness. My head feels clear. Other than a few body aches, I'm good."

Ryan gave her a crooked smile. He released her long enough to arch his back and raise his long arms above his head in a stretch.

As she admired the play of muscles over his magnificent body, she remembered more about their encounter with Zurvan. "Something knocked me down. Was it you?"

He shook his head. "No. Zurvan and the freaky hooded characters headed toward us, and the Nessie thing—they call it a Bantium—knocked us both down. I was knocked out immediately and woke up a few hours ago back in the room we slept in earlier." Ryan edged off the bed, but he leaned forward and kissed Gina on the forehead. "Sleep. I'll be back before you know it." His gaze landed on Nidia. "You'll watch over her?"

"Of course."

Ryan winked at Gina then departed through a white door across the room.

Nidia turned back to her, placing her hand on Gina's forehead. "Good. Your fever is almost gone. Within a few hours you should be completely well."

"What was wrong with me?"

"You had realm sickness. It's common to visitors who've never been here before. It sometimes reoccurs if a human comes back on another visit, but rarely."

"Can I have my clothes?"

"Not yet. We're making sure none of the bacteria that made you ill is on your clothes." Nidia smiled, and her expression held an angelic glow that went perfectly with those magnificent wings. "Don't worry. We are all watching over you. Your man will join you soon." Nidia turned and started to walk away. She turned back. "You have an extraordinary companion in Ryan. He's brave. He failed to tell you what he did to try and save you from Zurvan."

"I thought the Nessie creature saved us."

"Bantium saved you both, but Ryan pumped bullets into the Realm Guardians and Zurvan. He put himself between you and danger. He is very much in love with you."

Heady excitement flowed into Gina. Could he love her? She wanted his love, craved it to the last fiber in her being. She didn't say a word, uplifted by Nidia's revelation.

Nidia gave her an enigmatic smile. "Sleep and later on everything will be clearer."

She expected to see Nidia leave through one of the three doors in the room. Instead, she walked away and disappeared like a wisp of wind.

Lips parted in amazement, Gina stared at the space where Nidia vanished.

Too many bizarre things happened in a short period. Her eyelids flickered and a yawn cracked her jaw. *So tired. I'll just close my eyes for a few minutes.*

* * * * *

Gina awakened to a hard masculine body wrapped around her. She wasn't worried. She knew right away that it was Ryan. His left arm curled under her breasts along her rib cage, one hand possessing her right naked breast. Hairy, muscled thighs lay solid along her thighs, his relaxed cock pressed into the crease of her ass. His breathing, soft and deep, signaled sleep. She wanted to forget the bizarre and inexplicable world they'd landed within. Wrapped in his arms, she savored the moment and sank into a fantasy where they'd landed in Shangri-La and no harm could come to them. Reality, of course, could turn a different direction.

She shivered, and his arm tightened around her. His solid heat comforted, and she drifted in a hazy, relaxing world. Her thoughts jumbled as she ruminated on what they'd do next. He sighed into her ear then stirred. Ryan's fingers plumped her naked breast and pleasure zinged through her immediately. God, his touch wreaked havoc on her body with the slightest movement. Heat, dizziness and confusion ruled her world earlier, now she experienced a new flurry of sensation.

When his fingers traveled up to her nipple and tugged, she gasped softly as pleasure zinged through her breast. *God, yes.* That felt good. Nothing mattered but enjoying his touch and absorbing the pleasure. Both his hands cupped her breasts, his fingers stroking the undersides until she moaned and moved in his arms with frustration. She wanted more. She wanted it all.

"Ryan." She sighed as she grasped his hands.

He slipped his fingers up to her nipples and brushed with tender strokes.

Hard muscle, so solid and reassuring, pressed against every inch of her. She wanted and needed his firm presence behind her. When his hands brushed over her naked breasts, she shivered in keen appreciation. Tingles raced straight to her belly. Her clit sent out a tiny, aching throb. Restless, she shifted her hips and pressed back. Like a bar of hot, solid steel, his cock head pressed against her creamy opening. Longing made hot coils of desire build within her lower stomach.

He groaned softly and kissed the side of her neck. He sighed. "I'm sorry."

"About what?"

"That I didn't protect you." His voice ached with regret and his arm tightened around her waist.

"Oh, Ryan. You have protected me."

"Not well enough."

She snuggled back into his power and heat. "Please don't. You can't protect me from everything. It's just not possible."

His fingers trailed an exciting path along her thigh, then upward to linger on her ribs. "Intellectually I know that's true. Emotionally..."

He didn't finish, but she understood. More than once in her life she'd tried to alter a situation that couldn't be changed, then experienced the painful sting of regret.

Wordlessly he cupped her right breast, his palm and fingers gentle and oh-so warm. "I need to tell you now, before anything else happens. You're the most...the best thing that's ever happened to me."

Amazement, happiness and caution battled for supremacy inside her. "That's wonderful."

"I remembered how I kept you at arm's length for all this time."

Her gut tightened with apprehension. "Do you...do you regret any of it? Do you wish we hadn't moved our relationship forward with...sex?"

His breath ruffled the hair on her neck as he kissed her shoulder. "Shit, Gina. I was a fuckin' fool. I remembered that I've had feelings for you for since the day we met. I figured with my job in the military and then at SIA that I couldn't fit in a relationship. I know now I should have told you how I felt anyway. Even if you would have told me to go jack off."

She laughed. "That sounds exciting." A wicked grin flirted with her lips. "I mean, watching you jack off."

"Mmm." He tasted her shoulder again, his hands starting to move over her possessively. "Only if I can watch you play with your clit."

"It's a deal." As he cupped her breast and pulled on her nipple, she gasped. "Can I be honest with you too?"

"Of course."

Happy tears welled up in her eyes. "I wanted to be with you since I met you. I've fantasized about being with you. I haven't been upfront with you, either."

An exquisite tingling radiated from her nipple as he thumbed it. "How do you feel about me?"

His husky question freed Gina, and she didn't hold anything back. "You're the world to me."

His fingers lightly pinched her nipple. She shivered as his hands coasted with tender attention along her arm, then down to her hip where he caressed with slow, steady strokes.

He rolled her toward him until she could see the steady blaze of his eyes. Within them she could see an answering truth. Before she could speak, he took her mouth in a kiss so carnal, she writhed under the exquisite taste. His tongue moved in and out with plundering thrusts. Her heart pounded a new beat under his onslaught.

His kiss moved to her chin, to her cheeks, to her forehead as his lips pressed tender and delicious touches to each delicate surface.

His warm breath tickled her ear. "I want to fuck you."

Ragged and desperate, his voice asked for her surrender. More than that, it asked to share the deepest, most amazing act two humans could feel with each other.

She tangled her fingers in his hair and sighed deeply. "Yes. God, yes."

With slow movements, his hand wandered down over her breasts, brushing fire into her nipples. His mouth followed in a lingering, nibbling path down her neck, over her collarbone. Quivering, she enjoyed the heady sensation of his lips brushing featherlight over one nipple, then the other. As he tortured her breasts, his fingers slipped between her legs. One finger slipped between her folds and inside her.

Pure pleasure slipped high up inside her as his large finger caressed, then slipped away to leave her wanting. "Oh, Ryan."

With his lips he tugged at her right nipple, worrying it between his teeth then soothing with his tongue. Desperate for more, she clutched at the coverings. The need for sex roared inside her and drove her to writhe, to clasp his shoulders in heady need.

One swipe of his tongue over her nipple made her gasp. With a laugh of satisfaction, he licked repeatedly.

She whimpered, and he intensified his ministrations. With finger and thumb he manipulated her nipple while tonguing the other. Sucking deeply, he tugged sharply on the other nipple until she gasped on a sweet splinter of pleasure.

His fingers slipped into the wet folds between her legs and one long finger plunged inside. Exquisite torment lashed her as he slid another finger inside, then another until three of his thick fingers pressed deep. When his fingers thrust and caressed, she gasped.

"That's it. Come for me," he murmured around her nipple, and each brush of his lips over the hard tips sent shock waves down through her belly to pool deep in her pussy.

He started a rhythm, his fingers caressing aroused flesh deep inside while his mouth closed over one taut nipple and sucked hard. She cried out, uncaring whether anyone heard them.

Here, surrounded by this strange dimension of gentle light, pleasant scents and the warmth of his body, Gina knew nothing could interfere with her happiness in the moment. Nothing in the past or the future would erase these joyful minutes.

His lips traveled with stunning skill and attention to her belly, his hands following in their wake. Each brush of his flesh over hers echoed in her belly and warmed her body. Warm, wet heat flicked here and there as his tongue followed his hands on a path so thorough Gina thought she'd go mad before he released her from this glorious spell. His tongue dipped into her belly button, and a tug of pure excitement darted into her lower stomach and pussy. She ached between her legs with a growing fierce need.

Ryan looked up at her. "Whatever happens whenever we leave here, I wanted you to know how I feel."

Sweet satisfaction, as comforting as a blanket on a cold night, stole into her heart and mind. She smiled. "This is too good to be true."

He looked up at her. "It doesn't get any more real than this."

Full comprehension made her sit up, and when his hands trailed up her thighs and parted them, wicked intent quickened her breath and heart. For one of the first times in her life, she wasn't afraid to say what she meant. "This is a dream come true for me, Ryan."

He grinned. "Really?" One dark brow twitched upward. "Being stuck in a strange realm with creatures threatening to attack and not knowing when you can go home?"

"Anywhere is bearable if you're here."

The masculine, sexy curve of his lips formed into a sardonic smile. "Tell me more about this fantasy of yours."

"For the last ten years I've had these fantasies about what would happen if we were in bed together."

"You did?" The amazement in his eyes and on his face made her heart melt. This wonderful man had no idea the effect he could have on a woman.

"Yes. I spent a lot of time daydreaming about us together."

"Shit."

She frowned. "Shit?"

He edged down to the bottom of the platform. As he parted her thighs, his hands skimmed slowly downward, Inch by inch, he pressed tender kisses to her vulnerable skin. "Yeah, shit. For how long have you felt this way?"

Go ahead. Admit it. "Like I said before. Ten years."

His head jerked up and surprise entered his deep eyes. "The whole time we've known each other?"

"Yes."

He smiled. "I've spent most the last ten years wanting you under me with my cock buried inside you."

Her cheeks heated. Gina thought she'd gone beyond embarrassment, but his erotic words and husky voice threw that theory out the door.

"I want that more than anything," she said, her throat tight with emotion.

"Damn. Then let's not waste any more time." He dipped his head and flicked his tongue with gentle strokes over her wet folds.

She arched into his touch. God, nothing was better than his hands caressing her, his tongue reacquainting itself with her body. With warm touches his tongue licked over one fold, then the other, each stroke long and unhurried. The musky scent of arousal spilled over her senses. Sighs of pleasure left her throat. With a long, languorous lick, he massaged her clit, and sweet arousal built with steady waves. Sensation burst, every second pinpointed down to the continual flick, the heat and wetness as his tongue drove her higher and higher.

She panted as the crest rose. "I can't take it."

"You can."

He proved it, drawing more moans, more excited cries from her throat.

His fingers parted her folds and his gaze took in her most private area with an attention that set her on fire. His tongue dipped between her folds and plunged. She shivered and savored endless ecstasy.

His mouth found her clit, his tongue swiping with steady movements that lingered, retreated, drew her into a sensual dance. Her hips undulated as he caught her ass cheeks in each hand and urged her movements. As each flaming touch flicked over her clit, a new fire burned within her core. Her breath quickened the flight toward orgasm within a few seconds of success.

When he stopped the relentless licking, she whimpered. "Ryan. Please."

Releasing his grip on her butt, he parted her thighs and once more his tongue speared deep between dripping-wet folds. The sensation of his hot, clever tongue plunging in and out of her started her relentless rise to the top once again. His thumb passed over her clit with one stroke. She gasped and grabbed the soft cushion under her head. Writhing, she moaned for mercy. She couldn't take much more.

"Ryan." She gasped his name, almost unable to speak, her arousal was so strong.

"Mmm." His word muffled against her, the purring sound vibrating sensitive tissues.

His thumb passed over her clit with another tantalizing stroke, and the agony restarted. She'd never been stroked, tasted, tortured with sweet desire as she was this moment with Ryan. She'd remember this special event for as long as she lived.

With a swift flick, his thumb circled her pebble-hard clit.

Her world tore apart in blinding glory as climax slammed into her. A cry ripped from her throat. As her hips twitched and she panted, Gina opened her eyes. He skated up her body until he lay next to her. Ryan brought her close, his arms nestling her securely. His left hand clasped her ass cheek and brought her more firmly against him. His mouth found hers without hesitation, and she tasted her musky essence on his lips. Hungrily, she responded as Ryan plunged his tongue into her mouth, pumping and stroking in a wildfire possession she didn't want to deny.

With a gentle roll he moved on top of her, his hips lowering without hesitation between her thighs.

His cock found instant entrance, pressing high, hard and deep into her. Her eyes popped open as a gasp of half surprise left her lips. Delight shimmered like a wave over her body and all her senses. He felt huge. As if his cock grew with each second, hardening inside her flesh until he filled her so solidly she would come with the very first movement.

She squeezed her muscles and he gasped, the gust harsh as a groan rumbled in his chest. Satisfaction made her lips curl up. He moved the tiniest increment, and arousal sparked a conflagration in her lower belly.

Oh, shit. Yes. Yes.

Lubrication eased his passage as he drew his cock back. When the tip rested inside her, he stopped. He held her on the quivering edge of knifelike torture. He thrust hard, and she moaned at the exquisite pleasure. His balls rested against her ass, his pubic hair brushing against her clit. Then he started again. Easing in and out, he thrust.

So hard. So thick and demanding.

His body asked things of her that thrilled and yet scared her at the same time. Yet not a single coherent thought could make it past the way her body responded to his.

Trembling vaginal muscles quivered around his solid cock, the hardness thrust all the way to her womb unrelenting, its strength determined to control and plunder. His steady thrusts slipped in and out, arousing and subduing.

She twisted her hips, and his breath hissed out. His fingers tightened on her flesh, but nothing deterred him from the mission. The semidarkness of the room, so soothing and relaxing, lulled her into a sexual daze. She sensed their link growing and the way their bodies pulsed against each other sent ripples across her sensitive skin. His fingers brushed over her cheeks then released her. She shifted, groaned, pressed her breasts against his hair-rough chest. His cock rubbed high inside her, until she felt nothing but the stretch of her muscles as they gave way under his controlled insistence. Hard muscles tantalized her into touching. Gina clasped at the undeniable power in his shoulders. Sinew moved to her lightest touch.

Gina marveled once more at his masculinity. The tremendous fire as his cock moved inside her, with a schooled, measured thrust. His hot breath tickled her ear, his chest rising and falling.

He leaned down to suckle one nipple in time with his cadence, his tongue dragging over the hard tip. She shivered under the relentless attention.

The hot coil of climax built along with a rush of fluid as she soaked his cock. She moaned, planting her feet and lifting her hips, aiding penetration. Her hips bounced as she arched up, then retreated to the surface of the bed, the pace now steady but not yet hard. Mindless with passion, she moaned, begged with her body for a finish. His tongue snaked across her nipple, then retreated to paint a wet path over her neck.

Ryan's lips found her ear as he whispered huskily, "Fuck me."

Oh, yes. Yes. Yes.

Reaching down, she found his ass cheeks and urged him into a faster pace. No longer slow and sensual, his cock drilled her with beat after beat of thick flesh. She waited for the shivering climax to reach a zenith. She struggled to catch her breath, a light buzz filling her senses as she gasped and writhed under stimulation so high she didn't think she could stand it. A guttural sound left his throat as his thrusts quickened, now short, jabbing movements of his hips as he pounded out his lust. Ryan's hips drew back until his cock barely teased the entrance to her core, then slipped back inside and penetrated deep. Once more he stopped the tentative cadence and returned to a ruthless fucking.

In one explosive burst of pure ecstasy, her body coiled, her belly fluttered, her pussy tightened and released in mind-blowing orgasm. She shrieked, not caring if anyone heard.

Ryan buried his face in her neck and let the titanic waves of her climax overtake him. He didn't relent, continuing his fast, hard thrusts as he fucked her through the climax. As her body shuddered, he pulled from her tight, wet clasp. As she moaned in disappointment, he urged her over on her belly and lifted her hips until she knelt on the bed dog-style.

Ryan caressed her ass cheeks. God, they were beautiful. Round and tight and lush. Her soft pants of arousal brought an answering groan from deep in his throat. Animal needs coursed through his blood and refused to allow any thought but fucking her hard. Right now. Excitement pulsed within as he looked down at his tumescent cock. He placed his thickness against those plump, wet pussy lips and watched his cock slide slowly and firmly into her tight, slick clasp. As he pressed inside she groaned, the sound rising high as he pushed relentlessly. He closed his eyes and savored sensations of creamy wet heat clenching and releasing over his cock. His breathing quickened as he grasped her hips and started a slow but steady pumping into paradise.

She lowered her upper body to her forearms and tilted her beautiful ass higher. He clasped at her waist and drew his hips back.

He slammed deep inside, and she moaned. "Yes!"

Gina's acceptance made him move faster. Driving his cock into her silky warmth, he watched her move as she thrust back with every plunge he took. He drew her hips back, hunching closer until his cock ground inside her hot channel. Fucking her like a beast, he allowed the animal inside him to take over. He growled, he grunted, he fucked her harder and harder. As her cries escalated, he swiveled his hips with each thrust.

Her pleas roughened as she allowed passion to overtake her. "Yes. Oh, yes! Oh, please!"

Wanting to make sure she came before he did, he slowed his thrusts and concentrated on control. He didn't have to wait long. Her tight little passage rippled, the contractions growing faster and faster as her voice went high-pitched with a moan of pure soul-searing ecstasy. As her body shook, he continued to thrust, picking up speed. As her body shivered, his cock massaged her quivering core until he thought his head would explode from the spiraling pleasure. His balls tightened his cock stone-hard.

Climax seized, spurted inside her with blast after blast of cum. While his body quaked, shook with incredible pleasure, he kept thrusting. Her shout of answering orgasm kept his hips pumping and seeking to provide her that last bit of pleasure.

At last she eased down, and as Ryan held her close, he knew he'd never experienced a moment like this in his entire life.

He would abandon everything for Gina in one breath, in one second without the slightest hesitation.

Chapter Fifteen

ඍ

"You have a particle sword?" Ryan asked Nidia as he stood with her in one of the many rooms in the strange complex of tunnels.

Nidia shook her head and walked away from him, her eyes serious. "That is something the SIA invented for use."

"Yeah, but we got the idea from this dimension, didn't we?"

She nodded. "It was stolen from Realm Guardian technology to use against them and weredemons. We don't use them."

"What do you use to defend yourselves?"

She stopped pacing and turned back to him. "Marcanas soldiers use telekinesis to fight."

Ryan's mouth dropped open then snapped shut. "You're kidding me."

She allowed her arms to fall to her sides, and the long, billowing sleeves of her white garment fell down around her legs like a swirling wedding dress. "We renounce violence and only when necessary do we fight." Again, worry entered her light-colored eyes. She didn't look at all happy. "This is not wise, Ryan. You cannot do this alone."

"I don't have a choice."

"Yes, you do. At least travel with Marcanas soldiers by your side."

He grinned. "Okay. I thought you'd never offer. Now, when can we take on this fuckin' Zurvan and where the hell is he?"

She gave him an old map. Faded and worn, at least the map's sturdy linen-like material kept it from easy destruction.

"You'll need more than that primitive weapon you brought with you into the dimension," she said.

"I know. That's why I hoped you had a particle sword."

"They should have explained to you the origins of the sword."

He winked. "Guess that I missed that part of the briefing."

"Your irreverence shouldn't amaze me," she said. "We have something else, however." She reached into a desk drawer and brought out a thin, credit-card-sized device. She handed several of them to him in a stack. "You've seen these before."

"Hell, yes." He palmed the small devices and put them into his front jeans pocket for easy access. Regret stung him. "I had some of these, but when Zurvan attacked me and my partner, something happened to all of them. I thought you said you renounced these types of weapons."

Uncertainty flickered over her features. "We do as a society. I don't in this case. I received these from an SIA visitor not long after they were created more than ten years ago. Law here dictates I should throw these away. I decided to keep some for just such a situation."

Surprised, he said, "I never pictured you as a rebellious type."

She didn't smile. "Thankfully, in this case, I am." Her expression softened. "You must forget everything painful about your partner's death and this entire adventure. In fact, you must put mental traumas out of your mind from this point forward."

"Not exactly easy."

"It's imperative. At the heart of Zurvan's desires lies a craving for mental torture. If you fall into his clutches, you will endure tremendous pain and suffering through mental imagery. The Realm Guardians are adept at putting human beings through forced madness."

"Spectacular," he said with a sarcastic tone. "Anything else I need to know?"

"Not at present."

He squared his shoulders. "Let's round up these soldiers of yours and be on the way."

She closed her eyes and folded her arms. "I'll call them."

He waited while she took two deep breaths, then three. Impatience returned, but he wrestled with it until she opened her eyes.

"They'll be here in a moment."

Less than two minutes later, a pair of double doors swung open and eight stalwart Marcanas walked into the room single file. Surprise filled Ryan. Even the servants who'd attended them during the stay didn't look anything like these guys.

Close to seven feet tall, they towered over Nidia and Ryan. Their wings folded behind them. Each Marcanas had a rugged countenance, a face that said he would die defending the innocent. Some had dark hair, some various shades of blond, their haircuts varied.

Their garments fascinated him. Each wore what Ryan knew to be a chain mail bishop's mantle over his shoulders. Under that, they wore short red tunics with leather belts buckled around the waists. The leather "skirts" under the tunics looked like a Roman soldiers'.

For once, he thought maybe this ill-fated venture would work.

Ryan said in wonder, "This will be damned interesting."

* * * * *

Gina awoke to an empty bed. For a few seconds memories of beautiful lovemaking filled her heart and mind. She sighed with lingering pleasure, the thoughts starting a throb low in her belly. Oh yeah. She could use more of that. With that in mind, she reached over to touch Ryan.

Her hand met empty, cool sheets.

Puzzled, she opened her eyes. The ethereal light that illuminated these rooms with a nonstop glow, even through their sleep, suddenly seemed too bright. "Ryan?"

No sign of him or the backpack they'd brought with them on this adventure.

Instantly she knew what he'd decided. He'd gone hunting for Zurvan without her. *Damn his hide.* She sat bolt upright, panic choking her breath. Angry with herself, Gina decided to take action. She never pussyfooted around—she didn't need to start now. Yes, she'd always taken chances, but since this adventure something had changed. She'd feared more, felt more than any other time in her life. Perhaps, while she'd been jumping out of airplanes and bungee jumping, she'd tried to hide from the rest of her life. Feelings of inadequacy and her desire for Ryan haunted her for years. Now she understood she didn't have to hide from any of her emotions, good or bad. They were natural. Human.

God. What a time to start understanding herself.

Nevertheless, she couldn't let apprehension paralyze her.

You've never been a wimp before. You've jumped off cliff faces, jumped out of planes, done too many dangerous things in your life. What's stopping you now?

She knew, if she would admit to the worries lying buried deep within her.

Ryan's well-being came first. Maybe she should enlist Nidia's help to find Ryan. She took a deep breath and slipped from the bed. Surprised and gratified to feel steady on her feet, she quickly put on her clothes. Worried, she walked to the double door entrance that led to the adjoining hallway and the other rooms where she hoped to find Ryan. She opened the doors with caution and they swung open on smooth hinges.

When she stepped into the corridor, the air shifted, as if the cocoon of safety had lifted from this area. Her stomach dropped and her heartbeat quickened. Something wasn't quite right. What, she couldn't say for certain. Perilous waters lay ahead, whether she wanted to venture into them or not.

Might as well take the plunge.

When she walked into the passageway where she and Ryan had faced attack before, she kept her eyes open for anything unusual. She didn't hear a thing. Silent as the grave made an apt descriptor. While she hadn't heard much while staying there the last couple of days, she expected more activity. Perhaps one of Nidia's silent male counterparts who seemed to serve her every whim would show up.

"Nidia?"

Silence gathered around her like a smothering cloak. Damn it, where was she? Trepidation rose up, even though she didn't want it to appear. Seconds later, she heard a telltale noise, one that froze the blood in her veins.

Zurvan's roar.

She couldn't turn away from the sound. Ryan had to be here somewhere.

Before she could move, the door next to her burst open and two Realm Guardians plunged into the passage. A startled cry left her, but she turned full toward them. She wouldn't run this time.

"What do you want? Who are you?"

The creatures reached for her.

"No!" She flailed against their painful grip, kicking and thrashing as they dragged her into the dark opening. The door slammed behind her. She couldn't see a thing. Panic threatened, but she shoved it down and resurrected determination from within. Fear gave her strength. She broke their grip, and she fell to the hard floor. Pain jolted through her body as she hit. She cried out.

Silence surrounded her in a cocoon, and fright jolted straight through her like a lightning bolt. She sat straight up as pain sliced through her side. She gasped with incredible fear, anger and gnawing pain.

"Son of a bitch," she muttered.

Had she gone blind and deaf? Why couldn't she hear anything? Cold rippled over her skin as air brushed her body with icy fingers.

"God." The word came out as a plea, a whisper.

Terror crept up on her, a nightmare from one of the most frightening scenes in one of her books. Her hands trembled as she reached out and felt around her. Things started to register with more clarity. She sat on something hard. Her fingers and palms encountered unforgiving stone. What the—?

Where the hell had the cloaked cretins gone? An uncanny sensation built, her heart thumping a frantic beat. Panic threatened to send her into a realm of stark insanity. How had she ended up in this...this hellhole with no light or sound? Memories flashed at her. Tremors raced through her skin and shook her limbs as reaction took hold. As her eyes adjusted, she realized the room held a slightly gray tinge to it—almost luminescent. A loud cracking noise erupted around her, and she started. A few seconds later, a door opened in the darkness. Light shot through with such intensity, her eyes snapped shut and her hands went over her eyes. Pain throbbed behind her eyeballs. She groaned as the irritating sensation slithered through her hands, arms and then threatened her chest.

She dared to peek through her hands and saw the door open farther. Her breathing turned erratic, her heart pounding so furiously she couldn't catch her breath. Her mind tried to quiet her body.

Don't panic. Breathe slower.

Dizziness assaulted her, and she sucked in deep breaths to try stopping it. What was out there? Was it as horrible as what she experienced in this pitch-black room?

Beyond the now somewhat subdued light, a dark shape proceeded into the room. She blinked rapidly and tried to clear her still pounding head. All she registered was the grim-reaper cloak, and behind that, the hulking Zurvan beast.

Fear tried to assault her, but she swallowed it back. She understood if she surrendered to the unspeakable horror it would destroy her.

Be strong.

Besides, she must return to Ryan. Must find him. Must tell him how deeply she loved him.

The reaper-like creature came closer.

"Who are you?" she asked through a dry throat.

The hiss that came from Zurvan behind the reaper sounded like a warning. Gliding rapidly across the stone floor, the reaper latched on to her arm with gray claw fingers.

Pain sliced her arm, and she staggered as the agony took her breath.

* * * * *

The Marcanas followed Ryan through the confusing maze of tunnels. Torchlight flickered against the otherwise dark interiors. Like the corridors he'd traversed with Gina, these held a wealth of wonders. Colorful murals wrapped the ceilings, the blue, red and rust paintings calling to his curiosity. Mysterious pictures begged for explanation, their dancing nymphs, huge-cocked gods and sensual goddesses detailed strongly enough to seem almost real. Before he'd left with his winged companions, Nidia had emphasized once more that the Realm Guardians served Zurvan and they were underworld dwellers who rarely ventured aboveground unless something happened to drive them there. He cleared his throat and tried to clear his mind. Ruminating on the Realm Guardians and their proclivities didn't mean a thing.

Get a hold of yourself. Concentrate.

He kept on point, ahead of his winged companions. Determination lengthened his stride. Other than doing the job, he knew why he couldn't bear to leave this situation with Zurvan unfinished. It wasn't just doing the job or completing the picture. No, he needed to do this for the only woman he loved. Gina. Without her, without her love, he didn't think he wanted to escape the twisted world in this dimension. No. He'd go down with a fight, his sword and training readying him for any fight the evil threw at him. Eager to take down the monster and return to his Gina, he turned quickly down the next hallway and stopped. He consulted his watch. According to Nidia and the map, this was the most likely place for Zurvan to appear. When he'd asked why, Nidia refused to provide explanation. Again, she reiterated that he couldn't know everything about this underground dimension. It was too vast, too complicated for one man to understand. Deciding it made more sense to destroy Zurvan than to understand Zurvan, he plunged ahead with the plans. He ignored cold, lack of light, and a fear that tried to worm into his soul. A man without fear often died, while a man who possessed a sense of self-preservation would live. He would be the man who lived. For Gina. For himself.

"Stop," one of the Marcanas said behind him. "Zurvan is near."

Ryan almost turned around to ask how the man knew. Instead, he stopped and sensed the air. Something out there didn't feel right. Oh, yeah, the Marcanas was right. Something dense and evil lay within easy reach.

He pulled out one of the credit card-sized particle weapons Nidia had given him and held it at the ready.

"Yes," the Marcanas said at the same time.

And Ryan stepped forward.

* * * * *

"Bring her to the altar room," the low-pitched, almost sibilant voice said close to Gina's ear. "Zurvan must feed."

Bone-deep anxiety spiraled within her gut.

The two robed reaper creatures, their faces obscured within their hoods, pulled her mercilessly toward the bright opening. At least she'd leave this dark prison. But to what fate? Her heart kicked into ramjet speed. They both grunted as she tried to stall them by digging in her heels. Her right knee wrenched painfully as they yanked her forward again. Ah, shit. This was not good. Not good at all.

A few seconds later they stopped. She hung in their arms, limp with exhaustion and ready to throw the last of her energy into a desperate effort. Four torches sent flickering light over the chamber's many wall paintings and the niches all along the walls. She realized in a snap of a second that the niches held some of the symbols Ryan had mentioned to her in the Mithras religion. Her brain took note of the room's large size, the pretty paintings that covered every space, and the niches containing funerary jars. An altar, pristine fresh and white, sat in the center.

Her captors' cruel hands bruised her arms, and she raged within against their brutality. Tired of being treated like a sack of potatoes, she did the unexpected. She lunged backwards and barreled into the creatures with her weight. Ripped from their grip, she stumbled and fell onto her butt. Pain radiated up her tailbone, and she sucked in a breath. A groan slipped from her mouth as she scrambled to her feet. Before she could run, the reapers grabbed her arms.

"You bastards!" She writhed, wriggled, but it did no good. Rage mingled with a searing desire to survive, to see the man she loved again. "Ryan!"

One reaper clasped her shoulder and heat went through her skin. She gasped and feeling left her body. Panic surged and overwhelmed all logic and common sense. But she couldn't do a damned thing. Couldn't move. Couldn't scream. She sucked in a breath, grateful she could accomplish that much. *Thank you. Thank you. Thank you.*

The reapers lifted her onto the cold stone altar, and her arms fell limply to the side, hanging off the edges of the altar. She couldn't move other than to suck in desperate breath after breath.

I don't want to die this way. I won't die this way.

Seconds later, she heard the sound. A low, deep growling that reverberated off the walls. The rumbling sound increased until it hurt her ears. She blinked and winced. *At least those parts of me aren't paralyzed.* She wanted to groan, to thrash, to fight the inevitable. Because she knew the growling belonged to Zurvan.

A huge shadow fell over her body, and then the reapers moved back. This was it. She'd come to the edge of her life and Zurvan had chosen her as a meal. She cringed within, thinking of her fate. A gruesome, horrible end without dignity or even the ability to fight. She wanted that. Wanted the comforting knowledge that she'd done all she could to save herself.

No. It wasn't meant to be.

Zurvan's shaggy, golden lion head appeared over her body. She took in the creature without seeing it in full, without absorbing the completely honest horror. *No. Please no.* Her heart hammered in her chest, her breaths frantic. Tears came to her eyes and blurred the creature within her sight. Perhaps this was better.

Then a different growl burst through her consciousness. A man's anguished shout, with the underlying cries of other men.

"No! Gina!"

The angry denial burst from Ryan's throat. She'd recognize his voice anywhere. Relief mixed with continued dread. Fear for him. She couldn't move her head to see what he did.

Zurvan's slavering jaws and massive head moved back, turned away. Another ear-splitting roar ushered from the creature. Gina twitched, her muscles reacting to the cold, hard surface under her, her ears battered by the leviathan roar. Suddenly hands touched her head. She couldn't see who pressed her temples lightly, and a second later her paralysis disappeared.

With a gasp, she burst into an upright position, and she witnessed the insanity. Her heart pounded like a drum as she surveyed the scene in light speed. A Marcanas stood near the head of the altar, wings spread. She knew he must have been the one to remove her paralysis. Ryan stood near one corner, confronted by the massive body of Zurvan.

She'd never seen a more powerful, determined man, a more impressive masculine assurance. With feet spread apart and fists clenched at his side, he looked ready for the creature's attack. He held something in his hand, but it was small. She didn't see another weapon in his possession. The reapers had fled. The other winged men stood behind the massive monster as if ready to attack.

Ryan didn't look at her. Her attention riveted on him as he stared down the throat of almost certain death. Before she could help him, the winged man near her lifted her in his arms and ran out the opposite door with her.

"No!" she cried out, struggling in his strong grip. "Ryan!"

The man ran and didn't look back. He'd just turned a corner when a brilliant flash of white light erupted from around them. The Marcanas fell to his knees, his arms sheltering as she screamed. A sharp slashing noise followed the brilliant light, then a deep rumbling of falling earth and rock.

She knew down deep Ryan had sacrificed himself for her. Anguish roiled up with a sting, a terrible ache so devastating, she couldn't care less if she lived or died.

The pain exploded from her in howling denial. "No!"

Chapter Sixteen

ಎ

"Where are you taking me?" Gina's rusty throat felt as if she'd swallowed sand.

The Marcanas didn't speak, but continued to tread down the corridor at a fast pace that didn't quite reach a run. She couldn't believe the silent man's strength. He'd walked for what seemed miles through a brightly lit set of passageways. She couldn't stop the tears running down her face, nor the recriminations that also assaulted her. She should have stayed to help Ryan. Or stayed to die with him.

Ryan must be dead. The explosion—

No. God, no. She couldn't think of it. Agony lacerated her with biting teeth. Nothing penetrated beyond the searing intensity of her grief. Eternity passed before the Marcanas stopped at a double door, this one carved with elaborate swirling designs she thought might be Celtic. The idea barely registered. She swallowed hard and shivered in the man's grip. She didn't care anything about him, his name and his unending silence. Her heart sank until she couldn't find it anymore. So when the winged warrior set her on her feet, she didn't ask him why he'd brought her here or where they were.

She simply didn't care.

Her legs barely held her up. The man slipped his arm around Gina and she leaned against his side. In another time and another world she might have appreciated his strength.

"You are home," the man's deep melodious voice spilled over her.

"Home?" she managed to say around a raspy throat.

"Your dimension."

"But..."

Too many thoughts spun in her mind. Too much despair, too much confusion. Too much effort required to think passed the next second.

"Ryan asked Nidia and me to safeguard you home." He closed his dark eyes. He drew in a deep breath, and a few moments later, the huge doors started to crack open. Shaking, wary and yet not caring what happened next, she waited.

When the doors swung open completely, a woman stood at the opening. Her London blue topaz eyes caught Gina's attention at first—their kindness, their wise attention made her feel safe. Taller than Gina, with a fall of long, shimmering champagne and caramel hair that reached her waist, the woman didn't look like another of the Shadow Realm dwellers. Wearing blue jeans and a T-shirt, and holding a large leather volume to her chest, she represented the ordinary. Behind her were rows upon rows of bookshelves.

The winged man nodded at the blonde woman.

"Thank you for bringing her safely home," she said. Slightly husky, the sensual voice purred with a softness that comforted.

The winged man nodded and said, "It was my honor and pleasure."

He promptly disappeared into thin air. Gina gasped, startled. She gave a weak laugh. God, nothing should surprise her any more.

The blonde woman put her hand out to Gina. "I'm Dorcas Shannigan. Dorky to my friends. Come. Step over the threshold. You're safe now."

Gina trembled as she placed her hand in the other woman's warm palm. She pulled Gina gently through the doorway.

* * * * *

"Gina, you should eat something," Tara Crayton said as she watched her friend sitting silently at the dining table.

Gina shook her head slowly. She took a deep breath and tried to resurrect some enthusiasm for the oatmeal in front of her. She couldn't. She'd wakened this morning at Tara and Marcus' home without one desire to leave the cozy bed in the guestroom. She'd only crawled out of her cocoon because Tara had come into the room at ten a.m. to check on her. Gina's stomach had growled. She hadn't eaten anything in so many hours she couldn't remember the last time. Now, staring at the food in front of her, huddled into her robe and pajamas, she wanted everything to disappear. Her. The world. The nightmare her world had become.

"Gina," Tara said again. Her unusual eyes, one blue and one brown, deepened with worry. "You have to eat something, honey, or you'll become sick."

Gina smiled, but it was halfhearted. "I know. I just need..." She shook her head. "I don't know what I need."

Tara reached across the small breakfast nook table and pressed Gina's hand. Her eyes shimmered with tears, and it surprised Gina. Fresh grief pierced her heart. She recognized her friend's compassion and wished she could somehow erase what had happened in the darkness of a different realm.

"I don't know what to do," Gina said. "I don't know what to think."

"You're depressed. In shock. We're all worried about you."

Gina shivered and allowed the tears to come for what seemed the millionth time in the fifteen hours since she'd stepped into the strange basement world of the SIA and was taken under the wing of Dorky. Dorky. What a name. Yet the woman she'd heard so much about from Marcus and Tara had treated her with equal sweetness and concern. From what Gina understood, she was one of the few people who'd ever seen Dorky, the basement dweller and SIA agent extraordinaire.

"Ryan sacrificed himself for me," Gina said around tears. "I...he shouldn't have."

"He loves you."

"Loved." The word came out sharp and harsh.

Tara passed her a tissue, and she took it as the tears came like rain. She sniffed, her throat so tight she couldn't utter another word.

"Marcus will find him," Tara said.

"What? Marcus shouldn't go in there. Tell me he isn't."

Tara sighed. "Yes. Along with some other agents. A special team of the best. Ben Darrock, Mac Tudor among others."

Gina had heard the names before.

"They aren't just agents, Gina. They are supervisors and division heads. That's how important it is to find Ryan."

Gina sobbed and buried her face in a wad of tissues. She mumbled, "Find him dead."

She wanted to feel stronger, to keep a stiff upper lip, but she couldn't.

"No," Tara said as she pushed back a fall of her hair. She reached for her coffee cup and took a sip. "There is still a chance he's alive."

"What? How could he be?" A tiny ray of hope struggled within her riotous emotions.

"They think he is."

But Gina's tears wouldn't stop coming.

* * * * *

Gina dreamed of Ryan, and while she dreamed, her happiness was complete. No sorrow interrupted, no reality to destroy the golden glimmer of excitement and beautiful joy.

Gina? Gina, it's Ryan. I'm with you. I'll always be with you in your heart. Please don't be sad. I'll always love you.

She woke slowly, reluctantly. Such a beautiful dream should never end.

A light touch along her forehead, so gentle and sweet, made her sigh deeply.

"Gina?"

Oh, she didn't want to leave. This dream felt so real. So wonderful.

A kiss touched her forehead, warm and exquisitely tender. "Sweet colleen. I'm here."

Her eyes snapped open as she rolled onto her back. At first she couldn't believe her eyes. She blinked rapidly. Ryan was sitting on the side of her bed, a little ragged and dirty-looking, but as alive as she was.

"Ryan." She almost couldn't force the word from her throat. A huge grin broke over his face, and with a cry of pure joy, she sprang upright and into his arms. "Ryan!"

He held her tightly, his hands searching over her back with restless energy. "I thought I'd never see you again."

He peppered her face with kisses, and they fell into a passionate kiss that sent a wave of incredible heat through her. Happiness crowded out her depression, the horrible malaise that had threatened her sanity. Her hands ran over his shoulders and into his hair, and their kisses heated into a firestorm of need. Ryan urged her onto her back. He cuddled her in his arms and broke away from the kiss.

She pulled back enough to look into his dear face. "How? I thought you were…" Tears of happiness sprang into her eyes. "I thought…"

"I know." He kissed her forehead. "Before the SIA could come looking for me, the winged Marcanas led me from the maze. Dorky explained that you'd made it out alive. I was so damned happy. But then she told me that you thought I was dead."

"Of course. And so did almost everyone else. That flash was so loud and bright I didn't see how anyone or anything could survive it."

"A small particle weapon."

"How did you survive?"

His hands started a journey down to her breast. He cupped it with reverence. "I had enough time to escape before the weapon exploded. When I saw the winged man take you out of the room, I knew that was the time to take action. The Marcanas distracted Zurvan long enough for me to throw the weapon. I dived out of the other door I'd entered from originally just as the weapon exploded."

"The Marcanas were killed also?"

"No. They have this strange way of disappearing, in case you didn't notice."

She grinned. "I noticed." Her smile dissolved as she thought of something else. "It's been hours since it happened."

He kissed her mouth quickly. "I'm sorry. After the smoke cleared and the Marcanas reappeared, we hunted the immediate area for any sign of Zurvan. We didn't find him."

"He wasn't killed in the explosion?"

"We doubt he was eliminated. If it was that easy to kill Zurvan, someone would have done it hundreds of years ago."

His eyes warmed and caressed her. "When I realized Zurvan had you, I wanted to make certain you got out safe. Nothing else. I couldn't have taken it if anything happened to you. I love you, Gina."

Her heart soared, happiness complete in a way she never could have imagined a few short hours ago. "When I thought you'd been killed, I wanted to die. I love you so much."

His wide grin and sparkling eyes told her how much he liked her confession. Then his gaze heated, his possessive touch sweeping over her body and baring both breasts to his touch. She writhed in building ecstasy as they moved to a new beat of lovers rediscovering each other. Heat shifted, built. As he kissed her, she heard him struggling with his belt buckle. In no time at all, his pants were open and her hand slipped into his briefs to caress the steel-hard smoothness of his cock. He gasped and slipped his hands into her pajama bottoms to find the soft, wet folds between her legs. She moaned softly into his mouth.

When he pushed one finger into her depths, she writhed, her hips twitching, her body aching to have him inside. Desire coiled tightly in her belly. She sighed as his fingers tenderly brushed over her nipple and his kiss went deeper. Drugging, heated kisses that threatened to send her into a spiral of no return.

With a gasp, she pulled back. "Tara and Marcus."

"I locked the door when I came in, and they went out to dinner for the evening. I think they figured we'd want some time alone."

She smiled. "Oh, yes." She frowned. "There's so much more to learn about the Shadow Realm."

His eyebrows lifted. "You really want to know more?"

She shook her head and linked her arms around his neck. "Maybe not. I think I saw enough."

As his tongue rasped over her nipples, she held his head to her breasts and shivered under his skillful touch. Each long, lingering lick propelled her into a longing so fierce she writhed.

"Please, Ryan. I need to feel you inside me."

"I want you." His voice rasped husky and deep. Ryan's eyes looked moist, hot with emotion. "Marry me."

Her heart leapt with new excitement. "Yes. Yes."

His cocky grin and searching gaze heated her heart and body. "Then I'm the happiest man in *this* dimension."

She giggled.

He lowered his hips between her thighs as she helped him shove his pants and briefs down. She was so ready, so aching for his touch. He helped her slip out of her pajama bottoms. As his kisses became ravenous, he probed her wet opening with the tip of his cock. With a steady pressure, his cock tunneled straight into her. The iron-hard male flesh felt so wonderful, she knew she'd never forget this moment of incredible happiness for the rest of her life.

Ryan's heart wouldn't stop pounding like a jackhammer, his body sinking into her tight, hot womanhood. "Shit, that feels so good."

When he'd heard from Marcus that Gina believed he was dead, Ryan had wanted to call her right away. Then he realized that he couldn't wait to be with her, to touch her. He kissed her with unrestrained passion, eager to explore her taste and remember that silky seduction of her tongue against his. His hips started a motion of thrust and retreat, each stroke more powerful, more determined than the last. With a soft, sensual cry, she moved to his rhythm. Her hips rose and fell with his, her hands searching frantically over his shoulders and chest as he plunged deep into the hot well of her body. His breath took on a harsh, ragged pace against the overwhelming excitement shooting through his veins. Slick and tight, her body held him without mercy, taunting him into a quick, fierce completion. As he drove into her, all his tension concentrated on one goal. Bring her to a breath-stealing orgasm. He pumped harder and her cries built in rising excitement. Each thrust came harder, his breath harsher, his need stronger until all sensation centered on his final goal.

He plundered her like a madman until she shivered beneath him and her gasps for breath were punctuated by incoherent murmurs of ecstasy. With a last uplift of her hips, she shuddered and her pussy clenched around him. She cried out. Ripples pulsated out from her core to milk him, demand his release.

With a rough growl his body burst into the most heated orgasm of his life. He poured into her forever, his hips twitching, his throaty cries of completion echoing in the room.

As they rested in each other's arms, he finally felt a sense of peace, of finding himself whole in the embrace of the woman he loved.

The End

Also by Denise A. Agnew

ɞ

eBooks:

Bridge Through the Mist
By Honor Bound (*anthology*)
Clandestine
Dangerous Intentions
Dark Fire
Ellora's Cavemen: Dreams of the Oasis II (*anthology*)
Ellora's Cavemen: Tales From the Temple IV (*anthology*)
Haunted Souls
Jungle Fever
Major Pleasure
Maneater
Men To Die For (*anthology*)
Night Watch
Impetuous
Instinct
Over the Line
Primordial
Shadows and Ruins
Sins and Secrets
Special Agent Santa
The Dare
Treacherous Wishes

Print Books:
By Honor Bound (*anthology*)
Clandestine
Dark Fire
Ellora's Cavemen: Dreams of the Oasis II (*anthology*)
Ellora's Cavemen: Tales From the Temple IV (*anthology*)
Haunted Souls
Impetuous
Night Watch
Primordial
Shadows and Ruins
Sins and Secrets
The Dare
White Hot Holidays Volume 2 (*anthology*)
Winter Warriors (*anthology*)

About the Author

෨

Suspenseful, erotic, edgy, thrilling, romantic, adventurous. All these words are used to describe award-winning, best-selling novelist Denise A. Agnew's novels. Romantic Times Magazine called her romantic suspense novels DANGEROUS INTENTIONS and TREACHEROUS WISHES "top-notch romantic suspense." With paranormal, time travel, romantic comedy, contemporary, historical, erotica, and romantic suspense novels under her belt, she proves her gift for writing about a diverse range of subjects. (Writing tales that scare the reader is her ultimate thrill.)

Denise's inspiration for her novels comes from innumerable sources, but the fact she has lived in Colorado, Hawaii, and the United Kingdom has given her a lifetime of ideas. Her experiences with archaeology have crept into her work, as well as numerous travels throughout England, Ireland, Scotland, and Wales. Denise currently lives in Arizona with her real life hero, her husband.

Denise welcomes comments from readers. You can find her website and email address on her author bio page at www.ellorascave.com.

Tell Us What You Think

We appreciate hearing reader opinions about our books. You can email us at Comments@EllorasCave.com.

Why an electronic book?

We live in the Information Age—an exciting time in the history of human civilization, in which technology rules supreme and continues to progress in leaps and bounds every minute of every day. For a multitude of reasons, more and more avid literary fans are opting to purchase e-books instead of paper books. The question from those not yet initiated into the world of electronic reading is simply: *Why?*

1. *Price.* An electronic title at Ellora's Cave Publishing and Cerridwen Press runs anywhere from 40% to 75% less than the cover price of the exact same title in paperback format. Why? Basic mathematics and cost. It is less expensive to publish an e-book (no paper and printing, no warehousing and shipping) than it is to publish a paperback, so the savings are passed along to the consumer.

2. *Space.* Running out of room in your house for your books? That is one worry you will never have with electronic books. For a low one-time cost, you can purchase a handheld device specifically designed for e-reading. Many e-readers have large, convenient screens for viewing. Better yet, hundreds of titles can be stored within your new library—on a single microchip. There are a variety of e-readers from different manufacturers. You can also read e-books on your PC or laptop computer. (Please note that Ellora's Cave does not endorse any specific brands.

You can check our websites at www.elloracave.com or www.cerridwenpress.com for information we make available to new consumers.)

3. *Mobility.* Because your new e-library consists of only a microchip within a small, easily transportable e-reader, your entire cache of books can be taken with you wherever you go.

4. *Personal Viewing Preferences.* Are the words you are currently reading too small? Too large? Too... ANNOYING? Paperback books cannot be modified according to personal preferences, but e-books can.

5. *Instant Gratification.* Is it the middle of the night and all the bookstores near you are closed? Are you tired of waiting days, sometimes weeks, for bookstores to ship the novels you bought? Ellora's Cave Publishing sells instantaneous downloads twenty-four hours a day, seven days a week, every day of the year. Our webstore is never closed. Our e-book delivery system is 100% automated, meaning your order is filled as soon as you pay for it.

Those are a few of the top reasons why electronic books are replacing paperbacks for many avid readers.

As always, Ellora's Cave and Cerridwen Press welcome your questions and comments. We invite you to email us at Comments@ellorascave.com or write to us directly at Ellora's Cave Publishing Inc., 1056 Home Avenue, Akron, OH 44310-3502.

COMING TO A BOOKSTORE NEAR YOU!

ELLORA'S CAVE

Bestselling Authors Tour

UPDATES AVAILABLE AT
WWW.EllorasCave.COM

Discover for yourself why readers can't get enough of the multiple award-winning publisher

Ellora's Cave.

Whether you prefer e-books or paperbacks,

be sure to visit EC on the web at
www.ellorascave.com

for an erotic reading experience that will leave you breathless.

Hideaway
Special Investigations Agency

DENISE A. AGNEW

Ellora's Cave
Romantica Publishing